SHADOW IN THE BACKWATER

SHADOW IN THE BACKWATER

ACADEMY OF NECESSARY MAGIC™ BOOK SEVEN

MARTHA CARR
MICHAEL ANDERLE

This book is a work of fiction. All of the characters, organizations, and events portrayed in this novel are either products of the author's imagination or are used fictitiously. Sometimes both.

LMBPN Publishing
PMB 196, 2540 South Maryland Pkwy
Las Vegas, NV 89109

Version 1.01, August 2021
eBook ISBN: 978-1-64971-967-6
Print ISBN: 978-1-64971-968-3

THE SHADOW IN THE BACKWATER TEAM

JIT Readers

Dave Hicks
Diane L. Smith
Dorothy Lloyd
Zacc Pelter
James P. Dyer
Jeff Goode

If I missed anyone, please let me know!

Editor

Skyhunter Editing Team

From Martha

To everyone who still believes in magic and all the possibilities that holds.
To all the readers who make this entire ride so much fun.
To Louie, Jackie, and so many wonderful friends who remind me all the time of what really matters and how wonderful life can be in any given moment.

From Michael

To Family, Friends and
Those Who Love
To Read.
May We All Enjoy Grace
To Live The Life We Are
Called.

CHAPTER ONE

"Summer, I'm serious." Amanda Coulier folded her arms and scowled at her best friend before glancing over her shoulder at the front door. "He'll be back any minute."

"You're *way* too worried about what that stunted dwarf thinks, shifter girl."

"Stunted." Amanda snorted. "You mean like your common sense?"

"Relax." The witch closed the lid on a long metal box in Johnny Walker's home workshop with a *clang*. "What's he gonna do anyway, huh? Torture me?"

Scratching her head, the shifter girl muttered, "If he finds you going through his stuff, yeah. Probably."

After the entire summer of her torturing him, *he'll probably end up calling it payback.*

Summer stood and perused the shelves filled with modified tech pieces, neatly stacked tool boxes and supply totes, and a random yet impressive array of weaponry. "You know, I thought you'd be way more laid back. At least at home, right? But no. Apparently, the only thing the shifter girl's afraid of is her bounty hunter storming through the front door to find her going through his stuff. What, does he tie you up and not feed you for a week when nobody's around to see it?"

"What?" Amanda couldn't help but laugh. "Okay, first of all, how many times do I have to tell you he's not 'my bounty hunter?'"

"Until it's true, I guess."

"Whatever. Second, I'm not scared of him."

"Oh, yeah?" Summer turned and flashed her friend a mischievous grin. "So it won't matter to you if I reach into this box right here and take a look at—"

"Stop." Amanda abandoned her post as lookout in the hallway and raced into the workshop. "Get your hand out of there."

The witch laughed. "Or what? You'll *make* me?"

"Now. He was already this close to throwing you out two weeks ago when you tried to strap homemade rockets to the back of his truck. If he sees you in here going through his *things*..."

"He'll get pissed and stomp around like a poked bear, cursing and drinking, and he'll forget about it. Just like with the truck. And when I found his shotgun taped under the side of the house. *And* after I blasted the door off the shed out back—"

"Just listen to me and get your hand out of there."

"Wow. It must be *really* awesome if you're freaking out like this."

"Summer!" Amanda grabbed her friend's wrist and tugged the girl's hand from the box on the shelf. The lid banged shut again, and the shifter girl slapped her hand down on it to keep the witch from trying again. "Stop."

Summer's eyes widened. "Now I *have* to know what's in there."

"Explosives, okay? That's like...eighty percent of what he keeps in this room. So keep your hands to yourself."

"Seriously?" Summer snorted. "You think that's gonna make me *less* likely to open this box?"

"Yeah, okay. I should've known better." Rolling her eyes,

Amanda squeezed herself between her friend and the closed box of Johnny's explosive bolt tips. "So should you. Unless you wanna spend the next two weeks of the summer living with one of Johnny's swamp friends."

"Yeah, right." The witch scoffed and turned away. "No way does the dwarf who thinks he's Oriceran's gift to Earth have any friends. It's amazing he even has a *girlfriend*. You know what? I bet he pays her to keep up the act."

"You're the worst." Despite the difficulties of keeping her best friend out of all her guardian's highly sensitive explosives, Amanda couldn't help but huff out a laugh. "Honestly, I have no idea how he and Lisa got together, but I don't think she's going anywhere. And he *does* have friends."

"Fine." Summer spread her arms. "It can't get much worse than staying here in *this* dump."

"Let's see." The shifter girl counted on her fingers. "Darlene lives in a trailer behind her trailer. Leroy sleeps *and* cooks fake seafood for tourists out of a hut the size of an outhouse. Ronnie lives in a shack that'll probably fall on him if he shuts the door too hard."

Arthur's house is pretty nice, but she *doesn't need to know that.*

"Ha! The Wood Elf with no teeth?" Summer headed toward the tall worktable and poked around at the leftover pile of metal shavings from one of Johnny's projects. "You can't seriously expect me to think *that* old hick is worse than the dwarf."

Amanda pressed her lips together and tried to fix her friend with a perfectly serious, warning stare. "Yeah, the Wood Elf with no teeth. Who makes up for it with his shotgun. That he takes *everywhere*. And he's as good a shot as Johnny."

"Please. No one's gonna shoot a teenage witch—"

"He shoots everyone who walks onto his property without an invitation." Amanda folded her arms. "If Johnny throws you out, you definitely won't get an invitation."

"Whatever." The witch puffed out a sigh through loose lips. "I don't know how you can stand living all the way out here. There's nothing to *do* if I can't even get a good look at all the—wait a minute. What's that?"

Amanda crossed the workshop with wide eyes. "It doesn't matter. Leave it alone."

"It doesn't *matter*?" Summer burst out laughing. "All this crap and he keeps this teeny tiny little squirt gun in here with everything else."

"Squirt gun?" For a moment, as she peered around her friend's shoulder, Amanda almost forgot all her efforts to keep Summer out of Johnny's stuff. "I have no idea what that is."

"He keeps giving you tiny versions of his stuff." Summer grabbed the incredibly small silver pistol from the shelf and turned it over in her hand. "Like that useless knife. What is this? A gun for babies?"

"Don't—"

"It's not even loaded. No clip or anything."

Amanda frowned. "Since when do you know about guns?"

"Since forever, shifter girl." Summer swung the pistol across the workshop, squinting and taking aim.

Despite knowing Johnny kept all the *loaded* weapons either on the airboat, hidden at strategic points around the property, or tucked away into drawers inside the house, Amanda grimaced and ducked out of the way when her friend swung the weapon toward her. "Jeeze. Obviously not."

"Nah. Marianne used to take me to the shooting range. I know guns inside and out."

"Wow. So you and your mom *did* have some kind of bonding time."

Summer cocked her head and closed one eye as she aimed the tiny pistol at the doorway leading into the hall. "Bonding time. Right. With a rented ten-millimeter TRP."

"It's still something you guys did together."

"Oh, yeah. Sure. We bonded so much over me being stranded

on the other side of town with noise-canceling headphones while she took herself out to get her nails done or get wasted or whatever. The first time, the guy who owned the place called the cops because he thought I was trying to steal his shit."

Amanda bit her lip. "Were you, though?"

Summer shrugged. "Only the one time. But I got really good at hitting a bullseye after that."

The sound of tires crunching across gravel and the roar of Sheila's engine caught Amanda's attention. "Okay, time to put the gun down."

"Why? It's not like I'll hit something."

"He's back."

"Uh-huh." Summer studied the gun in her outstretched hand before closing her other eye for a different view.

"No, I'm serious. I can hear him outside." Amanda grabbed her friend's arm and tried to lower it. "Seriously, if Johnny walks in here and finds you with one of his *guns*, I can't even imagine what he'll—"

"You're such a buzzkill."

"Summer."

The witch snorted. "This thing probably wouldn't even fire anyway."

She squeezed the trigger, and the high-pitched screech drowning out everything else made Amanda clamp her hands down over her ears.

"Whoa. Whoa, hey. What's wrong with you?"

Amanda crashed to her knees and swatted at the weapon in her friend's hand before grabbing her head again. "Turn it off!"

"Jesus, you don't have to... Hey. Are you okay?"

No, my head's about to explode. What is *this?*

Yelps and squeals from the hounds outside the cabin barely registered.

"Johnny, make it stop!"

"We're gonna die!"

"What the hell's wrong with y'all?" Johnny bellowed.

"The death whistle, Johnny."

"My *head*!"

With a snarl, Amanda lunged for the gun in Summer's hand and ripped it away. As soon as the witch's finger left the trigger, the screech threatening to split her head open cut off immediately. She slammed the gun back down on the shelf and gripped the edge of the metal wiring for support, her chest heaving.

Summer stepped back. "Well, you don't have to make a huge show about it—"

"I *didn't*."

The front door burst open, and Johnny's bootsteps clomped across the wooden floors toward them. "Amanda! I *know* y'all ain't messin' 'round in my—"

He stopped at the entrance to his workshop to see a heavily breathing shifter girl and a wide-eyed witch looking back at him.

"Aw, hell. What'd I tell you?"

"I know." Amanda swallowed and finally released the shelf. "Sorry."

"Sorry? Y'all damn near broke my hounds. And you too, by the looks of it. Give me the gun."

"What gun?" Summer muttered.

"Don't play games with me, sunshine. Only one thing makes my hounds lose their minds like that. Hand it over."

The witch spread her arms and showed him her hands. "I don't have anything, man."

"Uh-huh. And I reckon you're as honest with me as every other idiot who takes you in for a whole damn summer."

"We were just looking around, okay?"

"That ain't all you did. Now I ain't a fan of repeatin' myself, so where's the—"

The high-frequency shifter gun toppled from the side of the shelf and onto the floor. The bounty hunter glared at it. Amanda grimaced.

Summer grinned and pointed. "Hey, look at that. It's like magic, right?"

Amanda stooped to grab the weapon and dejectedly slapped it into Johnny's open hand. "Sorry."

"Yeah, I bet you are." He shoved the gun into the back waistband of his jeans and sniffed. "You okay?"

"Probably."

"I'm not." Luther panted as he shuffled down the hall toward the living room. "Thought my brains were gonna burst out."

"Yeah, and you can't blame us for *that,* Johnny," Rex added, pausing to paw at his ears with a low whine. "Or tell us to clean up afterward."

"Y'all're fine. Ain't the first time y'all got caught in crossfire."

The hounds disappeared down the hall, and Summer snickered. "What are you *talking* about?"

"Private conversation that ain't your business." After looking both teenage girls up and down, Johnny stepped aside and snapped his fingers. "Get out."

"Okay, okay." Summer lifted both hands and side-stepped around the bounty hunter scowling at her. "What *is* that thing, anyway?"

"That ain't your business either. Just like my damn workshop. I step out for half an hour, and y'all're in here playin' with guns."

"It's not even loaded."

"Not with bullets." Johnny turned to chase her out of the workshop with his unwavering glare. When the front door opened and the porch's screen door banged shut against its frame, he looked back at his ward. "Come on, kid."

"I know. I get it." Amanda took a deep breath. "I couldn't stop her."

"Really? You tellin' me that delinquent witch has some kinda secret strength I don't know 'bout *keepin'* you from stoppin' her?"

She wrinkled her nose at him. "Are *you* telling me I should throw my best friend around because she won't stop touching your stuff?"

"If it'll get the job done, then hell. Throw her 'round some. I reckon she could use a little roughin' up to get a point across." When he noticed his ward staring at him in disbelief, Johnny growled out a sigh and rubbed his mouth. "You know I ain't serious."

"Yeah, I know. Can't believe you said it out loud, though."

He smacked his lips. "Remind me again why I agreed to let her spend the whole summer here."

With a wry chuckle, Amanda slipped past the dwarf and entered the hall. "Because she didn't have anywhere else to go. And because she's my friend."

"Huh. Then remind me later to make sure I got a better reason. That rainbow-haired headache's been terrorizin' this place too long."

"Well..." She grinned at her guardian and shrugged. "At least we'll be going back to school next week."

"Longest week of my life." Johnny squinted and scanned his workshop. "What else did she touch?"

"Nothing," Amanda called over her shoulder as she headed for the front door. "Just the gun."

"Uh-huh."

CHAPTER TWO

Amanda slipped quickly outside and found Summer lounging back in one of the Adirondack chairs on the front lawn. The witch drummed her fingers on the armrest, her eyes closed. "Is he sending me to the toothless Elf with a shotgun now?"

"No." Stopping beside the chair, Amanda drew a deep breath of the sweltering, obnoxiously muggy air of the Everglades in mid-August and rolled her shoulders back. "But he's pretty pissed."

"Maybe he shouldn't keep guns in the house."

"Or maybe you shouldn't go through everybody else's stuff."

Summer scoffed. "Come on, shifter girl. There's nothing else to do out here. Can't he at least let me *look* at all the exploding—"

"No."

Cracking open one eye, the witch looked her up and down. "Then what's the point?"

"Hey, if you wanna go back to campus and spend the rest of the summer *there,* I don't think Johnny would have a problem taking you back."

"Right. He'd probably bury me alive on the side of the road and say he had no idea what happened to me."

"What?" Amanda laughed. "Johnny wouldn't do that."

"You really believe that?"

The shifter girl glanced back at the front door of the cabin and fought back another laugh. "I mean, maybe to his worst enemy. Not a teenage girl."

"You know, I'm kinda getting the vibe those two things are one and the same right now."

The girls stared at each other, then burst out laughing.

"Okay, I have an idea. Come on." Amanda walked toward the side of the cabin.

Summer stayed where she was and called after her, "Are we gonna bury *him* alive?"

"Hey, you can try if you want..."

The witch turned to peer around the back of the chair, but the shifter girl had already disappeared. "It's no fun if I have to do it on my own."

Then she leapt to her feet and raced after Amanda.

"Johnny," Amanda called as she passed the back door. "We're taking the airboat."

A cabinet in the kitchen slammed shut, followed by the dwarf's barked response of, "You break it, you buy it."

Summer laughed. "With *what?*"

Amanda shook her head. "He's just messing around."

As if the bounty hunter had shifter hearing too, the back door from the kitchen opened abruptly. "If y'all get it in your heads for even a second that I ain't serious, go'head 'n try me." He pointed at the girls with one hand and lifted a half-full rocks glass of whiskey to his lips. "I'm watchin'."

"What's he gonna do?" Summer muttered. "Make us work it off as his slaves for the next fifty years?"

"I know one of y'all has a job already," Johnny called after them. "Don't do anythin' stupid."

Rolling her eyes, Amanda shook her head and took off across the back lawn toward the dock. "I know what I'm doing."

"Yeah, but what about that job?" Summer wiggled her eyebrows. "You've been hanging out with me all summer."

"You mean babysitting you?"

"Okay, yeah. I guess I can admit you're a serious cramp to my style, shifter girl."

"Oh, yeah. That's *exactly* what I am." Laughing, Amanda pointed at the airboat for her friend to hop aboard, then got to work untying the mooring rope. "And there is no job."

"So you *do* lie to your bounty hunter."

"He's not—" The shifter girl clenched her eyes shut and shook her head. "Forget it."

"Ooh, now I'm *really* intrigued." Summer dropped into one of two metal-mesh chairs Johnny had bolted to the deck of the airboat at the start of the summer—with an added threat of adding witch-proof restraints if their witch guest didn't keep her hands in her lap—and crossed one leg over the other. "I thought you guys were close."

"We are."

"I thought you told him everything."

Amanda looked sharply up at her friend. "Where did you get *that* idea?"

Summer shrugged. "I'm just prying. Now I know you don't."

"Definitely not. I mean, Johnny's great. It's not like he needs to know everything about what I do or…whatever. Why do you care so much?"

The witch sighed and gazed off into the swamp. "I don't. I'm still waiting for you to tell me about the job the big guy on the swamp totally thinks you have."

Amanda dropped the docking rope and glanced at the back of the house. Johnny still stood there in the open doorway at the top of the back stairs, watching them. For added emphasis, he raised his hand with the whiskey glass to point two fingers at his eyes before pointing straight at his ward and cocking his head.

Great. I bring one friend home, and it's like I just moved in all over again. Should've eased him into it with Grace first.

"He's talking about the internship."

"Oh, *yeah.*" Summer nodded sagely. "With your top-secret shifter gang."

"The Coalition isn't a gang."

"Really? Because that one guy pulled some serious gangster shit on me when he tried to tear me apart with his magic-wolf."

Amanda threw her head back and laughed maniacally. "You were *spying* on our meeting. The one we never actually got to have, by the way. You're lucky they didn't kidnap you after that."

"Oh, yeah? That's what they have you doing now at your *internship?*"

"You know exactly what I've been doing for them." Smirking, Amanda headed toward the stern of the airboat and the keys Johnny always left in the ignition. "They only *offered* me a job. I didn't, like, sign a contract or anything. I don't even know if Fiona was serious. It's hard to tell with her."

"Yeah, she's as crazy as the dwarf. Hey, how come *they* didn't get together?"

"Gross." With a quick jerk on the ignition, Amanda turned the throttle control stick to bring the airboat's fan up to a coasting speed. "They'd kill each other first. I'm pretty sure Lisa's the only magical on both planets who can be that close to Johnny and *not* kill him."

"Yeah, maybe there's something wrong with her too."

The girls laughed, and as the airboat pulled away from the dock, Rex and Luther barreled through the back door, jostling Johnny between them in their fight to get outside. He stumbled forward with a roar of frustration as what was left of his whiskey sloshed over the side of the glass and onto the small back patio. "Damnit. This is *my* house!"

The hounds howled and barked as they propelled themselves

off the stairs and raced across the lawn. "Hey, pup! Hey, wait for us!"

"Wait, wait, wait!"

"Whoa." Summer leaned away in her chair before Rex took a flying leap off the end of the dock first.

Amanda had already turned down the throttle when she saw them racing toward the airboat, and Rex landed on all fours, skittering across the deck before finding his bearings again. "You waited!"

"Me too!" Luther howled as he soared through the air. Instead of his claws clicking against the deck of the airboat, he landed with a *splash* and a yelp in the water two feet from the boat's edge.

His brother cracked up laughing.

Summer snorted. "There is something seriously wrong with that dog."

"There's nothing wrong with him." Amanda stepped toward the edge of the boat as Luther sputtered and doggy-paddled as fast as he could toward the craft. "He's just a little...special."

"Hey, pup. Hey." Luther whined and pawed at the side of the boat. "How about some help, huh?"

"I gotcha." She bent down to haul a fully soaked coonhound up over the edge of the airboat. "You know, we weren't that far away."

Rex cackled. "Are you going blind or what?"

"What? Bro, I'm way too young to go blind. It was the wind."

"The wind." Amanda laughed. "Must've only been right on the dock."

"Yeah, it totally was, pup. You didn't feel it or see it, 'cause it's...you know. Wind."

Summer let out a nervous laugh. "You know, if anyone else heard you out here talking to two—hey!"

Luther's brisk shake flung water all over the place, and he was completely oblivious to the witch glaring at him as he trotted toward the bow and sat beside his brother.

Amanda wiped the swamp water from her face and grinned as she grabbed the throttle again. "You were saying?"

"People would think you're nuts." Summer pulled a thin clump of waterlogged reeds off her sweater and tossed it into the river. "It sounds like you're talking to yourself."

"I told you I can hear them."

"That doesn't mean it's any less weird. They don't actually, like, have anything useful to say, do they?"

Rex looked over his shoulder at the witch and chuffed. "Look who's talking."

"Right?" Luther licked his chops. "Baby two-legs over here didn't even know what a chum bucket is."

Amanda smirked. "They're smarter than you think."

"Huh." Summer folded her arms and stared at the hounds. "Are they any good at sneaking into places they're not supposed to be?"

"Are you kidding?" Luther's head bobbed up and down as he sniffed the briny air. The boat picked up speed. "We get into everything."

"And we're *definitely* not supposed to," Rex added. "Like the trash. The fridge."

"Johnny's laundry."

"Johnny's shed."

"Johnny's room."

"What do you need, witch?"

"Yeah, we'll get it for you. For a price."

Luther snickered. "Lots and lots of treats."

Amanda forced back a laugh and steered them down the winding river. "It's not like Johnny trained two coonhounds to be superspies or anything. They're dogs."

"Uh-huh." Summer shook her head. "Just like you're the girl who lives with a bounty hunter and talks to animals."

"Hey." Luther looked back at the witch this time. "Who are you calling animals, huh? Rude."

"Yeah, you know what, two-legs? The deal's off."

Amanda bit her bottom lip and twisted the throttle to kick up their speed another notch.

Yep. That's all I am. Johnny Walker's shifter ward who talks to coonhounds and drives airboats on the swamp. Forget bounty-hunter school and the Coalition and having no idea how I'm gonna get through my last year.

CHAPTER THREE

"So." Looking up from her plate at the long table stretching across the back lawn, Lisa Breyer grabbed her glass of iced tea and smiled at the two teenage girls sitting across from her. "What did you girls get up to today?"

Johnny snorted. "That ain't the kinda question I wanna hear the answer to."

"That's fine, Johnny. *I'm* the one who asked it."

He looked up at his partner as he chewed and narrowed his eyes.

"Oh, you know." Amanda shrugged as she tore a big bite of roasted chicken off the bone between her teeth. "The usual."

"These two tried to blow themselves up," Johnny grumbled.

"What?"

The shifter girl shook her head. "No, we didn't."

"If I hadn't come home when I did, I reckon there'd be no house to come home to. First time in my life anyone's gotten close enough to consider razin' my property to the ground, and it's two fifteen-year-old girls."

Summer cleared her throat. "I'm almost eighteen, actually."

"Even better."

Lisa sipped her tea and looked back and forth between Johnny and the girls. "What happened?"

"Nothing."

"Got a trigger-happy witch stayin' with us, darlin'."

"Johnny, I thought we agreed you'd put the guns *away* while we had guests."

He shot his partner a disgruntled frown, then grabbed another chicken thigh off the platter. "I did."

"It wasn't loaded or anything," Summer offered.

"Honestly, in this house, that doesn't really mean anything." Lisa shook her head.

"It made the dogs freak out." The witch jerked her thumb toward Amanda. "And her."

The half-Light Elf lowered her fork to her plate and stared at her partner again. "The frequency gun, Johnny? Really?"

"It ain't like I left it out for anyone to find. These kids got no clue what *off-limits* even means."

Summer leaned forward over the table and widened her eyes. "You know what would keep us out of your stuff for good?"

"Us?" Amanda snorted. "Please."

"Okay, fine. Me."

"I don't wanna hear it." Johnny shook his head. "Ain't happenin'."

"You *could* pull out all those super-secret bombs you keep inside and let us shoot off a few."

Lisa choked on her food. "While most of what you own has a tendency to explode, this is the first time I'm hearing about actual bombs."

"'Cause there ain't any bombs." Johnny gestured toward their dinner in the center of the table. "How 'bout we eat dinner like normal folks and quit talkin' 'bout what ain't applicable to eatin'?"

Amanda and Lisa met each other's gazes across the table, then they both broke into poorly restrained laughter.

"What?"

"Like normal folks?" The shifter girl spread her arms. "Since when did you want to be *normal?*"

Lisa cleared her throat to try covering up another laugh. "Honestly, I think we're past the point of no return on that one."

"I ain't seein' the funny part."

"Hey, go with what's normal for *you,*" Summer added. "Like, being all grumpy and making fun of everybody."

Johnny narrowed his eyes at the witch. "That's enough outta you."

Amanda snorted.

"You know what?" Summer pointed at him. "I'm pretty sure shooting off some explosives in the middle of the swamp is your kinda normal."

"Jesus. Do I gotta take my plate somewhere else and go eat in private?"

"I'm just saying..."

"No. No bombs. No explosives. No guns. Hard enough as it is keepin' Amanda away from all those. Ain't enough backup in the world to handle the two of y'all put together, and my insurance policy just expired. Forget it."

"Okay." Lisa wiped her mouth with a napkin and smirked at the table. "That sounds like the cue for a topic change. Do you two have everything you need before school starts?"

Summer chugged her tea and set the glass down with a sigh. "Like what?"

"I don't know. Supplies. Clothes—"

"Darlin', if you're fixin' to take these two shoppin', I ain't gonna interfere. But I ain't payin' for it."

"Nobody asked you to, Johnny." She widened her eyes at the girls and minutely shook her head. "But if they need things for school..."

"I'm pretty sure the Academy has a budget for all that stuff anyway," Amanda muttered around a mouthful. "We're good."

"Seriously?" Summer shot her a disbelieving glance. "If Boss Lady wants to take us out and buy us whatever we want, why would you say no?"

"I...didn't say whatever you wanted," Lisa clarified. "And I'm not quite sure why you still won't call me Lisa."

Amanda reached for the pitcher of tea to refill her glass. "Yeah, nicknames are her thing. Don't ask."

"You got one for everybody?" Johnny asked.

Summer shrugged. "Pretty much."

"Even me?"

Amanda stared at the table and tried not to make the same face the hounds did when someone caught them snooping around the wrong trashcan.

"I guess," Summer muttered and crammed her mouth full of chicken.

"Well, go on, then." With a snort, Johnny dropped his forearms onto the table and nodded. "Let's hear the fancy nickname you whipped up for the dwarf. 'Cause if you're callin' *Lisa* Boss Lady, I oughtta have somethin' real good."

"They're not good," Amanda cut in. "Seriously. I mean, I've been shifter girl since freshman year."

"Then there's Romeo, Woody, Blondie, Ladykiller—"

Lisa burst out laughing and had to turn away from the table before she sprayed her mouthful of dinner everywhere.

"Who's *that*?" Amanda asked.

"Take a wild guess," Summer teased, waggling her eyebrows.

I know she's talking about Matt, and she better cut it out before Johnny and Lisa start asking questions.

Fortunately, the bounty hunter was far more interested in his own Summer-formulated pseudonym than anyone else's. "I'm waitin', girl. Been called a lotta things in my life, but this'll be the first time a teenage witch came up with somethin' all on her own."

"It's...not really something to talk about over dinner," Summer muttered. "Don't want anybody to lose their appetite."

Lisa laughed again after having recovered from her last outburst, and Johnny glared at her. "All right. This is how y'all wanna show some appreciation for the fella openin' up his home to every wayward magical comes knockin' on my front door. I see how it is."

"Maybe I'll tell you later." Summer pressed her lips together. "If you let us shoot off some of your—"

"I ain't makin' deals with a pyromaniac teenager." Johnny pointed at her. "Nice try."

Lisa cleared her throat. "Anyway. You don't need anything for school. We've got that covered. Any idea what's coming up for you two this year?"

"No idea." Summer shrugged and pushed her food around on her plate. "I can tell you right now it'll be the most boring nine months of my life."

Johnny snorted. "You hate it that much, huh? Figured the kids from L.A. might've needed some time to get used to the place, but you came in after that, right?"

"I guess."

Amanda wrinkled her nose.

Great. Now he's sneaking on private Summer territory. I told her not to push him.

"You ain't said what brought you to that school in the first place." Johnny sipped from yet another glass of whiskey. "Feel like sharin' that little fun fact?"

"I got kicked out of SoNM."

"Huh?"

"The School of Necessary Magic," Lisa whispered. "In Virginia."

"No kiddin'. Place's been 'round a long time. What's it take to get kicked out of a fancy school like that?"

Summer met the dwarf's gaze and raised her eyebrows.

"Apparently, they can't handle witches and explosions any more than you can."

Johnny froze, blinked twice, then cleared his throat and muttered into his rocks glass, "Reckon I shoulda seen that comin' a mile away."

"Summer's done blowing things up, though." Amanda shot her friend a warning glance. "Learned our lesson on that one freshman year, didn't we?"

"I mean, not if we include the stuff you and Blondie whipped up in the greenhouse last year."

"Summer."

"Hold on now. What *stuff*?" Johnny pointed at the girls. "I ain't heard 'bout this one."

"*Technically*, it wasn't me." Summer snickered. "Which was a first. You should've seen this stuff when it hit the plastic bucket and the whole—"

Amanda kicked her friend's shin under the table.

"Hey. What—"

"They have scouts come to the school second semester to pick who they wanna hire out of the senior class," Amanda blurted, ignoring Summer's deepening scowl. "Glasket's trying to get everybody jobs after they graduate."

"Uh-huh." Johnny raised an eyebrow. "Sounds *real* excitin'."

Now I'm gonna get an earful about how I never told him about exploding buckets and making stuff in the greenhouse. Illegally. With my friends. After stealing school property...

"That's a pretty great idea," Lisa said. "Where are these... scouts from?"

Summer puffed out her cheeks and blew a raspberry. "No clue. Probably not the best places. I mean, who wants to hire a bunch of high school graduates from the *Academy*?"

"Watch it," Johnny warned. "Only school of its kind teachin' the kinda real stuff y'all're learnin' there. I knows plenty of folks who could do with an extra pair of hands. Maybe not as bounty hunters *yet*, but y'all're the ones with a head start."

"On what?"

He stared at the young witch, cleared his throat, then returned his attention to his meal. "Reckon that's what you're there to find out."

Summer scoffed, but her poorly hidden smirk betrayed her amusement.

"I think we all have a pretty good idea of what Amanda will be doing after graduation," Lisa said. "Which I honestly can't believe is right around the corner already."

"Yeah, she's already got an 'in' with the mafia, right?"

Johnny choked on his chicken. "Say what, now?"

"She's talking about the Coalition," Amanda clarified. "With another nickname."

"What about you, Summer?" Lisa folded her hands on the table and smiled at the witch. "What do you think you'll end up doing after high school?"

"Uh..." The girl frowned. "I don't see the point in thinking that far ahead."

"You got no plans and nowhere else to be after you finish with school." Johnny *tsked*. "Sounds like someone's fixin' to learn the hard way."

"Says the guy who takes every case and goes into every life-threatening situation without a plan." Lisa playfully nudged him in the arm. "Sounds like she's taking a page from *your* book, Johnny."

"I got plans."

"Hey, that's a good idea." Summer grinned and perked up at the table. "That's what I could do."

"Trust me, kid. You don't wanna end up like me."

"No, but I could do the same kinda thing. Except you couldn't pay me anywhere near enough to work for the FBI."

He snorted. "You'd be surprised."

"Maybe I'll do some consulting stuff, you know?" Summer nodded, her grin widening by the second until she looked as half-crazed and happy as if she already had a bomb in her hand. "You guys need any help around here?"

Johnny grimaced at her. "With what?"

"You know, consulting stuff. An extra pair of hands, like you said."

"No. Hell no."

"Oh, come on." Summer laughed. "Why not?"

"We already tried that a few years back. Didn't work out."

Amanda frowned at him. "With who?"

"Someone who didn't work out. That's it."

"If you need help finding a job right after graduation," Lisa cut in, "we'd be happy to help you out. Not that you'd have any trouble with it if Dean Glasket's already inviting potential employers to the campus."

Summer gave her a crooked smile. "She has *you* calling her Dean too?"

"Isn't that her title?"

"Listen, shifter girl." The witch shook her head. "It's been real hanging out with you for the summer, but you've got some weird parents."

The table fell silent, and Summer was the only one who didn't seem to notice as she shoveled bite after bite into her mouth.

Johnny looked up at Amanda with a smirk half-hidden beneath his bushy mustache. Lisa dipped her head to hide her amusement and briefly set her hand on the dwarf's shoulder.

Amanda immediately focused on her dinner again, but her smile had a way of breaking through her surprise too.

First time anyone's called them my parents. *I guess that's what they are. If Summer's trying to get her hands on Johnny's explosives...*

She choked back a laugh and buried her face in her cup of iced tea.

That might've worked.

CHAPTER FOUR

There were no bombs, guns, or explosions of any kind during the last week of the summer, although Summer did everything she could think of to convince Johnny it was a good idea.

It didn't stick.

The Saturday before classes started, the girls packed up all their things, collecting them both from Amanda's room and the private space they'd carved out for themselves in the houseboat. Soon after lunch, they were ready to head back to the Academy's campus for their final year at bounty-hunter school.

Amanda lugged her duffel bag into the back seat of Johnny's red Jeep and looked around. "Where is he?"

"You know what I think?" Summer tossed her backpack into the Jeep and stuck her hands on her hips. "I think he's avoiding us."

"Huh. I wonder why."

"Nah, I'm done asking about blowing stuff up."

"Wait." Amanda narrowed her eyes. "Now I actually *do* wonder why."

"Lost cause anyway, shifter girl. I bet he's hiding away somewhere so he doesn't have to see us go."

"Yeah, but we need to get to school."

"That's what I'm *saying*." Summer spread her arms. "He doesn't want us to leave. I mean, can you blame him? We're kinda the best."

"Okay... Well, if *you* wanna stay here with him, go for it. I'm sure that's what's going on right now. *I* wanna get to school." Laughing, Amanda headed back toward the house. Summer stayed where she was and leaned against Sheila's rear bumper, folding her arms and nodding like she owned the place.

There's no way Johnny wants us to stay. He probably got too involved in making something.

She stepped into the house and headed for the workshop. "Johnny?"

The room was empty, and only then did she hear the quick scuffing and muffled laughter across the hall. Coming from Johnny's bedroom.

Ew. Come on...

Fighting back the urge to gag, she tiptoed back down the hall toward the front door again. The *clack* of the dog door came from the kitchen a second before the hounds raced through the cabin.

"Johnny!"

"Hey, Johnny! Time to get on the boat!"

"Time for a ride."

"Yeah, there's this *giant* turtle out in the swamp, Johnny. All dried up and shriveling."

"Smells even better than the crab traps. You should totally come—oh." Rex skidded to a stop and panted at Amanda, his tail thumping against the entryway of the workshop. "Hey, pup."

She grimaced and put a finger to her lips, shaking her head.

"Rex, what does that mean?"

"I don't know."

"You hungry, pup? The kitchen's back that way. We'll help you find something."

"She doesn't need our help, bro."

Luther cocked her head. "Hey, that's right. Then why are you standing here like you don't want Johnny and Lisa to know you're—*Oh…*"

Rex snickered. "You know what they're doing in there, right?"

"Ain't doin' nothin'," Johnny grumbled from his room. "Y'all git on."

Amanda hurried toward the front door but was too late. Lisa opened the door and poked her head out of the bedroom. "Everything okay?"

"Yep. Totally. Everything's fine. Just getting a glass of water. Now I'm going back outside."

"Really?" Luther sniffed around on the floor. "Where'd it go?"

Lisa smoothed her hair away from her face, then jolted and looked at her watch. "Oh. You're ready to go."

"No. It's fine." Amanda jerked open the door. "I'll just—"

"We said noon," Johnny groused.

"It's twelve-thirty, Johnny," Lisa whispered.

"Huh. Well hell. Should've set an alarm."

"Just…um…" Lisa shot the shifter girl an embarrassed smile. "We'll be right out."

"Yep." After that, Amanda booked it as fast as she could out of the house, both hounds racing out on either side of her and laughing.

"Wow, pup. Was that awkward or what?"

"Yeah, I bet Johnny can't *wait* to get you out of here. *We'll* miss you, though."

"You can always count on us, pup."

Amanda walked straight toward the Jeep and puffed out her cheeks.

Summer looked her up and down and laughed. "What happened to you?"

"Nothing. They're coming."

"You look like you walked in on somebody... Oh." The witch made a face. "Whoa. Really? Who *does* that?"

"Just...get in the Jeep." Amanda opened the front passenger-side door and slid stiffly into it.

This is officially the worst way to start the school year before it even starts.

The front door opened, and Johnny stormed out before throwing open the screen door too. "What're y'all doin' with Sheila?"

Summer snorted. "That was fast."

"Back away from the Jeep, witch."

"We have to get to school *somehow*," Amanda muttered. "Kinda hard to do *outside* the Jeep."

"Uh-huh. Here's what I wanna know." He stopped beside the driver-side door and folded his arms. "Y'all're grown-ass adults now, ain'tcha? Last year of high school."

Amanda turned in the passenger seat to stare at him. "I'm fifteen."

"Well, you're the exception to damn near every rule."

Summer rolled her eyes. "It's not technically a real high school..."

"It is right now. Y'all should be drivin' your own selves to school."

Amanda sighed. "I *would*, but I missed the whole 'learning how to drive' thing last year."

"*I* didn't."

Johnny pointed at Summer. "You ain't drivin' nothin' of mine."

Lisa walked down the front porch steps and finished tying her dark hair up into a ponytail. "How about some driving lessons at home, then?"

He turned to stare at her. "You gotta be kiddin'."

"For Amanda." Lisa shrugged. "I don't think it's a problem. She missed out on an integral part of her junior year because of...

well, stuff most juniors don't have to deal with. It's not that hard. I bet she'll have it down after the first try."

"Oh, I totally will." Amanda leapt out of the passenger seat and crawled across the center console to slip behind the wheel. "Piece of cake."

"I ain't said yes," Johnny grumbled, grimacing at his ward's hands all over the steering wheel of his Jeep. "Can't we get you a go-cart or somethin'?"

"We'll be fine." Lisa kissed him quickly on the cheek and rounded the vehicle's front to climb into the passenger seat. Then she slipped on her sunglasses and grinned at him. "I promise to bring her back in one piece."

"Sure, but what 'bout Sheila?"

Amanda laughed. "I won't break your Jeep, Johnny. Probably."

"Jesus, I can't watch this."

Summer shot him the guns with both hands as she backed toward the rear door. "If she does, I get to come back here and play with your bombs."

"No!"

Lisa and the girls laughed, and Johnny turned away to storm back toward the house. "Have a great semester."

"it's gonna be *way* better now." Amanda grinned and tried to turn the key in the ignition, but it wouldn't budge. "Why won't it—"

"Okay, first lesson." Lisa tapped her shoulder. "Buckle up."

"Right."

Both girls strapped themselves in. Then Summer slapped her thighs. "Let's go, shifter girl. Light her up."

"I said no," Johnny called over his shoulder. "Nobody lights up my Jeep."

"You need your foot on the brake before you can start the engine," Lisa added.

"The brake. Which one is that?"

"For cryin' out loud!" Johnny spun and headed toward them

again. "Never mind. I take it all back. Y'all move aside, and I'll drive the damn thing mys—"

The engine roared to life under Amanda's hand, and she whooped in excitement. "I got it. I got it."

"Shift into drive."

"That's the D, right?"

Johnny ran a hand over his hair. "You're killin' me, kid."

"Yep. That's it." Lisa smiled at him, then gestured toward the pedals. "Now ease forward on the gas and—"

Sheila lurched away down the gravel drive, making Lisa gasp, and Summer burst out laughing.

Johnny groaned as his Jeep fishtailed violently before taking off in a mostly straight line toward the side road. "Don't drive down the middle of the road!"

Amanda raised one hand to throw him an excited wave.

"Damnit. Keep your hands on the wheel!"

"We're all gonna die!" Summer cackled as the Jeep disappeared behind a cloud of dust and dirt, the thick bushes on either side of the road fluttering madly in their wake.

"Hell." Johnny rubbed his chest and scowled at the dust cloud. "One of us's gonna die, and it'll be me with a damn heart attack."

"Okay, now brake," Lisa suggested half an hour later. "Brake. Amanda, use the brake. Brake! Stop!"

Amanda slammed her foot down on the brake, and the Jeep lurched to a shuddering jolt at the end of the gravel drive on the Academy campus. Pebbles sprayed in every direction, and all three of them jerked forward in their seats.

"Yes!" She pounded a fist on the steering wheel and jolted them all even more with a violent honk of the horn. "Whoops. I did it."

"Yeah." Lisa grabbed the gearshift and shoved it forward into park. "Time to get out."

In the back seat, Summer puffed out her cheeks and leaned forward. "I think I'm gonna be sick."

"Oh, come on. That was *good*." Amanda nodded at Lisa, still grinning. "I did good."

"You didn't kill us. So…" The Light Elf leaned over to turn off the engine, then unbuckled her seatbelt. "It's a start."

"I can *drive*…" Amanda bobbed her head and danced out of the car before grabbing her duffel bag from the back. "So when do I get my car, huh?"

Lisa smoothed her disheveled hair away from her face with both hands. "When you're twenty-five."

"Ha. Very funny."

"I'm not sure I was joking."

Summer stumbled out of the back seat and raced toward the bushes before losing her lunch on the side of the drive.

"I don't get it." Amanda spread her arms. "That's how Johnny drives."

"That's…" Lisa frowned at the sounds of Summer's continued retching before shaking her head. "That's not the point. Johnny also knows the difference between the gas and the brake, and he…" She rolled her eyes. "Okay, maybe we should have had *him* teach you."

"Nah. You're way better at teaching." Amanda slung her bag over her shoulder and grabbed Summer's too. "You can tell him I said that."

"Ha. That'll go over well. You okay, Summer?"

"What does it look like?" The witch finally emerged from the bushes and grimaced. "Maybe shifters aren't meant to drive, huh?"

"You heard Johnny. I'm the exception to the rules." Grinning, the shifter girl grabbed a bottle of water from the back of the Jeep and handed it to her friend. "Here."

"Thanks."

"Okay." Lisa clapped her hands together. "I'm taking this vehicle back home so you don't have another chance to get behind the wheel, and...good luck with your first semester."

Laughing, Amanda hugged her and squeezed extra tight. "Thanks. Johnny would never have let me drive the Jeep."

"Oh, trust me. Now I know why." With a tight smile, Lisa squeezed the shifter girl's shoulders and nodded. "Call us if you need anything."

"Yep."

"Bye, Summer."

The witch stumbled forward and jerked her chin up at Lisa. "Thanks for...you know. Letting me crash with you guys."

"Anytime." Lisa opened the driver-side door to get behind the wheel. "Yes, I'm talking for both Johnny and myself when I say that."

"Cool." Still looking green and feeling wobbly, Summer raised her hand in a weak wave before stalking after Amanda.

Lisa pulled away from the school and disappeared down the drive through the Academy's front gates.

Amanda waited for her friend to catch up, her grin unfading. "How cool was *that*, huh?"

"It wasn't." Summer took a long drink of water, swished it around her mouth before spitting it out onto the grass, then chugged half the bottle. "Like, not even a little."

"Oh, come on." She nudged the witch with an elbow and laughed. "You've been through way crazier stuff than that."

"Like what, shifter girl?"

"Like the Starbucks train, for one. I always get nauseous on that thing. G-force or whatever, right?"

"Pretty sure the train goes in a straight line, though." Summer finished off the water, crumpled the empty bottle in one hand, and held the other out toward Amanda. "I'll take my backpack."

"Oh, yeah. Here."

With a sigh, the witch slung one strap over her shoulder and shook her head. "You know, I think I changed my mind."

"About what?"

"About you being gone most of last semester. I mean, yeah, it was boring as hell without you, but if you'd been here for driving lessons, I'm pretty sure you would've killed the driver."

Amanda laughed. "What are you talking about?"

"That old wizard. The one who likes you." Summer smirked. "He would've keeled over and croaked right there with you behind the wheel."

"Whatever."

"Maybe even a few students too. Glasket would've pulled all her hair out."

"My driving isn't *that* bad."

"Says the shifter girl who's never driven anything but boats." Summer smacked her lips as they headed across the central field filled with students of every age milling around and enjoying the outdoors before their summer of free time officially came to an end. "Now I'm hungry all over again."

Amanda nodded and smiled at a group of juniors giving her hesitant waves. "Well… Dinner's in a few hours."

"Or we could go to your fairy friends right now and get a little snack."

"They're pixies. No, I'm not busting down the kitchen door in the middle of the day before classes even start because *you* don't know how to keep your lunch where it belongs."

"Not even to make it up for me?"

Amanda folded her arms and gave her friend a playful glare.

"Yeah, what was I thinking? Of course not. Maybe I'll go—"

"Coulier! Hey!" Jackson Pris waved wildly over his head as he hurried toward them from the other side of the field.

"Or not." Summer sighed. "It was a lot quieter at that dumb cabin on the swamp."

Amanda laughed. "Yeah, that's what Johnny says too. Like, all the time."

CHAPTER FIVE

After dropping off her things in room 228C on the third floor of the girls' dorms, Amanda spent the rest of the afternoon with her friends, catching Grace, Jackson, and Alex up on her summer. Which, this year, included Summer.

She hadn't expected her friends to be so incredibly curious about the whole thing, and they asked way more questions this year than at the start of previous semesters. Oddly enough, they directed most of those questions at the witch instead of the shifter girl.

"So what's he like?" Grace leaned over their regular picnic table in the outdoor cafeteria during dinner. "I mean, over a few months and not only when he shows up to drive Amanda home."

"He's a jerk."

"Hey." Amanda playfully nudged Summer's arm with a fist. "You could at least *try* to be nice."

"Why? It's the truth, shifter girl. And you know it." Summer shrugged and lifted her plastic cup to her lips. "He's not the *biggest* jerk I've stayed with for more than a few hours, but he's not exactly all warm and fuzzy."

Wow. Johnny Walker summed up by a teenage witch who barely knows him. Didn't think that was possible but okay.

"But what's he *like*?" Grace asked again.

Jackson snorted. "Why do you care so much?"

"Why do I care?" The blonde witch stared at him and widened her eyes. "Oh, I don't know. Maybe because he's one of the best three bounty hunters *in the world,* all of whom just so happened to *form this school*. Seriously. It's useful information."

"You've never drilled *me* about Johnny," Amanda said. "But you want Summer's opinion all of a sudden?"

"Well yeah. No offense, Amanda, but you're a little biased."

"Ha!" Jackson pointed at Summer. "You think *she's* the best source for completely objective information?"

"*She's* not his kid."

Summer slammed a fist down on the table and grinned. "You know what? I kinda missed you guys. All the bickering. Takes me right back to the good old days when I wished I'd never been shipped off to the middle of nowhere to spend the next four years with *you* crazies."

Jackson blinked in surprise. "That changed?"

"No way. I just have something to compare it to now."

Amanda shook her head and focused on her dinner.

Good to know a summer spent at Johnny's cabin didn't change her.

"Okay, so you covered that he's a jerk. Great." Grace folded her arms. "Is that all you have to tell us?"

"Yeah, I wanna know what you guys did," Jackson added. "Did he take you hunting?"

"Nope."

"Why not?"

Amanda chuckled. "He didn't trust her with the guns."

"Huh. Fair enough. What about all the cool stuff Coulier says he makes? Did you get to make something with him?"

Summer took a bite of pasta salad, her deadpan expression unchanging. "Nope."

"He didn't trust her with his tools," Amanda added.

"What about fishing?"

"Nope."

"Catching bad guys?"

"Nope."

"Any backwoods swamp parties?"

"No."

"What about—"

"No. No. No. Not even that. And definitely not." Summer eyed the curious wizard with complete detachment. "Guess your bubble's just gettin' burst all over the place, Romeo."

Jackson groaned in frustration. "Then what did you *do* all summer?"

Amanda shrugged. "We went out on the airboat a lot."

"A *lot*."

"And ate at Darlene's."

"Who's that?" Grace asked.

"Big ol' lady who runs a diner out of her trailer." Summer chuckled. "And cooks all the food."

"What kind of restaurant is run out of a trailer?"

"The kind that doesn't have a license. For food *or* liquor, and yeah, she was selling that too."

Grace balked. "Please don't tell me you spent the whole summer getting drunk at an illegal diner."

"Hey, you're right." Summer smacked Amanda's arm with the back of a hand. "Why didn't *we* think of that, shifter girl?"

Grace pointed at her. "Don't start."

"So you guys ran around in the swamp for three months." Alex stared blankly at his plate as he shoveled a huge forkful of mashed potatoes into his mouth. "Sounds pretty boring."

"It's not," Amanda corrected. "I mean, was it as exciting as it normally is? No. But we had a good time."

"Sure." Summer bit off a chunk of dinner roll and shrugged. "The houseboat was pretty cool."

"He has a houseboat." Grace's eager smile widened. "In the middle of the swamp."

"I told you guys that, didn't I?" Amanda spread her hands. "He's had it since freshman year."

"It's *huge*." Summer spread her arms wide for added emphasis. "Fully stocked too. There's a deck up top, giant kitchen, surround sound. Has some weird parts covering up what *I* think were giant explosions—"

"You think everything's a giant explosion," Grace interrupted.

"No, I just wish it was."

Alex snickered. "Cool."

"Yeah, that part was pretty cool," Amanda added. "We camped out on the houseboat for a while. Pretty sure that's what kept Johnny from killing us both."

"And you can't tell us anything else," Jackson muttered. "Like, anything?"

"Not really." Summer pursed her lips and shook her head in a businesslike and very un-Summer manner. "It's all top-secret stuff, you know? Like, the bounty hunter didn't want us seeing what was going on, but he can't exactly hide it from anyone living in his *house* with him. So whatever else happened, we can't talk about it."

Grace leaned forward over the table. "Top-secret stuff? Like what?"

"Did you hear anything I said, Blondie?"

"Oh, come on. Amanda told us about all her work with the Coalition—"

"Yeah, and it took her years to spill the beans on *half* the crap the shifter girl's been keeping to herself."

"There's no top-secret stuff," Amanda said. "Promise."

"Then why the hell did the dwarf keep yelling at us to stay out?"

"Okay, correction." Smirking, Amanda turned toward

Summer and pointed at her. "It's only top-secret now because he doesn't like teenage witches rifling through his stuff."

"Maybe he should've thought about how labeling anything as off-limits is an invitation to come check it out."

"Wow." Grace pushed herself away from the table and shook her head. "You really know how to talk up a whole bunch of nothing."

Summer shrugged. "Yeah, it was an okay summer. What did you guys get up to?"

Jackson drained the rest of his drink and set the cup on the table with a sigh. "The same stuff as the last three summers. We did make a few trips out to the kemana, though."

Alex puffed out a sigh through loose lips. "And there went all the extra money from last year."

"Really?" Amanda looked back and forth from one of her friends to the next. "What did you guys get?"

The Wood Elf gestured across Jackson's chest toward Grace. "What do you think?"

"Hey, I didn't spend *all* my leftover cash on HardPull." The blonde witch folded her arms and smirked. "Just most of it."

"I bet it's all gone now too, huh?" Summer tossed her napkin onto her plate. "I think you might have a problem with the legal kid-booze, Blondie."

"I really like it, okay? That doesn't make it a *problem*."

Jackson cocked his head. "Yeah, but when you start begging us to buy you more..."

"I didn't beg." She smacked his arm, and he burst out laughing. Alex chuckled beside him and shook his head. "You could've told me no."

"And risk you hitting me even harder? No thanks."

Grace gathered up her dishes. "Anyway, it's good to see you guys. I can't believe this is our last year."

Summer stood and stepped over the bench. "Don't remind me."

"Aw. Are you getting sentimental? Wish you could stay longer?"

"Have you met me, Blondie? I'm talking about having the *entire* year still ahead of us. Like, what else do we need to stick around a whole other year for?"

"If you go into it with that attitude, you're not gonna learn much of anything."

"I've had this attitude the whole time."

Laughing, the witches headed off together to throw away their trash and dump their dishes in the bus bin.

Amanda looked up at the guys. "I kinda missed that too. Their weird frenemy thing."

Jackson snorted. "I didn't. But now they're gonna be at it all year, and we get to smile and nod and pretend they're both not completely insane."

Alex hissed out a laugh. "Different kinds of crazy, dude."

"Crazy is crazy. Just because you have a thing for Summer doesn't mean one kind's better than the other."

"Wait, what?" Amanda forced back a laugh as the guys looked up from their plates and stared blankly at her. "You have a thing for Summer?"

Alex stuck his thumb out toward Jackson and muttered, "He's crazy too."

Then he stood and left to clear his plate.

So she focused her amusement on Jackson. "When did *this* happen?"

The wizard shrugged, his unignorable flush creeping up the sides of his neck again. "No idea what you're talking about, Coulier."

"Really? 'Cause you said it, like, two seconds ago."

"Maybe you should get your hearing checked." Jackson looked up at her and snickered. "You know, your shifter hearing. The kind that picks up literally every single sound no one else can... Whew. It's so *hot* here. I gotta take a shower."

He scrambled quickly away from the table, dumped off his dishes, and hurried to catch up with Alex.

Amanda sat alone at their picnic table, her face morphing between a frown and a bubbling smile.

Okay. Starting this year like I ended last year. Doing my thing while my friends run off and do theirs. If I don't hear from the Coalition soon, maybe I won't miss as much school as I thought.

CHAPTER SIX

It was impossible to go to sleep that night. Beyond the excitement of starting a new school year and all the unknowns that came with her first semester as a senior, something else kept Amanda awake in a way that confused her at first.

She kept looking at her door, listening for any sound on the other side of Summer's door opening or the young witch heading across the hall.

Why do I care so much about what she's doing right now?

She tried to ignore it, but that only made it worse.

Then she realized what it was.

We spent the whole summer together. Same room, same adventures. I haven't done that with anyone since Claire...

The thought of her twin sister even now, over three years since the Boneblade murdered her family, brought angry tears shimmering in the shifter girl's eyes before she quickly blinked them away. In so many ways, it had been easy to forget she was a twin—that she had a sister who would have been the same age right now, going through the same things right at her side. Her life had become more than a little chaotic, especially last year. Even the pieces of who she'd been before her run-in with New

York criminals and becoming Johnny Walker's ward sometimes got brushed aside.

But her sister and her parents were always with her, weren't they?

It's not like things would be exactly the same, but with a twin. If I still had Claire, I wouldn't have met Johnny and Lisa. I definitely wouldn't have come to a bounty-hunter school in the middle of the Everglades.

She tossed and turned for another fifteen minutes but couldn't get rid of the feeling that something was missing. After three years of being alone during the summer and over break and having her own space here on campus and at home, that missing piece was having somebody right there with her the whole time.

I can't believe this is bothering me so much. I'm not twelve anymore.

With a frustrated sigh, Amanda whipped the covers off herself and got out of bed. She padded silently to the door of her room and listened for any other movement in the hall. Of course, there wasn't anyone else out this late at night. Senior and junior girls already used to sleeping in a dorm room on campus filled the third floor.

Except for me, apparently.

She snuck out of her room and headed across the hall toward Summer's. Then she knocked gently and listened.

The rustle of movement on the bed rose through the door, but that was it.

"Summer?"

"You're still up?"

"Uh...yeah."

The witch's footsteps moved quickly across the room. Then the door opened a crack and Summer peeked out with one eye. "What?"

"I just..."

"Jesus, shifter girl. You look like you saw a ghost or something." With a snort, Summer opened the door all the way and turned to head back toward her bed. "Close the door."

With an amused frown, Amanda stepped into the room and did as instructed. Then she sat beside her friend at the edge of Summer's bed and sighed.

A long moment of silence passed, then Summer turned to sprawl out on the bed and folded her hands behind her head. "Spit it out, already."

"What?"

"You came here for a reason. What's going on?"

"Just can't sleep. That's it, I guess."

Right. Because talking about my dead twin on our first night back at school is such a great way to start off the year.

"Me neither." Summer clicked her tongue and stared at the ceiling. "It's weird being back."

"Really?"

"Kinda, yeah. I mean, other than being held prisoner in *this* place nine months out of the year, that dinky little cabin in the swamp is where I've spent the most time in one place. Like, ever."

"Dinky little cabin." Amanda huffed out a laugh. "What kinda places have *you* been staying in?"

"Shitholes, mostly." Summer sighed. "I guess the place was starting to grow on me. That's what I get for coming to spend the summer with you, right?"

"Yeah, it really sucked."

They both laughed, and Summer sat halfway up to smack her friend's arm with the back of a hand. "Hey, there's one good thing about this, though. At least we don't have to share a tiny room anymore."

There's the real Summer, trying to hide how she really feels by saying the exact opposite.

Amanda nodded. "Yep. That's a plus."

"I know, right? I got all this space to myself, and you don't get to keep me up all night talking about random crap that doesn't even matter."

"I kept *you* up?"

"You talk a lot, shifter girl. Hey, it's not a bad thing. I get it. Some people talk a lot. Maybe I'm just happier being by myself, you know?"

"I totally get it."

"No offense or anything."

Amanda chuckled. "I'm not even a little offended."

"Good."

"Good."

Mentioning all the space we had on the houseboat would only make this more awkward. I know what she means.

After another long silence of Summer clicking her tongue at the ceiling and Amanda sitting hunched over her lap, swinging her legs back and forth over the side of the bed, the shifter girl slapped her hands down on her thighs. "Okay. Well...I guess I'll have to go force myself to sleep. You know, since you like being alone so much."

"Yeah, thanks."

Amanda headed toward the door.

"Hey, feel free to knock on my door whenever you can't sleep," Summer blurted as she sat up. "You know, in case it helps. If I only have to sit here and literally do nothing for a friend, I'm totally fine with it."

"Ha." Grabbing the door handle, Amanda looked over her shoulder and grinned at her friend. "If the least amount of work possible helps out a friend, it's worth it, huh? Good to know."

"Yeah. I mean, it's the best of both worlds."

"Okay, Summer. Good night."

"Yep."

Amanda got halfway through the door before one more question popped into her mind. "Hey, do you still have that—"

Summer jerked her hands behind her back and sat up straight, her eyes wide. "The what?"

"What are you hiding?"

"Nothing."

"Summer, you're hiding something behind your back."

The witch snorted. "I don't do that."

"Yeah, you do." Amanda wrinkled her nose. "Now you smell *really* nervous."

"You can't do that. You can't tell me what I smell like and use that as an excuse."

"Since when?" Pulling the door closed again, Amanda headed across the room. "Show me."

"Forget about it."

"Yeah, right. Like that's even possible now."

Summer scooted away on the edge of the bed. "It is if you quit trying to butt into none of your business. You were about to ask me something completely different."

"That was *before* you start looking like the guiltiest witch on the planet."

"Stop."

"Just—" Amanda grabbed her friend's wrist and pried it from behind Summer's back.

The witch immediately opened her hand to reveal nothing but air. "See? Told you it was nothing."

"Show me your other hand."

"Damn, you're really on a mission, huh?" With a sarcastic huff, Summer whipped out her other hand and opened it to reveal yet more nothing.

Not before Amanda's shifter hearing picked up the sound of something small and hard dropping onto the mattress behind the other girl.

"Right." She pointed at Summer's empty hands. "So you're just trying to screw with me."

"Duh. That's what I do. And you make it so easy—"

Amanda moved in a blur and lunged toward the mattress to snatch up something cold and hard and metallic off the bedspread.

"Hey!" Summer spun and clamped her hand down on the bedspread, but Amanda was already stepping back across the room. "Cheap shot, shifter girl."

"That's weird. I was about to say the same thing to you." Amanda stared at the glass-encased bolt tip with the metallic base resting in her palm, the liquid inside glowing a bright orange. "What's this?"

"A…souvenir?"

"This is Johnny's."

"Oh, yeah?" Summer scratched her head and let out a self-conscious chuckle. "Huh. Small world."

"You stole it from that box in the workshop, didn't you?"

"What?"

Amanda cocked her head. "Are you insane? Johnny never lets anyone into the house. Like, not even his friends. You can't just steal things from his workshop."

"Hey, *you* take his crap all the time."

"I'm his kid." Amanda glared at the glowing bolt-tip. "You're the delinquent thief I brought home for the summer and tried to convince him that's not what you are."

Summer held out her hand. "It's not that big of a deal."

"It will be when he finds out."

"Come on, shifter girl." The witch stood and walked toward Amanda before nodding at the contraband. "The guy has a million of these things. He's not gonna miss *one*."

"He missed the accelerant I stole from him, and he only let that one go because, again, I'm his kid."

"See? This is why I didn't wanna tell you. I knew you'd freak out." Summer snatched away the bolt tip and shoved it into the front pocket of her sweatpants.

"You're gonna get us both busted."

"It's not like I'm gonna run around campus tomorrow waving this around and telling everybody I stole from Johnny Walker the bounty hunter."

Amanda pointed at her. "You better not. If Glasket or any of the teachers see that—"

"Yeah, big trouble. I get it."

They stood there staring at each other, then Amanda sighed. "Don't use it."

"Why? Is this one of the exploding ones?"

"You're insane."

"It *is*." Summer grinned and rubbed her hands together. "I knew it. I *knew* I could find something awesome."

"Oh my God." Shaking her head, Amanda headed for the door again. "It's our senior year, Summer. *Please* don't blow anything else up."

The witch *tsked*. "I can be careful."

"Okay, well, if you're not and that thing goes off, don't expect me to take the fall with you this time."

"Because you'll rat on me at the first sign of a boom?"

"No. I won't cover for you."

Summer folded her arms. "Fine."

"Fine."

Before Amanda could get out the door, her friend cleared her throat. "What were you trying to ask me, anyway?"

For a moment, the shifter girl considered dropping that part altogether because now her best friend had *two* items of Academy-forbidden contraband, and they'd both technically come from Amanda.

If I don't ask, I won't know how to handle a repeat of last year.

Turning slightly, she shot her friend a deadpan stare. "Do you still have that phone?"

"The crappy flip phone? Yeah. It's in my bag. Don't tell me you want it back, shifter girl. Yours is way cooler." Summer grinned. "Hey, you wanna trade?"

"No. Just hide it and keep it in your *room,* okay?"

"I'm not an idiot. I hid it last year."

"Okay."

"You think your shifter gang's gonna call again and summon you back to the base?"

Amanda rolled her eyes. "I have no idea. This is just in case."

"Sure. Whatever."

"If Johnny sends any texts, don't answer them."

Summer laughed. "Man, the look on his face when he realized it was me—"

"Summer."

"Yeah, yeah, I heard you. No talking to your bounty hunter with the phone he gave you. I got it."

"Good." She tried to give her friend another warning look, but a small smile cracked through her frustration. "You're unbelievable. You know that, right?"

Summer pressed a hand to her heart and pretended to be thoroughly touched. "One of the best compliments I've ever had, shifter girl. You know, if I had any self-esteem issues, that would've wiped them right off the map."

"Good night."

"Uh-huh."

By the time Amanda made it back into the hall and closed the door to Summer's room, she was fighting back even more laughter.

It's not funny. None of this is funny at all, and I shouldn't be laughing.

A choked snort escaped her.

Good thing I got to drive the Jeep before *Johnny found out about this. And my best friend's a chronic thief. Maybe she'll make a decent bounty hunter when we graduate.*

CHAPTER SEVEN

It had been hard enough over the summer not to check her Coalition phone every waking second for news from Fiona or Dr. Caniss or anyone else at Omega Industries. Now that Amanda was back on Academy grounds, it was even harder. She still kept the phone in her back pocket the next day and planned to carry it around with her the entire semester.

The last thing I need is for Fiona to pop up looking like she's about to kill somebody because I forgot to answer a text.

She and her friends spent the next day speculating about what their senior year would entail and joking about how terrified this year's freshmen class looked.

"You think they know what they're in for yet?" Jackson nodded at a group of freshmen who looked incredibly small compared to the other students.

Across the field, Tommy Brunsen and a group of his other senior friends playing magical-light hacky-sack all turned at the same time and startled the new kids watching the game. Two boys practically leapt out of their skin, one stood stock-still with his fists clenched at his sides, and a fourth giggled nervously when the seniors burst out laughing and clapped the new students on their shoulders.

Grace stuck her hands on her hips, trying not to laugh. "I don't think anything they could've possibly heard about the Academy before now is even *remotely* close to what happens here."

"Look at them." Summer snorted. "Completely clueless."

"So were we when we first showed up here," Amanda added.

"Yeah, but we were the *first* freshman class." Jackson pointed at the lowerclassmen trying to regain at least some of their dignity. "Once we're gone, this place doesn't belong to the homeless kids who used to live under L.A. anymore."

Alex nodded as if the realization had filled him with awe-inspiring wisdom. "It'll belong to them."

Grace burst out laughing. "Why do you say it like it's such a bad thing?"

"Just won't be the same anymore. That's all."

That thought stayed with Amanda for the rest of the day, especially when a group of freshmen girls got lost on their way to the outdoor cafeteria for lunch and stopped to ask her where they were going. They didn't have a clue that she was a senior and not a sophomore like the other Academy students her age, and they clearly had no idea she was a part of the school's incredibly low shifter population.

Not the only shifter anymore, though. Unless Matt Hardy decided he didn't want to stick around this place until graduation. Where is he?

That night, preparing for classes to start in the morning, Amanda stared at her Coalition phone and swiped through the different lists of names and contact info for the other shifters around the country who were all part of the Global Shift app's network. Part of her tried to rationalize it as an attempt to distract herself from the fact that she still hadn't gotten a call from anyone with the Coalition. It was mostly an excuse to have her phone on hand just in case.

It's not like they're known for perfect timing.

When she glanced at the alarm clock on her nightstand to find it was almost midnight, her dependable shifter restlessness drew her out of bed. If she couldn't get to sleep by lying in bed, going for a run would help.

Probably.

Amanda snuck quickly through the dorms and out the back door on the first floor, out of habit more than anything else. The security enchantments and Lights Out for upperclassmen had been done away with for years. As she headed toward her favorite stand of tall reeds at the edge of the grounds beside the swamp, her stomach let out a furious growl, and she clapped a hand over it.

I can run after a snack. After all, this is *the last time I'll show up for the start of a new year. Better get in all the time I can, right?*

So she switched directions and headed across the training field toward the outdoor cafeteria and the kitchens building. A thick, muggy wind kicked up, blowing toward her as if pushing her toward the building and urging her to step inside. When she reached the kitchen door, she paused and snorted. "Fairies. How does Summer even get those two confused?"

She knocked on the door, looking forward to seeing Fred's giant smile and hearing Carlos and Gloria bickering about ridiculous pixie things. As soon as the handle turned in the door, the wind died, and the smell hit her before anything else.

"Amanda," Fred boomed. "How you doin', girl? Man, it feels like forever, huh?"

"Sure," Carlos called from his seat at the table stainless-steel prep table. "Almost like an entire summer."

Amanda stared past the giant pixie in front of her and lifted a finger, though it didn't exactly point as directly as she'd intended. "What's he doing here?"

Matt Hardy grinned back at her, his blue eyes crinkling around the corners, and lifted the paper plate of double-chocolate cake in his hands. "Getting a midnight snack."

Carlos glanced at his watch. "Okay, *now* that would be literally." Gloria's high-pitched laughter came from the back corner of the building hidden by the door.

The shifter boy stuck a forkful of cake into his mouth and said around it, "Want some?"

"Don't just stand there, girl," Fred boomed. "Come in! Come on. We haven't seen you in months. And we hardly saw you at all last semester. Get inside."

Suspecting the giant pixie might grab her arm and haul her inside this time, Amanda smiled weakly and saved him the trouble.

"Talking about hardly seeing you," Carlos added, "where *were* you last year, huh? You didn't write. You didn't call. You didn't stop by in the middle of the night so we could test out our newest recipes on your tastebuds..."

"I was pretty busy."

"Yeah, I'll say. You still managed to get all your ducks in a row before the summer." Fred clicked his tongue. "I don't know how you do it, kid. You blow my mind."

She gratefully accepted a piece of cake he all but tossed into her hands, but she still couldn't eat it. Not yet.

What the heck is Matt doing in here? This is my *thing. There's not enough room or time for two shifters sneaking out in the middle of the night.*

"What's the matter?" Fred scrutinized the cake on her plate. "You're not allergic to chocolate."

"No, but I think she might be allergic to Mr. Blue Eyes over there." Carlos hissed out a laugh and pounded a fist onto the steel table.

"You stop that," Gloria chided, rocking back and forth in her chair. The smile she gave Amanda, however, looked a lot like she agreed with him.

"That's pretty impossible," Matt said. "Otherwise, she'd be allergic to herself, too."

"Hey, that's *right*." Fred thumped his massive, muscular belly with a hand and let out a booming laugh. "I keep forgetting there are *two* of you now. Now, don't take it personally, Amanda. You'll always be our honorary pixie shifter girl."

Carlos scoffed and shook his head, smirking.

"But we can't turn away a hungry student knocking on our door in the middle of the night," Fred continued. "And while you were gone…"

The pixies all chuckled good-naturedly, and Matt stared at Amanda as he kept shoveling cake into his mouth. "It's really good. You should eat it."

"Yeah…"

She couldn't think of a single thing to say to that and had no idea how to respond.

They'd settled their differences a little last semester, but coming out here to see the pixies at night was taking it too far.

"If you don't," Matt added, "I will."

"Hoo! Kid talks a big game over here, doesn't he?" Carlos ran a hand vigorously through his bright-orange hair. "Are you willing to put your money where your mouth is, shifter?"

Gloria cackled. "No, he's putting his cake where his mouth is."

The pixies howled with laughter again, and Amanda was finally able to crack a smile that didn't feel like she'd stolen it from someone else.

"All right, all right. Come on, you useless waste of wings." Fred stalked toward the table, fluttering both his huge hands at Carlos as he approached. "Move. Move over. Let these two have their cake and eat it, huh?"

"Bet others have only ever told you that's not possible, huh?"

Carlos jumped off the high stool at the center of the table and climbed up onto another one.

Amanda laughed when Fred gestured for her to take the newly emptied stool. "That's why pixies are the best, right? You guys especially."

"Ooh, honey. Would you listen to her?" Gloria pushed herself out of the rocking chair, her sequined boots sparkling under the lights, then headed for the table to join. "I always knew there was a reason I liked you, girl. Get me a slice, Fred, will ya?"

"Another round it is, then." The bald pixie turned to grab more plates and slice more cake, pausing only to point at Matt and attempt to look stern. "You. To the table. If the cooks are sitting down, we're all sitting down."

"Man, Gloria's *always* sitting down," Carlos joked.

"Gloria's an exception."

"Thank you." The blue-haired pixie woman lifted her colorful skirts to climb up onto a stool across from Carlos.

Fred bustled through the kitchen and returned with more cake for everyone before taking his seat. That left only one stool open. Right beside Amanda.

He kept grinning at her.

"Seriously, Amanda. You should really try the cake."

"Oh, don't you worry about *her* cake," Gloria teased. "There's plenty to go around. Besides, she knows what'll happen if she doesn't eat what we give her."

For the first time, Matt's smile faltered. "What'll happen?"

All three pixies stared at him and deliberately lifted forkfuls of warm, gooey chocolate cake to their mouths.

Amanda fought back a laugh.

Okay, maybe I am still their favorite midnight shifter.

"Seriously." Matt leaned toward her, looking incredibly concerned now. "What happens?"

She cut off a piece of cake with her fork and shook her head. "You don't wanna know."

The pixies exploded with laughter. Gloria's high-pitched shriek startled Matt so much, he almost fell off his chair, and that made the pixies lose it even more.

"He doesn't wanna know!" Carlos howled. "He doesn't!"

Fred chuckled and clapped a hand over his mouth to keep from spewing cake everywhere.

Matt ran a hand through his short, dark brown hair and flashed Amanda a crooked smile. "You guys are totally messing with me."

"Probably." She finally took her first bite of cake and instantly widened her eyes. "Whoa."

"I *know*, right?" Fred cleared his throat before falling into softening laughter again and digging back into his dessert. "This was supposed to be for dinner tomorrow."

"It's not gonna make it," Carlos muttered between bites.

When Amanda looked up at the shifter boy sitting beside her, Matt was staring at her with that unwavering smile. She pointed at his plate with her fork. "If you don't eat that, I will."

"Ha!" Carlos slapped a hand down on the table and fell into another fit of barking laughs. "Stop. Just stop it. You're killing me."

"Eat your cake," Fred growled.

Gloria smiled at Amanda and darted a knowing glance at Matt, who was too focused on eating to notice a thing. "Good to have you around, honey. We sure did miss you."

"Yeah, I missed this too."

CHAPTER EIGHT

The entire cake was gone in under thirty minutes, mostly eaten by the pixies, as they went around the table and shared a few highlights from their summer. Then Fred ushered both young shifters out of the kitchen as if he thought someone would catch them sneaking out for secret desserts.

"Now, I don't really care what you two get up to after this, but *we* need some decent shuteye. And knowing Carlos..." Fred looked over his shoulder at the orange-haired pixie furiously scrubbing out the cake pan over the sink. "Well, that chocolate'll keep him up way longer than any of us want. But it was worth it."

"Thanks, Fred. You should definitely make that again."

"Then I suppose I'll have to put in an official request with the boss."

Matthew frowned in amusement. "Isn't that you?"

"You know what? It sure is. And this goes without saying, but a little reminder never hurt anybody. You kids stop by anytime. I mean it."

"At the same time," Carlos shouted from the sink. "It's way more fun with *two* shifters to pick on."

"You hush." Gloria snapped a towel at him, and he flinched away with a sharp laugh.

"Good offer," Matt said. "Thanks."

"You bet. Good night." Fred closed the door, and his shout carried easily on the night air. "Carlos, if you don't get away from that sink right now, I'm throwing you down the stairs. Remember what happened last time you tried to clean the whole kitchen in one night?"

Amanda and Matt laughed and walked away from the kitchens. It seemed like an aimless stroll, but she remembered all too well the last time they'd come out this way together at night. Once they'd escaped Matt's weirdly crushing admirers—A.K.A. every girl in the school—during the Spring Fling dance, they'd made their way out to the edge of the swamp on the northeast side of campus. That was exactly where they were heading now.

Matt stuck a thumb back over his shoulder. "I think they're just looking for an excuse to eat cake. Not like they need one. They made it."

"They probably get bored in there."

"With all their dessert experiments and having to cook for an entire school three times a day?"

Amanda snorted. "Bored with each other. I know I would if I stayed crammed into one building with the same magicals day in and day out. You know, except for one time Fred came out to set up refills on the banquet tables, I'm pretty sure I haven't seen any of them leave."

"Well, they're pixies." He shrugged. "You wouldn't see them anyway, right?"

"I guess."

This is a weird conversation that's going nowhere. Why am I staying awake for this?

"So." Matt scuffed the sole of his shoe against the grass and stuffed his hands into his pockets. "How was your summer?"

"Were you hiding from me?"

Her question came so quickly on the heels of his that he laughed and stopped to look at her. "What?"

"Summer and I got back yesterday. I haven't seen you anywhere until I go out for a run, and you're already hanging out in one of my favorite spots."

"Oh. That." He glanced up at the stars and looked like he was about to laugh again. "I got here a few hours ago."

"Oh. No Starbucks train for Mr. Hardy, then, huh?"

"Starbucks train? No." He wrinkled his nose. "My dad would kill me if he found out I was riding that train."

"Why?"

"Oh, I'm sure he'd come up with some stupid reason about it being too *public*. Whatever that means."

Amanda wiped her palms on the legs of her knee-length jean shorts. "So how'd you get here?"

"Private jet. Then a private car. Then a private escort back onto the grounds."

"Seriously?"

They reached the water's edge and turned to keep walking north. "Seriously. I know, it makes me sound—"

"No, I get it. Johnny has a jet."

"Oh, yeah?"

"A *present* from the FBI. Or so he says." Amanda lowered her voice and couldn't keep her amusement out of it. "I kinda have this feeling it was payoff for blackmail."

Matt drew a sharp breath. "Your… What do you call him?"

"Um… I don't know, actually. Johnny. Calling him anything else would be way too weird."

Unless it's Summer calling him and Lisa my parents. Then apparently it's all good.

"Fair enough." He reached out and plucked a few loose reeds swaying toward them in the breeze. "You really think he blackmailed the FBI?"

"Probably. I mean, all in a few months, he got the jet, the

houseboat, this weird satellite hub computer thing you can walk into that he named Margo."

Matt choked on a laugh.

"Yeah, it was a weird few months freshman year. That's pretty much when he stopped working with the FBI too. So I'm putting two and two together."

"Knowing all that, I'd probably say the same thing."

"I'm guessing *your* dad didn't blackmail anybody for his jet and private car and everything, though, right?" She'd meant it as a joke, but when Matt stiffened beside her, and the loose reeds dropped from his hand to flutter to the ground, she immediately knew she'd gone too far. "Sorry. I was just—"

"No, it's fine. He, uh… He doesn't blackmail government agencies. As far as I know." The shifter boy ran a hand through his hair and drew a deep breath. "He's just really…"

"Private?"

"Ha. You picked up on that part."

"A little."

An owl hooted from somewhere overhead, followed by a soft *splash* in the swamp and the burble of some creature going under. They both turned to study the dark water shimmering under the sky, then Matt shrugged. "So what about you? Are you gonna be around more this year, or is that a weird assumption to make?"

Amanda wrinkled her nose and rubbed the back of her neck. "Honestly, I have no idea. Still waiting to hear back on that one."

"I'm guessing you still can't talk about it."

"Not really. Sorry."

"Don't be. It's not like there's a rule about the only two shifters in the whole school having to share all their secrets or anything." He laughed and kicked the ground as they kept walking.

Amanda's smile felt way too tight.

He's right. I can't just blab to this guy I barely know about all the crazy shifter stuff I've been doing lately. It's none of his business anyway.

Still, his comment about them being the only two shifters made the idea of talking about their magical race in general seem a lot more plausible.

"Hey, speaking of shifters." She thrust her hands into her back pockets and tried to look casual about it. "Have you heard of the Coalition?"

"As in 'of Shifters'? Yeah. I've heard of them."

"Oh. Cool." Rolling her shoulders back, she scanned the dark overhanging branches of the swamp trees and tried to figure out how to approach this in the best way. "Do you know anybody who's a part of it, or..."

"Nah, not really. I tried looking into it a while back, but my parents shut that one down really quick. We're not all that involved in pretty much everything outside of the family business, honestly."

"How come?"

"No idea." He tried to give her another laid-back, crooked smile, but it didn't quite have its usual effect. "My dad's a little crazy about who we talk to. Who we know. I was surprised he even let me come to the Academy in the first place, but I think part of that has to do with how hidden it is out here. And that this is a school for *bounty hunters* and not, you know, shifters or anything else."

"So he has serious privacy issues and wants you to learn how to get into other people's private lives. Interesting."

Matt let out a wry chuckle. "Is *that* the point of being a bounty hunter?"

"I mean, besides the actual bounty part? Probably. You would know. Since you're the guy who got our entire team for Petrov's dumb game off the hook for finals last semester." She didn't even think about it before playfully knocking her shoulder against his, then immediately regretted it.

What am I doing? I'm not supposed to be hanging out with a shifter boy in the middle of the night. I told him I was way too busy. And now I have no idea.

He lowered his head and rubbed his mouth before shooting her a sidelong glance. "It wasn't all that hard."

"Yeah. That's what I mean." She cleared her throat and tried to subtly put a little more distance between them as they kept walking along the water's edge. "So hey, if your parents thought sending you here would teach you something you didn't already know, they're probably gonna be pretty disappointed."

"Ha. Right. Honestly, I think they sent me here to prove a point."

"That you're good at finding enchanted objects and shaking down other kids to turn them in for credit?"

"Very funny."

Amanda pressed her lips together to hide a smile. "Sorry. They sent you here to prove a point. Keep going."

"I don't know. Something about how everything won't always be easy for me because of who I am or where I come from." Matt shrugged. "The only thing that feels hard here is pretending everything isn't so stupidly easy."

"Plus hiding from every other girl in the school."

He stopped and gave her an amused frown. "Yeah. That's part of it too, I guess."

"And part of who you are and where you come from?"

"Yeah." With another deep breath, he nodded once and kept walking. "What about you? Why are you here?"

"Besides the fact that Johnny built the school and no one else was taking twelve-year-old freshmen?" Amanda shrugged. "I wanna be here. Simple as that."

"Really?"

"Yeah. But it's a lot easier than *I* thought it would be too. I mean, at least the school part, anyway."

He raised his eyebrows. "So when you were gone last semester, that had nothing to do with school?"

"Not really…"

"Oh."

They kept walking in silence, and Amanda couldn't figure out whether it was better to look at him or the ground in front of her or the quiet but still very active wildlife moving around in the swamp.

Guess we ran out of things neither one of us wants to talk about. Or can't talk about. And now it's awkward.

"Hey." Matt's wide eyes glinted in the light when he stopped abruptly and grinned. "Wanna go for a run?"

"What?"

"You know. What shifters do."

She blinked furiously and almost couldn't feel her face. "I know what a run is. I just… I mean, isn't that a little weird?"

"Why would it be?"

"You know. Shifting on campus and running around. Together."

"Oh, I get it." His smile widened, and he leaned toward her. "You've never actually run with anyone else before."

"That's not it. Come on." Amanda rolled her eyes and hoped it was convincing enough.

Apparently, it wasn't. "Well, now it's obvious."

"I've gone on runs with someone else before. Plenty of times."

"Like who?"

She spread her arms. "I mean, it was a long time ago."

"That basically means never. Come on." He started to take off toward the north end of campus.

"Wait."

Matt spun and gave her the kind of look that felt both condescending and wildly encouraging. "For what?"

"Just for me to find a spot to leave my clothes, okay?"

"Why?"

"Because that's how I do it, and I've been running around this swamp a lot longer than you have, by the way."

He chuckled and lifted both hands in surrender. "Okay. Don't let me ruin your groove or anything."

Trying to frown but only wrinkling her nose, Amanda turned and muttered, "That already happened when you showed up at this school."

Matt laughed and folded his arms.

Her favorite stand of reeds was way far behind them, which would have been ridiculous to return to now only to hide her clothes. So she stepped through a thick clump of ferns and forced herself not to look at the shifter boy standing on the grass and waiting for her to "get her groove back."

Since when did I care about who sees me? Besides wanting to be alone. *I shifted in front of the whole dumb* school *after the boar attack. Piece of cake.*

It made no sense at all why her face burned red-hot, and her palms hadn't stopped sweating since she stepped into the kitchens and found Matt there among her pixie friends.

Just do it. He's a shifter. Like he even cares.

After drawing a deep breath, she let her magic take over completely. Her clothes dropped to the ground in the reeds, then she padded back out of them again, searching for Matt.

His scent was everywhere, floating all around her with much more intensity than when she was on two legs. And his clothes lay in a heap right where he'd been standing.

He didn't wait. Awesome. Now I have to—

A streaking blur of black leapt from another clump of ferns and darted in front of her. Then the black wolf who now shared Amanda's territory at the Academy pounced forward with a *yip* and stopped with his snout inches from hers.

She growled.

What is he doing?

Matt lowered his muzzle, his ears swiveling in all directions, then chuffed and took off toward the swamp. He stopped again to turn back and look at her before stepping down into the water and sniffing around.

Okay, fine. I have no idea how to run with another wolf. This is so—

A fox darted out of the reeds up ahead and skittered across a broken log reaching over the water.

Amanda's instincts took over completely, and she raced down into the swamp before bounding after the fox for fun.

Matt *yipped* again behind her, his scent and his nearly silent padding growing closer and stronger.

Right. Like he could catch me.

She leapt off the log and onto a berm sticking out of the swamp before a loud scrabble of claws against wood made her spin. It gave her a split-second view of the black wolf scrambling for purchase on the log before he slipped forward and splashed into the swamp.

Amanda froze.

Maybe I haven't run with anyone else, but at least I know how to run on a log.

He raced out of the water toward her, leapt up onto the berm, and covered her snout-to-tail with briny swamp water as he vigorously shook himself. Amanda snorted and backed away.

For a moment, they stared at each other. Then the black wolf pounced at her, lowering his front paws and chest toward the ground while his hind legs stuck straight up.

If wolves could laugh, Amanda would have. Instead, she sprinted across the berm, zigzagging around low-hanging branches and draping ivy before leaping across the water and splashing her way all along the northeastern bank of the school grounds.

Then she heard the sound that had drawn her into more than a little trouble the summer she'd come home with Johnny, and this time it was much, much closer.

A wolf's howl.

She stopped abruptly in the shallow water, all four paws completely submerged, and sniffed the air as a rippling shiver coursed across her fur.

He was howling. Was it at her or for her?

Did it matter?

Matt let out another long, drawn-out howl that echoed seemingly forever across the water. Whatever it meant, Amanda's instincts took over again, and she didn't even try to hold back.

A low, warbling call rose from her throat. The power in her voice surprised her. It was nothing like the only other time she'd let loose like this. That had been years ago when she'd fought her way out of a magical gang's van to howl for help on the Brooklyn Bridge.

This wasn't a cry for help.

This was fun as hell.

Matt's soft panting grew closer behind her, and she turned to see the black wolf padding forward, watching her intently.

Okay, fine. This is awesome.

He cocked his head, then they both took off through the swamp again, splashing and leaping and crossing in front of each other through the dark underbrush.

Amanda had freed herself from so many other constraints when she learned how to use her ghost-wolf and her shifter magic. But the freedom she felt now, running through the swamp she knew like the back of her hand with another *shifter* instead of only her own shadow, was something else entirely.

She didn't think she'd ever stop.

CHAPTER NINE

Amanda's first thought the next morning—when the Academy's obnoxious wakeup alarm blasting an obnoxiously fast-paced flute solo across campus ripped her from sleep—was that she should've finished her run a lot sooner.

Oh, man. Way to start the school year, Amanda. On two hours of sleep.

Getting ready for the day she'd been looking forward to was a lot harder now that all she could think about was crawling back into her bed. She didn't. By the time she shuffled out of the girls' dorm and finally made it to the outdoor cafeteria for breakfast, her friends were already at their table beneath the pavilion and well into their meals.

The shifter girl was the only Academy student standing at the buffet table to pile her plate with whatever was closest.

Her friends stared at her as she stumbled toward them with her plate and a glass of orange juice. Summer snorted and leaned away when Amanda tried three times to lift her leg over the bench before taking a seat. "You look like crap."

"Hey." Even raising the plastic cup of orange juice to her lips felt like too much of an effort.

"You know, normally I'd tell her to mind her own business," Grace said, "but Summer's right. You look like you got run over by a train."

"And you got…" Summer reached toward the shifter girl's head before scattering bits of plant debris onto the ground. "Grass in your hair."

"Oh my gosh." Grace leaned forward across the table. "Did you sleep *outside* last night?"

"No." Half of the biscuit Amanda bit into dropped from her hand to clatter onto the messy pile of scrambled eggs. "I went out for a run."

"Must've been *some* run, Coulier." Jackson looked her up and down and grimaced. "I don't think I've ever seen you look this much like a zombie."

"Wolf zombie," Alex muttered. "Fits."

"Yeah, I just…stayed up later than I thought." Amanda washed down her mouthful with more juice and almost dropped the cup before setting it down. "I'll be fine."

"You're not gonna make it 'til lunch." Grace laughed, then clamped a hand over her mouth. "Like, I'd bet on it."

"You're on." Summer extended her hand over the table toward the blonde witch. "Twenty bucks says she passes out halfway through the first class."

Grace snorted. "I'm not taking that bet. And you should give her more credit."

Amanda groaned. "I shouldn't be getting credit for anything. That was a stupid move."

"Yeah." The blonde witch narrowed her eyes and pursed her lips. "The kind of stupid move you usually don't make. What exactly happened?"

"I told you. I went for a run." The shifter girl stared at her plate and didn't have to try making her face a blank mask. Even smiling would have exhausted her too much.

I can't tell them I was running with Matt. They'll take it to a whole new level, and Jackson's sitting right there, and it's just weird on so many levels.

"Uh-huh." Summer leaned toward her and scrutinized her profile. "You're full of shit. That's what I think."

"Whatever."

"You're not gonna do this every night, right?" Jackson asked as he vigorously ruffled his shaggy, dirty-blonde hair. "I mean, this is rough to watch."

"Okay, thanks for the input, guys. Feel free to quit interrogating me so I can eat."

"Whoa." Summer snickered. "Tired shifter girl has a lot more bark than normal. Noted."

Amanda glanced up at each of her friends, then dropped her gaze to her plate again. "Sorry."

"Sure." Grace stuffed the last strip of bacon in her mouth and flashed the other girl a sympathetic smile. "You should probably go to bed early tonight."

"Trust me. I'm passing out right after dinner. If I even make it that far."

Summer nudged her arm. "Twenty bucks says you don't."

"Shut up."

Despite eating a full meal she hardly tasted, it was even harder to stay on her feet when the entire student body moved away from the outdoor cafeteria. They crowded around the stage in the central field for the yearly start-of-the-school-year announcements from Principal Glasket. Amanda swayed on her feet, blinking heavily as the noise from all the students around her morphed into one warbling, indistinguishable tone.

She only realized Glasket had taken the stage when the witch cleared her throat, and Mr. LeFor's enchanted speaker system carried the sound halfway across campus.

"Welcome, everyone, to another year at the Academy of Necessary Magic." Glasket spread her arms and smiled at the crowd of students. "A special welcome goes out to this year's freshman class and all the new faces joining us for the next four years. I also want to recognize another class at the start of this semester. It's a little bittersweet for the Academy's faculty and staff, and I'm sure for many of you here today as well.

"This year's senior class came in as the very first freshmen at this school's founding three years ago. They've watched this academy go through growing pains alongside theirs, and they've helped create a safe, inclusive, and hopefully still fun environment for all the students calling the Academy home while classes are in session. We'll celebrate the end of the year when our seniors take their places in the world as graduates of the Academy of Necessary Magic, but I want to recognize them today as well. So let's hear it for our seniors."

Glasket started clapping, and the teachers lined up beside the stage joined. For a moment, the student body was silent—either out of confusion or complete lack of excitement.

"Get ready to party, seniors!" Tommy shouted in the middle of the crowd, pumping his fist in the air. "We're almost free!"

That elicited an explosion of laughter from the entire student body and a surge of shouts and cheers from the senior class. The juniors caught onto the excitement, but the underclassmen hesitated to celebrate. Of course, the freshmen still looked completely lost, and Tommy's mention of freedom probably only made their trepidation that much stronger.

Amanda swayed on her feet again within the cheering crowd, her eyelids drooping over and over.

Grace nudged her with an elbow as she clapped. "You don't look even a little excited."

"I'm thrilled."

"Come on, shifter girl. This is the year we *really* get to slack off." Summer grabbed Amanda's wrist and thrust her hand into the air before wiggling it around. "Time to party!"

With a snarl, Amanda jerked her hand back down and shook her head. "This is the year I really need to sleep."

Her friends laughed and cheered some more, then Glasket spread her arms to quiet everyone down again.

"Now, I have a few more announcements. First, Mr. LeFor has informed me that tryouts for the Louper team will be the *third* week of this semester instead of the second. Yes, freshmen are also encouraged to test out their skills if any of you are interested.

"The second announcement is that we'll be having a very special guest joining us before the end of the semester. They'll share some knowledge, tips, and advice with those of you interested in hearing from the generation of bounty hunters that came before you. So I want each one of you to keep that in mind as you go through the first few months of classes. Gather your questions and think about what you'd really like to learn from one of the best. I imagine there will be a Q&A afterward—"

"Who is it?" one of the junior boys shouted.

"That, Mr. Hark, will remain undisclosed until this special guest arrives. With that, I wish you all good luck with your studies this year. Please join your teachers with your respective classes. Freshman, you'll start the day with Mr. Petrov. The rest of you know how this works."

Glasket nodded once, then stepped off the stage and headed off the central field toward the main building.

"Freshman!" Petrov roared, sending green sparks flying five feet in the air above his head. "Fall in line and keep up! If I see any stragglers, you're running laps." He stalked across the field toward the training building and the obstacle course set up for first-year students in the training field.

The rest of the student body filtered away into their various classes toward their teachers throwing different-colored sparks and shouting out the class names. This year, Amanda and her friends headed toward the edge of the field beside the stage where Ms. Calsgrave threw red sparks into the air.

The shifter girl blinked wearily against the flashing lights of the Illusions teacher's spell, stumbling across the grass as the other seniors moved quickly ahead of her.

Nope. I'm walking through invisible mud. This day is never gonna end...

Calsgrave smiled at the senior class and took stock of all the familiar faces. "What a nice tribute, huh? And you lucky students get to start the first day of your last year with me. Keep up."

The witch turned and hurried toward the main building while the other teachers gave their brief introductory announcements to the other classes.

Grace grabbed Amanda's shoulder and hauled her forward. "Do you need somebody to carry you or what?"

"That's the last thing I need."

"It hurts to see you like this." The other girl's twitching smirk betrayed her statement as mostly a joke. "Seriously. Maybe you should stick to only running around at night on the weekends."

"Trust me, Grace. That's already the plan."

They followed the rest of the class into the main building and down the west wing toward the Advanced Illusions and Advanced Alchemy classrooms. The seniors filtered into Calsgrave's class, and Amanda reached into her pocket for the key to the greenhouse before the Illusions teacher reached out to stop her.

"Miss Coulier, step into the classroom first."

"What?"

Calsgrave gestured toward the open door.

"But I have the greenhouse—"

"Oh, I know. You'll get there, I promise. We have a few more announcements for seniors first, and I don't want you to miss them. Come on."

Puffing out a long, slow sigh, Amanda shuffled into the classroom, and Calsgrave closed the door behind them as she brought up the rear. The Illusions teacher leaned toward her shifter student and muttered, "Are you feeling all right? You look a little...out of sorts."

"Just couldn't sleep. I'm fine."

"Sure. I know it's all very exciting. That should settle down in the next few days." Smiling curtly, Calsgrave walked away down the side of the room toward the front.

Amanda slumped into the closest desk at the end of the very last row and frowned at Calsgrave's back.

I really hope she's talking about me not sleeping and not the excitement. Unless senior year is supposed to be the most boring year of my life...

She folded her arms on top of the desk and leaned forward to prop her chin up on her forearms.

Oh, man. I could fall asleep right now.

"All right, seniors. Listen closely."

Hearing Principal Glasket's voice at the front of the room instead of Calsgrave's made Amanda jerk upright again. She had to peer around Corey Baker's giant body to double-check. The half-Kilomea kid was sitting directly in front of her.

"In a few minutes, you'll be starting your Senior-Level Illusions class with Ms. Calsgrave. Before you officially begin your studies, I want to take the time for some important updates specific to your class alone."

"Yeesh." In the desk beside Amanda, Tommy leaned toward her and rolled his eyes. "Looks like this year's nothing *but* announcements, am I right?"

She could only give him a sluggish, half-hearted shrug in reply. The boy looked her over, snorted, and faced forward again.

"We've had two years to work out the kinks of preparing the Academy's graduating class for their life beyond school and as adults out in the real world," Glasket continued. "This year, I'm incredibly confident that the process will be the smoothest yet with all of you. As seniors, you have the opportunity to…restructure the foundation of your classwork across both semesters. Of course, this is optional, but I *highly* recommend you take advantage of the opportunity. Your teachers will tell you the same."

Grace's hand shot straight up in the air.

"Yes, Miss Porter?"

"What do you mean by restructure?"

Glasket smiled tightly and dipped her head. "If you'll allow me to continue, I'm sure it'll answer all your questions. I'm happy to address anything I haven't covered once I finished. Uninterrupted, if you don't mind."

"Right. Sorry." The blonde witch shifted in her seat and yanked a notebook and pen from her backpack, thoroughly prepared to take notes before their first class had even officially started.

"Thank you." Glasket paced in front of Calsgrave's desk as the Illusions teacher sat back in her chair and cracked open her weird black book with nothing but a gold-foil pentagram on the cover. "Think of this as an introduction to what most human colleges would call 'building your own major.' A bit of a precursor to trade school, if you will.

"Since institutions of higher education specifically dedicated to magicals, not to mention those looking to start their career as a bounty hunter, have yet to exist, this year will be your chance to select an area of study specifically. Any area you wish, as long as it falls into the boundaries of what you've learned over the last three years, what type of work you think you would enjoy most, and your skill sets, of course."

Annabelle raised her hand.

"Miss Lamar, please—"

"Do you have a list we can pick and choose from?"

"I…" Glasket blinked quickly and cleared her throat. "I wasn't calling on you, Miss Lamar, but that's an excellent question.

You'll have more information from Ms. Ralthorn when you get to your first History of Oriceran class this week.

"Now, if any of you have already adopted the notion that 'building your own major' as seniors might not be of any benefit to you, I want to offer one more point as to why I believe you should. Narrowing down your field of expertise according to your preferences and skill sets will also help you prepare for your evaluations at the end of the year when the agency scouts arrive to find...new talent.

"Most of them will be here to select their newest recruits and employees directly from the Academy, meaning you may walk away from this campus at the end of the year with gainful employment. Many of last year's seniors have already started their new careers with these large companies, and from what I've heard, they're doing very well."

"Will we know who's gonna be here?" Katie asked. "Before they show up to take their pick, I mean."

Glasket briefly closed her eyes and let out a small sigh. "I might be able to gather that information once we get closer to the end of the year, Miss Price. But for now, I highly recommend focusing on the areas in which *you* excel so you can hone those skills and put your best foot forward when the time comes. And Mr. Brunsen, I didn't want to call you out in front of the whole school, but I would be remiss if I didn't take the time to correct your misconception about what your senior year entails."

Tommy perked up beside Amanda, his eyes wide. "No parties?"

"As long as they abide by school rules, I have no issue with *parties*." Glasket folded her hands in front of her. "Still, that shouldn't be your focus. This year, you'll have less free time than you're used to."

The class exploded into resistance and outbursts of disbelief.

"What?"

"Less free time?"

"We already made it this far. Give us a break."

"Seniors are supposed to have it easy."

"If you'll all settle down," Glasket barked, "I'll explain what this means!"

The shouting stopped, although students still grumbled their discontent and gave each other exasperated looks.

"You all knew this was coming. As the final class of this school's original student body, you, more than anyone else here, will benefit the most from the mandatory extracurriculars added to your schedule this year. So, in addition to your regular classwork, you will be *required* to take these additional classes covering practical knowledge and real-world applications."

"Like what?" Evan grimaced.

"Like Money Management. Interview Etiquette. An overview of socially acceptable behavior as adults living and working and thriving on your own. General life skills."

Brandon snorted and folded his arms. "We already have life skills."

"Yes, Mr. Everly. I would call those *street skills*. Knowing how to survive underground in a bustling metropolis by stealing and lying your way through adolescence will hardly serve you once you graduate. These classes are to prepare you for how to be law-abiding and at the very least morally acceptable magical citizens. They are *not* optional. Any other questions?"

Grace's hand shot up in the air again.

"Yes, Miss Porter."

"Who's going to be teaching these?"

"Oh, Christ," Summer muttered beside her. "Please don't say Petrov."

Glasket smirked. "I'm happy to say I will be teaching you these courses myself. Once a week after your last class of the day on two-class days. Which is Senior-Level Alchemy, I believe. We'll alternate between Thursdays and Wednesdays, depending on the week. I hope you're all as excited for this year as I am."

That garnered nothing but absolute silence and wide-eyed stares as the entire senior class struggled to absorb the new information.

"Ha." Summer leaned forward over her desk and grinned. "Good one. Who's really doing it?"

"I'm doing it, Miss Flannerty. To be perfectly honest, I very much enjoyed overseeing the preparations for the Academy's first-ever graduating class, and I imagine I'll be taking up the role for seniors every year moving forward."

"Oh." Summer's grin faded instantly into a scowl of distaste. "Great."

"I'll see you all in my office on Thursday after lunch. Now I'll let Ms. Calsgrave get back to teaching her class." Glasket turned to smile at the Illusions teacher.

Calsgrave was so thoroughly engrossed in her reading that the principal had to clear her throat to get the other witch's attention. With a start, Calsgrave slammed her book shut and tossed it onto the desk. "Yes. Thank you, Dean Glasket. We're all looking forward to it."

"I can see that." Smirking, the principal turned and shot the entire class a gleaming grin. "Welcome back, seniors."

Then she strode briskly across the room, her heels *clicking* loudly in the strained silence, and slipped through the door.

Amanda stared at the surface of her desk and pressed her lips together.

Yep. Senior year is officially the most boring year of my life.

CHAPTER TEN

Once Calsgrave finished giving out instructions to the class—which included grabbing new textbooks from the front of the room and perusing the contents on their own to find specific areas of Illusions that interested them most—the teacher headed for the door and lightly tapped Amanda's desk. "Now you can go."

"Okay." Amanda grabbed her backpack and lugged it wearily over her shoulder before heading for the door. She felt the teacher's presence right behind her and turned. "I'm pretty sure I can find it on my own."

"Of course you can. I'm coming with you." Calsgrave opened the door and gestured into the hall.

Amanda glanced at her friends. Grace diligently flipped through the pages of her textbook, simultaneously scribbling in her notebook. Summer sat perfectly still with her arms folded. Even from behind, she was clearly fuming.

Then her gaze landed on Matt. He stared straight at her, smiling and completely oblivious to Katie and Emma sitting behind him and staring dreamily at the newest senior they probably didn't even know was a shifter.

Half-shifter. Whatever the other half is, it doesn't mean he can stare at me like that.

"Miss Coulier?"

"Yeah." Amanda blinked furiously and hurried out of the room. She almost tripped on her sneakers and overwhelming exhaustion but caught herself before Calsgrave closed the classroom door.

"Just a few things I want to go over with you before you start doing your thing in the greenhouse."

"Couldn't you tell me right now?"

"I *could,* but I prefer using visual aids." The teacher headed down the hall, and Amanda fought against the feeling of weighing a million pounds to keep up with Calsgrave's pace.

When they reached the greenhouse at the end of the west wing, the shifter girl fumbled in her pocket for the key and practically tore the door down trying to get it open. It banged against the inside wall and instantly bounced back again. She grabbed the handle just in time to save herself from a wooden slap to the face, then staggered inside and dropped her backpack on the floor.

Calsgrave raised an eyebrow as she entered. "Are you sure you're feeling all right?"

"Yeah. Just tired."

"All right. If it keeps up like this, I'd visit Nurse Aiken. She might be able to help you with a sleep potion—"

"Just a one-time thing. I promise. Won't happen again."

Amanda brushed her hair away from her face and tried to smile at her teacher.

Definitely won't happen again. I don't care how fun it was. I can't run with a shifter boy if it's gonna turn me into the walking dead.

"It's *your* senior year, Miss Coulier." With a shrug and a knowing smile, Calsgrave crossed the room toward the worktable in front of the center trough and waved Amanda forward. "This year, Dean Glasket and I decided you've earned a break in the...strenuousness of having grown so many magical plants for us over the years. I'm not entirely sure of the status with your work outside of school..."

When Amanda realized the teacher meant that as a weirdly framed question, she shook her head. "Me neither, honestly."

"Okay. Either way, your list of required plants this year is only a fraction of what it has been. At least as far as what we need at the school. Those would be the DarkSkull and the Angler's Root." The teacher gestured toward the trough closest to the curving wall of windows, still filled with the fully matured plants from last year. "Everything else, though, is entirely up to you."

"Wait, what?"

"There's nothing wrong with your hearing." Calsgrave chuckled and tapped the book resting on the worktable.

It wasn't the *Magical's Guide to Magical Greenery,* which had been moved to the next table over. This one was a thick paperback of the same size, with a highly glossed front cover on which at least twelve different ads had been squashed together beneath the title in large red letters: *Orion's Plant Emporium: Fifth Edition.*

"Right now, Miss Coulier, *this* is the approved list of plant seeds you are free to request and grow here in the greenhouse. Within reason, of course. It would be helpful for us if you curated a list by the end of the week, including the order number and how many packets you want. Anything not available directly from this catalog needs a written request with a full explanation of why. Dean Glasket was clear on infrequent allowances as long as you can make a convincing argument, in writing, as to why growing additional plants would be beneficial to you, the school, and your future career."

"I..." Amanda frowned at the catalog. "Couldn't I go up to her office and ask her in person?"

"She also stressed the importance of documentation from here on out. Something to do with missing supplies from Mrs. Zimmer's alchemy storeroom. That part was incredibly vague."

Swallowing thickly, Amanda forced herself to look up at the Illusions teacher and pretend like that wasn't a direct reference to her desperately delinquent acts at the start of last semester. "Okay. A written request. Um…how long does it have to be? Just hypothetically."

"As long as necessary to make a convincing argument. I'd say two pages at the very least, but you might have to revise and improve your requests if Dean Glasket doesn't think it's enough to warrant an approval."

"Two *pages?*"

Calsgrave gave her a sympathetic smile and nodded. "Get used to paperwork, Miss Coulier. Welcome to adulthood."

"Everyone keeps talking about *being adults.*" Amanda folded her arms and grimaced. "I'm fifteen."

"Ah. Right." The teacher hummed out a laugh. "I'm always amazed by how easy it is to forget that about you. I'll look for your order list by Friday."

Calsgrave headed toward the door, and Amanda's groggy, swimming brain settled on the weirdest question possible at that moment.

"Ms. Calsgrave?"

"Yes?"

"Um…I know I was gone a lot last semester, so I didn't see what was happening most of the time." The girl shrugged. "But I thought with another shifter kid at the school… I mean, I kinda figured you'd be sticking us both in the same non-magical classes, right?"

"I assume you're referring to Mr. Hardy."

"Yep."

Calsgrave nodded. "Mr. Hardy manages his magical classes perfectly well."

"But he's a shifter. We can't do everyone else's kind of magic—"

"Oh, he can perform magic."

As exhausted as she was, Amanda still felt like her eyes were about to pop out of her head. "What?"

"It's not my place to divulge other students' personal histories, Miss Coulier. I'm sure by now you've realized Mr. Hardy is only half-shifter. I'd focus on your abilities if I were you."

"He..."

When Amanda couldn't get anything else out of her mouth, Calsgrave nodded and opened the greenhouse door. "Happy catalog shopping."

Then she was gone, and it took another ten minutes for the shifter girl to wrap her head around what she'd heard.

Matt can do magic. Like actual magic. *What the heck is his dad?*

The thought was even stranger than learning shifters did have a form of magic and that Amanda could learn to harness and use hers under Fiona Damascus' instructions. It brought a lump to the girl's throat.

Okay. I'm not the only shifter here, but I'm still the only kid who can't do what everyone else can do. Not sure if that's better or worse than being drooled over by every girl in the school...

She turned, scanned the three cleared-out troughs and the final two holding healthy, flourishing plants, then went to the back wall and grabbed one of the metal folding chairs. Just lugging that across the room toward the worktable made her entire body ache, but she sat in front of *Orion's Plant Emporium: Fifth Edition* and pulled the heavy, floppy volume down onto her lap.

Whatever I want, huh? Pretty sure I won't find Fatethistle for wolf magic in this thing. Would've been really nice to get this last *year.*

When the grating alarm blared across the campus to signal the end of class, Amanda snorted and jerked her head up off her arms folded on the worktable.

Okay. That was maybe two more hours of sleep. And...ten pages through this gigantic book she wants me to read by the end of the week.

With a massive yawn, she struggled to her feet and left the chair there before grabbing her backpack to head to the next class. Which, unfortunately, was Combat Training with Petrov.

She met her friends outside the main building as the central field filled with sweaty, panting, red-faced freshmen on their way back from hell on an obstacle course.

Summer snickered. "Man. I do *not* miss that."

"Who would?" Grace asked. "Did *we* look that broken our first day?"

"Probably worse," Alex muttered. "At least they had a heads-up. We had no idea."

Jackson vigorously scratched his head and grimaced. "Just watching them is giving me PTSD."

Grace shoved him away from her. "That's not how PTSD works."

"Whatever you wanna call it. It's still trauma."

"You know, Blondie," Summer pointed at Grace, "if you *had* taken that bet, I'd win right now. There's no way shifter girl's gonna make it through this class. Not looking like that."

Grace eyed Amanda up and down and wrinkled her nose. "You slept through Illusions, didn't you?"

"It's not like anyone's in there to make sure I'm flipping through magical-seed catalogs. I think I feel even worse now."

"Oh, man." Summer grinned and rubbed her hands together. "The sarge is gonna lose his shit when he sees you sleepwalking your way through Combat Training. This is gonna be good."

Amanda rolled her eyes and let out a low growl. "This is gonna suck."

Petrov was nowhere in sight on the training field, so the seniors dropped their bags along the wall of the training building and headed inside. The bald Combat Training teacher stood in the center of the room on the sparring mats with his arms folded, scowling as the Academy's smallest class of only twenty-six filtered through the door. They fanned out as they had last year during their infrequent meetings for Petrov's Bag the Bounty game, waiting for the next bit of torture they were all sure was waiting for them.

"All right, seniors. Listen up!" The teacher didn't move but eyed each of them in turn. "The juniors are scrambling around this year in their clueless teams for Bag the Bounty like you did. You've finished with that. Now, you bunch get to enter the big leagues."

"It's not another game, is it?" Mark asked.

"You'd like that, wouldn't you, DeVolos? A second chance to screw it up and lose points for your team, huh?"

A handful of boys around Mark snickered, while those who'd been on his team for last year's Bag the Bounty grimaced and shook their heads.

"No," Petrov barked. "This year, you're focusing on sparring. With *me*."

The tension in the training building boiled to intolerable levels, but the entire senior class knew enough by now to keep their mouths shut.

Amanda blinked heavily and couldn't focus on one of the two Mr. Petrov's standing in front of her.

There's no way this is gonna turn out well. Not today.

Petrov pursed his lips. "Look at that. You finally learned how not to ask stupid questions. Feel free to get yourselves a cookie after lunch. Now here's how it's gonna work.

"Every class for the rest of the year, *one* of you gets a one-on-one session of two and a half hours with me. Alone. We're rotating through all twenty-six of you three times before you graduate. First rotation is hand-to-hand. Second rotation will include your weapon of choice from the rack."

He gestured toward the side of the training room, and the large weapons rack holding all manner of potentially deadly items—excluding long-range projectiles. "That'll fill up your first semester. After break, *if* you haven't killed yourselves first, we'll get to the good stuff."

"What...does that mean?" Evan asked.

"That's for me to know and you to lose sleep over, Hutchinson." Petrov pointed at the back wall of the training building, where his tiny box of an encased office took up the corner. "The list is posted on the door. And yeah, I laminated it so nobody tries to mess with the dates. Your name and the date you spar with me *will not* change. If you have an excuse to get out of your scheduled date, tough. There *are* no excuses, and nobody's getting out of this. No trading places, either. Write that date down, people. Tape it to the wall by your bed. Tattoo it on the inside of your eyelids. If you miss any of your sessions, you're not passing my class."

A collective but muffled groan filled the room.

Petrov smirked. "Now that that's out of the way, here's the fun part. The rest of you get to work on your skills, or lack thereof, on your own time. I don't want to see all of you crowding around on my mat because you think you should be here. You shouldn't. You should be preparing yourself physically and mentally for getting your ass kicked by your teacher. But if anyone wants to sit in on someone else's session, that's fair game."

"Shouldn't they be, like..." Annabelle shrugged. "Private?"

"You think a bounty out on the street's gonna come willingly with you into an enclosed space to fight? Just so you don't embarrass yourself? No, Lamar. That's not how it works. It's an open building during your class period. Show up and watch your friends if you want. Or don't show up at all. Just know I'm not going easy on any of you. You've learned enough by now to handle it."

The seniors turned toward their neighbors with wide eyes. Amanda let out a massive sigh of relief.

I'm so glad we're not actually fighting today. One good thing going for me.

Petrov scowled and snapped his fingers before pointing at the door. "Find your name. Remember your date. Then get out."

The class shuffled forward as one, weaving around Petrov standing squarely in the center of the room and giving him plenty of space. Then they crowded around the giant laminated poster tacked to his office door with nothing but a list of their names and two dates beside each.

"Aw, man…" Corey groaned and scratched the side of his hairy face. "I have to do this *tomorrow?*"

Tommy nudged him in the ribs. "Wednesday, dude. We don't have this class tomorrow."

"That's even worse. Now I have *two* whole days to think about it."

Nobody stayed very long in front of the list once they'd found their names, and the training building quickly cleared out. Amanda found her name and her preordained sparring sessions with Petrov—the first week of September and the first week of November.

At least I have more time to get ready, I guess. Not like anyone can ever be ready for fighting an angry bald teacher who enjoys throwing kids down onto the mat.

Petrov didn't say another word as the last of the seniors hurried out of the building to collect their bags. Amanda was among the last, but her friends were waiting for her when she emerged.

"That was definitely not what I expected." Grace handed Amanda her backpack. "But at least we all get a break today."

"Thanks." Amanda slung the strap over her shoulder and cursed herself for filling it with her supplies for every single class.

"Yeah, *especially* you, shifter girl." Summer nudged her friend in the ribs. "Guess you're gonna make it to lunch after all."

Grace clicked her tongue. "I should've taken that bet."

"Can you guys *believe* he would do something like this?" Blake Lively came up beside them, her usually meek demeanor replaced now with an alarming grin. "Sparring with Petrov one-one-one?"

Summer looked her up and down. "I gotta admit I'm seriously creeped out by how happy you look right now."

"Because it's *awesome*." The mousy witch clutched her book bag to her chest and bopped along as the senior class wandered off with almost a full two and a half hours of free time before lunch. "Hey, what do *you* guys think we're doing next semester? That was a pretty weird hint to make and not say anything about it, right?"

"Super weird." Grace nodded. "Not for Petrov, though."

"Right. I heard Tommy and Evan and the other guys talking about what it could be. 'Getting to the good stuff,' right? They think Petrov's keeping some kind of monster locked up on the grounds that we'll have to fight. Or maybe like some giant, angry, scary dude we have to bring down on our own."

Jackson looked Blake up and down and shook his head. "You're way too excited."

She ignored him completely. "Seriously, what do you guys think?"

"You taking a poll or something?" Summer asked.

"Hey, good idea."

"I have a better idea. Make it a bet."

"A what?"

The witch snorted. "You know, have all the seniors put down what they think it is and bet on it. Winner gets the whole pot when we find out."

"Wow." Blake widened her eyes. "That's fun."

"So that's your new obsession, huh?" Grace flashed a playful smile at Summer. "Betting?"

"Sure. Why not?"

"It's better than explosions."

"Hey, a witch can have more than one obsession, thank you very much. I'm not giving anything up here. Just…expanding my horizons."

Blake ignored the conversation completely and sidled up to Amanda. "So, what do *you* think, Amanda?"

"I think it's impossible to guess what Petrov's gonna do. And probably bad for your health."

Alex snorted. "Knowing him, he'll probably throw us into the swamp and declare a battle royale. Gladiator-style."

Blake squealed. "Oh my God. That's the best one yet. Yes!"

Amanda and Summer exchanged a glance, then burst out laughing.

CHAPTER ELEVEN

Their last class of the day was Augmented Tech with Mr. LeFor, and his overview of the rest of the year made the current status for seniors a running theme.

"You're basically on your own this year." The redhead teacher walked between the high tables in the workshop and dropped sheets of paper in front of every student. "This will start you out with what you need, but beyond that, building your work kit is a solo project you'll have to figure out on your own."

"A work kit?" Mark asked. "Like, a suitcase?"

Some of the boys around him snickered.

LeFor shot him a scathing glance and kept passing out papers. "You'll be building tech kits this year. Everything on this list will be part of those kits. Now, they may or may not be required for bounty hunters across the board, depending on which avenue you take when you graduate and what kind of professional you want to be. *But* a professional is always prepared. I believe every one of the items on this list is essential to have on you at all times. You never know what you'll have to come up with at the last second or what you'll have around you to work with."

Amanda slid her paper toward her and peered down at the two full columns stretching from top to bottom. "Holy crap," she muttered. "This is…a lot."

"Yes, Miss Coulier. It's an extensive list. That's only the beginning." LeFor spun beside the last table and headed back toward his desk surrounded by shelves of labeled tech gear. "Next week, we'll take a trip to the kemana during class. The Academy budget has allowed for each of you to buy everything on this list, plus a few extra items. Each of you needs to pick *two* other devices or gear you want to keep on you with your kit. No more, no less. We'll pick up those supplies for you to build the entire kit here during the semester."

"*Anything* we want?" Jack raised his eyebrows.

"No weapons, Mr. Perlin. And they have to be approved. So I want each of you to draw up a list of what you think you might need *in addition* to what's already on the list I gave you. That includes a write-up of each component, why it's necessary, what you plan to engineer during class, and how you'll use it in your career to be prepared for as many different scenarios as you can imagine. I expect those on my desk by the end of the day Friday so I can approve them all over the weekend."

"Wait." Jasmine shook her head. "That's like…an entire report in one week."

"Yes, it is. You didn't spend the last three years at this school not knowing how to write up reports. It shouldn't be that hard."

"I don't get why we need all this stuff anyway." Brandon ran a hand through his hair. Flakes of ice crystals fell from his head and tinkled across the worktable in front of him. "If we're getting jobs right after we graduate, what's the point?"

LeFor folded his arms and leaned back against the edge of his desk. "I honestly thought you all knew this by now, but I guess you need a little reminder. Life isn't a *007* movie, Mr. Everly. You won't have all the gadgets laid out for you to start playing with once you show up at your first job.

"This is about independence, self-sufficiency, and the ability to improve upon whatever you have around you at any given time. If you don't have a kit, *how the hell are you supposed to do any of that?*"

By the time the teacher finished his tirade, he was shouting at them. The entire senior class stared back in complete silence.

Jeeze, he's really touchy about his tech kits.

"That wasn't a rhetorical question!" LeFor barked.

"I don't know," Brandon muttered. "No clue. I was just wondering."

Blinking quickly, LeFor cleared his throat and stepped away from his desk again. "I suggest you start wondering about what you might need and the components you'll be shopping for next week. So get to work."

He slumped into the chair behind his desk and opened a clunky laptop to start typing something.

The seniors muttered to each other, asking what else they could need and how they were supposed to know what it was.

Grace leaned across the table toward Amanda and whispered, "Have any ideas?"

"Not yet."

"Okay, well..." The blonde witch looked over her shoulder at LeFor, but the teacher apparently wasn't paying attention to his class. "If you come up with more than two, let me know? I don't even understand the assignment."

Summer snorted. "Maybe you should build yourself a tiny computer that comes up with new ideas for you."

"Shut up."

Amanda fought back a laugh and studied the ridiculously long list of "kit gadgets."

I can probably come up with a million ideas. Still have the crossbow they made me for my birthday. Maybe I'll take a few pages out of Johnny's book and make explosive tips.

She glanced across the table to see Summer sitting back in her chair with her arms folded and her eyes closed.

And keep it completely secret from Summer until it's time for us to turn in this project.

Grace annoyed everybody over dinner that night by asking what they were planning to add to their tech kits, but no one had an answer. That only made her storm away from the table in a huff so she could race to the library and start looking up ideas on her own.

Amanda could hardly keep her eyes open at that point, so she finished her dinner as quickly as possible and grabbed her backpack.

I need a shower and twenty-four hours of sleep. Guess I'll have to settle for ten.

"Yeah, go sleep it off, shifter girl," Summer called after her. "You look dead already."

"Hey, thanks a lot." She turned to make sure the witch saw her eye-roll as Alex and Jackson chuckled.

"You don't look dead."

Amanda whirled around and found Matt standing right behind her with what had to be a plate of second helpings. "What?"

He flashed her that carelessly crooked smile and leaned slightly toward her. "Trust me. I'm feeling it too. Next time, we should start earlier."

"Next time." She swallowed and grabbed the straps of her backpack so she had something to do with her hands.

"I don't think—"

"And on the weekend." Matt raised his eyebrows. "Guess I got a little carried away on my first night back, but this is way too rough. So let me know."

"I..."

The shifter boy flashed her another grin, then stepped past her to head toward his table of other senior boys and a few juniors.

Blinking furiously, Amanda stalked past the kitchens and turned to head for the girls' dorm.

A new year, and I can already feel every single girl glaring at me behind my back. He should quit talking to me at all where anyone can see.

Still, a small smile bloomed on her lips when she thought about their run. When she reached the entrance to the dorms, she shook her head and growled at herself.

Nope. No next time. I can't keep running around in the swamp with another shifter when I have no free time.

That last part wasn't exactly true because Amanda still had no idea when the Coalition would call her in for another assignment or if they even would. The frustration that brought swirled over and over in her head as she took a shower with the water turned up as hot as she could handle, hoping it would relax her enough to match how exhausted she was.

Still, when she returned to her room, she couldn't keep herself from snatching up her Coalition phone and checking for new messages.

Nothing.

Great. Not a word all summer. Now I don't even know if I have *an internship, and I can't make plans unless somebody tells me something.*

Dressed in a tank top and shorts, Amanda climbed into her bed, sunlight still streaming through the blinds on the window, and pulled up a new text to Fiona.

I know I'm supposed to wait until someone reaches out, but this is driving me nuts. Am I still on with the Coalition?

For the next fifteen minutes, she tried to keep her eyes open in case Fiona decided for once to respond to a text. Amanda's eyelids drooped, the words she'd typed blurred on the screen, and she passed out without crawling under the covers and with school contraband toppling out of her hand. She was already out by the time it hit the floor.

CHAPTER TWELVE

The next morning started a million times better, and Amanda was back to her usual self. Which was a good thing because she couldn't have handled the weirdness of her classes that day if she'd still been asleep on her feet.

After breakfast, they headed into the main building to start their day with History of Oriceran. Ralthorn stood behind her desk with a pert smile as the seniors filtered into the class and grabbed their seats. She waited for at least five minutes of complete silence and students coughing and shifting around in their chairs before she finally began the day's lesson.

"Things are a little different for you this year if you hadn't already picked up the trend from your classes yesterday. You have more freedom, which also means you have more responsibility. That's what we'll be covering in my class this year. *Recent* Oriceran history, specifically when it comes to the industry most if not all of you will be entering after graduation."

"Wait, isn't Glasket teaching the dumb life skills stuff?" Evan asked.

"Mr. Hutchinson, if you're already calling the very important aspects of being an adult *dumb*, I'd venture to say you won't make it very far off Academy grounds. Yes, Dean Glasket will be guiding you through those extracurricular courses. *This* senior-level class is effectively 'How to Be A Bounty Hunter In Today's Society.'"

Summer groaned and mashed her hand against one cheek. "Super exciting."

Ralthorn ignored her and pointed at the pile of textbooks on her desk. "That includes learning about the *modern* bounty hunters and following the example of those who paved the way after the reveal of magic. You also need to know the laws that will apply to everything you do in your budding career. So I suppose, in a way, we could call this senior-level class a mix of history, economics, state and federal law, and a unique study of the best in your field. Fine. Maybe even throw a little sociology in there too."

Jackson leaned toward Alex sitting beside him and muttered, "Dude, what is she *talking* about?"

"I don't even think *she* knows."

"In a little bit, you'll come up here to grab a textbook and read chapters one and two. Whatever you don't get through before the end of class, I expect you to finish the reading before you return on Wednesday. First, we—sit down, Mr. Brunsen. I said in a little bit."

Tommy plopped back into his seat with a lazy smile and shrugged.

"Before you start the in-class reading," Ralthorn continued, "I want to go over this semester's overarching assignment with you. This is a self-directed research project within these parameters. I'll start by saying you most likely won't find any books in the school library about these specific individuals. You'll have to dig a little deeper. I believe the Everglades kemana has what's considered an extensive array of texts on the subject. Seeing as there's really nothing else to compare it to."

The history teacher tapped another thin stack of loose papers on her desk. "When you come up here to get your textbooks, you'll also grab one of these sheets. This is a list of the most prominent and well-known magical bounty hunters over the last fifty years.

"You'll pick one this semester and one next semester. I expect a total of no less than twenty pages in a thoughtful, well-organized, *coherent* presentation about the contributions these magicals have made to our world since magic's reveal.

"On Wednesday, you'll receive a rubric for all the elements your research papers *must* have to pass your final year. You might find you have an interest in certain fields you may never have considered without learning about these bounty hunters' lives."

Sighs and muffled groans filled the room. Summer slumped in her chair and tipped her head back, her arms dangling at her sides. "This is torture."

"This, Miss Flannerty, is knowledge and preparation. Which all of you absolutely need if you're going to succeed after graduation." Ralthorn blinked quickly, shoved her glasses back up the bridge of her nose, then clapped her hands. "Okay, *now* it's time to come up here and grab your materials. Let's go."

The dejected senior class shuffled forward in a mess of a line, none of them looking forward to reading textbooks on modern bounty hunters, economics, law, and sociology all smashed into one. Amanda almost laughed when she grabbed a textbook and read the title: *The Modern-Day Marshall: An Exploration of the Magical Law Enforcement In the Twenty-First Century* by Bernice Ralthorn, Ph.D.

Ph.D. in what? Glasket already told us there aren't any magical colleges.

She whisked a sheet of paper off the stack, then hurried back to her seat and watched her friends return to theirs.

"Look at this." Summer flicked the cover of her textbook and snorted. "I mean, how caught up in yourself can you get?"

"Hey, maybe you should say it a little louder." Grace slid into her seat and glanced at Ralthorn, who was already deep into reading something and completely oblivious to the conversations filling her classroom. "You know, so she hears you."

"Listen, Blondie. If she cared what any of *us* thought, she wouldn't be teaching her own textbook in class and making it required reading."

"I think it's pretty cool." Grace shrugged. "I mean, it has to take a lot of time and effort to put together something like this. Not to mention the research."

"She sure as hell better not expect a textbook out of me." Summer slapped her list of bounty hunters down on top of the book, skimmed the few dozen names, and barked out a laugh. "No shit."

"Language, Miss Flannerty." Ralthorn didn't look up from her book. "You should all be reading right now."

"Hey, shifter girl." Summer swung her arm out behind her and smacked the top of Amanda's desk. "Hey. Did you see this list?"

"Not yet. Why?"

"Tell me I'm not hallucinating."

Frowning, Amanda looked over the names and didn't recognize any of them until one name stuck out like a neon sign.

No way. She put Johnny on the list.

She fought back another laugh and kept reading.

Johnny Walker. James Brownstone. Leira Berens. Jamal Dupree.

Amanda raised her hand. "Ms. Ralthorn?"

"Yes."

"Are these names arranged in any kind of order? Like by how famous they are or their track record or anything like that?"

Ralthorn's gaze flickered up from her book and landed on the shifter girl over the top rim of her reading glasses. "That's something to consider when choosing your report subjects."

"Yeah, but if we know first—"

"I'm saying you'll have to find that out on your own, Miss

Coulier. That's what research is." The teacher returned her attention to her book and left no room for more argument.

Amanda dropped both hands into her lap and shook her head. "Thanks for the help."

"I'm not crazy, right?" Summer turned in her seat again and grinned. "You see who's on there?"

"Yeah. And?"

"I mean, that's an instant A for you right there, shifter girl. Write up a report on the dwarf. Man, the look on his face when he finds out his name's on a list with all these other chumps in a *history* class—"

"Shh." Grace shot the other witch a scathing glance. "Some of us are trying to read. You know, like we're supposed to."

"Yeah, I'm not touching this." Summer slid the textbook away from her and folded her arms. "You get why it's funny, though, right?"

"I have no idea what you're talking about."

"Shifter girl can tell you."

Grace turned and raised her eyebrows at Amanda. "Just say it so I can get back to reading."

Pressing her lips together, Amanda pointed at the paper. "Johnny's on the list."

"And?"

"That's it."

The blonde witch rolled her eyes and turned back around. "I need to change my seat."

Summer spun nearly all the way around in her chair this time and hooked her arms over the back. "You're gonna do it, right?"

"What, write a report on Johnny?" Amanda huffed out a laugh. "Kinda sounds like writing a biography, and that's just weird."

"Oh, come on. You'd kill it."

"No. I'm not doing research and writing a bounty-hunter report on my—on Johnny. I'll find someone else."

"Thank you," Grace whispered.

Summer leaned away from the blonde witch beside her and looked Grace up and down. "For what? You're supposed to be reading."

Holding her place with a finger digging down into the page, Grace looked up and replied curtly, "I don't know about Ralthorn, but I'd consider that cheating. Amanda's got enough integrity not to take the easy way out of this assignment. Which I appreciate. Hence the thank you."

Amanda leaned forward over her desk. "I'm pretty sure it would be *harder* to write about Johnny than any—"

"It's the principle of it, okay? That's what I'm talking about." Grace hunched over her textbook and sighed. "Now please, stop talking so I can read."

Summer made a face at her, then mimed straightening a tie and turned in her chair.

Amanda stared at the cover of Ms. Ralthorn's latest publication, then bit her lip as she opened to the first page.

There's no way this is more exciting than her lectures. At least we don't have to listen to her read it out loud.

Ralthorn's textbook did end up putting several students to sleep, and they were all rudely awakened by the obnoxious alarm at the end of class. Their history teacher didn't bother to wish them luck or offer any other assignments as the seniors scrambled to get out of the room and head to their second class of the day.

With her backpack heavier than ever and bulging under the weight of the new textbook, Amanda clutched the straps against her shoulders and wound her way through the sea of other students swarming through the main building. Senior-level Alchemy was next in yet another advanced classroom down the west wing.

I'll be really surprised if Zimmer doesn't give us a DIY outline for the year too.

As it turned out, Amanda wasn't surprised at all.

Zimmer stood beside her desk as the seniors filed in, one boot propped up on a plastic tote and her arms folded. Her gaze flickered back and forth across the room, sizing up the energy of her oldest students and raising an eyebrow when anyone looked at her.

At least that part hasn't changed.

Amanda slid into a chair at the third row of long black tables stretching across the room, watching Zimmer intently and waiting for the Wood Elf's next startling demonstration that usually started the first class of every semester. Her attention, however, was immediately diverted when another student brushed past her and dropped into the chair on her left.

She smelled Matt right there beside her before she even turned to look at him.

Staring at Zimmer, he leaned toward her and muttered, "I heard she blows things up on the first day of the year. Does she, or is Evan a moron?"

A tiny smile flickered at the corner of her mouth. Amanda might have laughed if she wasn't so caught off-guard by the shifter boy sitting next to her in any class at all. "She usually does, yeah. Not sure what that says about Evan."

Matt chuckled and pulled a notebook out of his backpack. "Yeah, he might still be a moron."

"Dude." Evan leaned forward on the other side of Matt and spread his arms. "I'm right here."

"Yeah, I know." Matt snickered when the other boy shoved him in the shoulder.

Then Mrs. Zimmer stepped off the plastic tote and turned to face her class head-on. "Here's the deal. You've made it through the last three years without blowing yourselves up, seriously maiming your classmates, or razing this school to the ground."

Summer turned at the table in front of Amanda, grinned, and pumped a fist in the air.

The teacher cleared her throat. "*Most* of you, anyway. In my class, making it through without digging yourselves an even deeper hole is a plus. I assume you're ready to start handling your projects without needing a babysitter, so don't prove me wrong."

She grabbed a stack of plain white folders off her desk and nestled them in one arm before walking down the first row of tables. A folder *slapped* down onto the table in front of each student.

"Inside the folder you're getting is a manufactured scenario. A problem to be solved and the obstacles to solving it. Every folder has a different writeup. No two are the same. This semester, you'll focus on formulating and constructing an alchemical solution to these problems within the scenario's given parameters."

Zimmer turned to walk down the next row of tables. "All on your own. No teams this year. No partners. And no trading."

Jack looked up from his folder. "You don't even know which ones you gave us."

The teacher stopped and looked over her shoulder at him with a raised eyebrow. "There's no possible way for you to know that, Mr. Perlin. If you try to get smart and shop around for someone else's assignment, I *will* know."

He frowned and leaned away from her before she carried on with distributing the folders. "That's creepy."

"This is not a group effort, and I can't emphasize that enough. You might be on a team when you graduate and move on to your new roles as employed adults who *contribute* to society. However, nobody's looking for bounty hunters who can play nice on a team without being able to think outside the box on their own. When the scouts show up next semester, they'll be looking for what makes you stand out. What makes you *different*."

Zimmer turned to walk down the final table, glancing at each of her students without any expression whatsoever. "Time to focus on that. If you can't figure it out, you'll have a hard time convincing an employer you're worth the effort."

"Wow," Jasmine McVar muttered.

Beside her, Annabelle nodded and whispered, "Yeah, that was harsh."

Zimmer returned to the front of the room and took another long moment to survey the class. "The first stage is writing up your solution, including a list of the materials you think you might need. Extra points if you get it right on the first try. If not, you'll repeat the process until either you *do* get it right or the semester ends. Whichever comes first. I don't have to tell you how that reflects on your grade this year if you take too long."

"So we have to write it all down?"

"This isn't a writing class, Miss Price. Once your write-up is complete, and you've given me a list of alchemical reagents and agents I can in good conscience approve, you'll be testing out your solutions in class. I'm grading this assignment on timing, ingenuity, and an ability to adapt to whatever may or may not go wrong. Any questions?"

Summer jerked her chin up at the teacher. "Yeah, when are you gonna show us something cool?"

Zimmer's face remained expressionless. "You're seniors now, Miss Flannerty. 'Something cool' is no longer the priority. if you haven't found alchemy to be exciting enough as it is, a demonstration hardly matters at this point."

She looked up at the rest of the class and nodded. "For the rest of the semester, I suggest you use this class period to work specifically on your projects. However, you'll only join me here for the first class of every month so I can check on your progress.

"In the meantime, consider my class period open office hours. No, I'm not here to help you come up with the solutions. But I *will* be here once you finish your writeups and will make myself available to help you collect your materials when you're ready to test out your theories. So I'll see you next month."

She gestured toward the classroom door with a sweep of her hand as she lowered herself into the giant office chair behind her desk.

For a moment, the class froze where they were, waiting for Zimmer to tell them she was joking. She didn't.

"So…you're not gonna—"

"I wasn't only speaking to Miss Flannerty, Mr. Baker. This year, you're doing your own demonstrations."

The seniors collected their things and rose from their seats, casting wary glances at their teacher. The Wood Elf watched them all with narrowed eyes, her arms folded, and didn't say another word.

"Man. Kinda disappointing." Matt slipped his notebook into his backpack and sighed. "I thought I was gonna see alchemy in action."

"Because you weren't here first semester last year." Amanda nodded. "I forgot about that."

"So it feels like I've been here forever, huh?"

"That's not what I meant."

He grinned at her and stood. "Okay."

Evan shoved him forward from behind, and a group of boys converged around the shifter before they burst into the hall, joking around with each other at obnoxiously loud volumes.

"This blows." Summer followed Amanda through the door, grunting in frustration. "We have to do all this crap on our own, and she can't even fix a few things together to at least make it *seem* awesome."

Amanda smirked. "You really need somebody to *show* you how to blow something up?"

"Just because I know how doesn't mean I don't like watching someone else do it now and then. I would've taken notes."

CHAPTER THIRTEEN

"This is so cool." Grace absently bit into her sandwich at lunch and flipped through the pages of her Alchemy assignment. "Definitely the best thing we're doing this year."

"What did you get?" Jackson asked, standing to lean over the table and get a better look.

She slapped the folder shut and glared at him. "It's mine."

"Whoa. Okay." He sat back down again and snickered. "She didn't say we couldn't *look* at someone else's...scenario."

"Yeah, well, we're supposed to be doing all this on our own, and knowing you, you'll accidentally come up with some kind of solution to *my* assignment just by saying something completely unrelated."

"Seriously? You really think I'm that good?"

Grace shrugged and slid her folder to the side to replace it with her plate. "Only when you're not trying."

Jackson's shoulders slumped. "Great."

"So what happens if someone accidentally finds your solution *without* looking at your special file?" Summer asked. "You gonna run to Zimmer and tell her to scrap the whole thing?"

"That's ridiculous. Though *technically,* if I didn't come up with the idea on my own, that would count as cheating anyway."

The rainbow-haired witch snorted and shook her head. "Figures."

Grace tried to hold back a smile and failed. "I don't think that'll happen. I already have so many ideas for this. I am *so* glad we finally get to work on all these projects *alone.* No more team efforts."

Amanda swallowed her bite of apple and looked her friend up and down. "Because we're the worst partners, or…"

"No. Because I finally get a chance to really *shine.*" The blonde witch's face lit up with an ecstatic grin. "To really show everyone what I can do. All on my own. Without having to share the credit for it. You heard what Zimmer said. Nobody's looking for bounty hunters who can play nice on a team."

Alex pointed his sandwich at her. "Yeah, 'without being able to think outside the box.' That was the other part."

"Whatever. I can think outside the box *and* do it all on my own."

The Wood Elf shrugged and looked back down at his sandwich. "Just more homework, if you ask me."

"Right there with you, Woody." Summer pointed at him. "Homework without all the cool stuff like watching Zimmer pour some crap on a thing and making it explode."

He snorted and kept eating.

"I can't do this." Jackson shook his head, staring with wide eyes at the table. "I'm done."

Amanda chuckled. "What do you mean?"

"No, I mean it, Coulier. I'm gonna fail."

"Dude." Alex looked him up and down. "You're getting intense—"

"Because I'm intensely screwed!" Jackson pounded a fist on the table and startled himself. "We have to do all this crap *on our own.* With no help. No talking to anybody else. And we have to 'use our skill sets' to make it happen? What does that even mean?"

"It means doing what you're good at to—"

"I know what it means, Grace," he snapped. "I don't have any skills. Not the real ones. Like, the only thing I can do is summon lights. That's it."

"That's not—"

"Are you kidding me? Freaking *lights*?" Jackson spread his arms and smacked Alex's shoulder in the process. The Wood Elf shrugged away with a frown, but Jackson didn't even notice.

"I'm completely useless. Then I'm gonna fail out of this school, and I won't graduate, and I won't have a job, and I'll just be...I'll be...that *guy* who couldn't finish bounty hunter school and now lives in all the abandoned tunnels under L.A. because he can't do *anything*!"

"Whoa, okay." Amanda half-stood. "Maybe drink some water."

"I'm so screwed. So freaking..." The wizard kept shaking his head, staring at the table.

Summer lifted a finger. "Do we have, like, some kind of mental-breakdown police on campus or something?"

Amanda flashed her a disapproving frown and shook her head. "Jackson, you're gonna be fine."

"Yeah. Easy for you to say. You have everything all figured out, Coulier. You live with a bounty hunter, you already have a job, and apparently, everyone's totally cool with you leaving for almost a whole semester. *I* can't do that."

"I don't have everything figured out—"

"At least you can *do* something!"

"Dude," Alex muttered and dropped his sandwich onto his plate.

"Compared to everyone else here, I'm dead weight," Jackson shouted. "I'm never gonna be able to handle all this before the semester's over. I'm gonna fail. I'm gonna get kicked out with nowhere to go. Then I'm gonna die."

In the blink of an eye, Alex turned away from his food and shoved the wizard roughly with both hands. Jackson toppled backward off the bench and *thumped* to the ground with a grunt.

With wide eyes, he turned his head to stare up at Alex and swallowed. "What—"

"Get it together, man." The Wood Elf stared down at him. "Or at least get it out of your system somewhere else, if that's what you gotta do."

"Out of my system?"

"If you were completely useless, they would've kicked you out a long time ago." Alex turned back toward the table, picked up his sandwich, and took a large bite.

"Right there." Summer pointed at him. "Woody's our mental-breakdown police."

Amanda and Grace shared a surprised look before the shifter girl peered over the other side of the table. "Are you okay?"

"Actually..." Jackson pushed himself up off his back and grabbed the edge of the bench with both hands. "I think I feel better."

"Yep." Summer grinned at Alex. "You know what you should do? Start charging people for private sessions. Hell, *I'd* pay for shove therapy."

Grace rolled her eyes. "Instead of paying for people to let you shove *them*? Seriously?"

"Blondie, I can do that whenever I want. Takes a special kinda something to push *me* around."

Alex gave her a crooked smile and lowered his sandwich from his face. "Hey, thanks."

Summer froze, wrinkled her nose, then quickly looked away. "Yeah, whatever. I'm just saying."

Jackson stood, stepped over the bench to sit, and let out a long, slow sigh. "Okay. I guess that's over."

"As in, you're not freaking out anymore?" Amanda asked. "Because it's okay if you're worried about—"

"Nah, I'm fine. Sorry about that, guys." He nudged Alex. "Thanks, dude. I needed that."

"All good." They bumped fists and went right back to their lunches.

Grace shook her head. "I don't get it. That's a guy thing, right? It *has* to be a guy thing."

Alex shrugged. "It works. That's all I know."

She stared at them, then opened her folder again and returned to reading. "You do you, I guess."

Amanda couldn't help but watch Jackson a little longer.

I've never seen him freak out like that before. Or maybe he has and I always missed it.

He looked up at her briefly to give her a self-conscious smile, and another deep flush crawled quickly up the sides of his neck to his ears. "Didn't mean to freak out on you like that, Coulier."

"That's okay. I didn't think it had anything to do with me." She wrinkled her nose. "Unless it does..."

"Nope. No way. Just my issues that needed a good beating. We're good." Jackson gave her a sheepish thumbs-up before snatching up his water and draining the whole thing at once. Then he cleared his throat. "How's the whole internship going, anyway?"

"Oh. Um...fine, I guess. Nothing going on right now, so I'm staying on campus." Amanda shrugged. "Never know when something might pop up, though."

"Right. Yeah. Cool." He dropped his gaze to his plate and shoveled mac 'n cheese into his mouth.

Everyone but Summer went back to focusing on their food—or in Grace's case, food and the Alchemy assignment—but Summer didn't have to say anything. Amanda felt her friend's stare crawling along the side of her face, and she gave the witch a sidelong glance. "What?"

"Just trying to picture you in that *internship*, shifter girl."

"Okay, well, you can picture it without staring at me, right?"

Summer snorted out a laugh and went back to eating too.

Yeah, I know I haven't told anyone else I might or might not still be on with the Coalition. Internship or paid job or anything else. Doesn't mean she has to stare at me like that.

Her hand reflexively went to her back pocket, and she froze. The Coalition phone wasn't there.

Crap. That was so stupid*!*

"Hey." Grace frowned at her. "What's—"

"I gotta go." Amanda spun on the bench, snatched up her backpack, and turned only to grab a handful of grapes off her plate before shoving them all into her mouth. Then she grabbed the plate too and headed for the trashcan.

"Everything okay?"

"Yep." Her plate clanged into the empty bus bin. "I just…had an idea. For my project. Gotta look into it."

"Huh." Grace cocked her head as the shifter girl broke into a jog. "That's usually *my* thing."

"What, you mean running away from everyone else to go do homework?" Summer asked.

"Yeah. Do *you* know what's going on with her?"

"Oh, sure." Summer tossed her hands in the air and rolled her eyes. "You just gave that whole speech about *principles,* and now you're asking me if I know what the shifter girl's big ideas are? How the hell does that work?"

Alex laughed through his mouthful and ended up choking on his sandwich. Jackson didn't waste any time bringing the side of his fist down into the Wood Elf's back before Alex finally brushed him off. "Dude, I got it."

"Hey, no worries. Just trying to return the favor."

Alex chugged his water and slammed the cup back down on the table. "Not even close to the same thing."

Grace stared at the guys but spoke to Summer. "I'm not trying to figure out what her idea is. She's acting a little weird."

"Yeah, I noticed too." Jackson nodded. "Hey, you spent all summer with her. What's really going on?"

Summer shot both hands up in front of her. "I plead the Fifth."

"So you *do* know what's going on."

"Please. It's not like we stayed up all night together swapping stories and painting each other's nails."

Grace raised an eyebrow. "You know what pleading the Fifth actually means, right?"

"Duh. But you can be totally clueless and still use it."

Jackson scrunched up his face. "Because you...*want* everyone to think you know something?"

"It's way more fun like that, Romeo. Trust me."

CHAPTER FOURTEEN

Amanda barreled into her dorm room and threw her backpack against the wall. Then she headed straight for her bed and swiped her hands across the covers, under the pillow, and the sheets.

"Crap. Where is it?" She looked in the bedside table drawer and one more time under her pillow before dropping to her knees. "I had it last night, and now this stupid..."

There was her Coalition phone, right under the bed. With a massive sigh of relief, she got down on her stomach to swipe the device toward her. She didn't bother to get up before checking her messages.

Nothing.

"Oh, jeeze." Drawing a deep breath, she pushed herself up to sit against the edge of the bed, then went through her texts one more time to make sure she'd sent the one to Fiona.

Of course, I did. And of course, she didn't get back to me.

For a moment, she considered calling the anonymous hotline at Omega Industries that was apparently answered by whoever happened to be closest to the phone at the time. The number was right there.

No. That would look desperate. I'm not desperate. I think.

Still, it was tough to put the phone down and wipe her expectation of a call or text or any kind of communication from the Coalition out of her mind.

It's all this talk about jobs when we graduate. That's why I'm thinking about this. Last year, I would've been totally happy not thinking about it at all.

Her fingers poised over the touch screen as a million possible questions raced through her mind—what would and wouldn't get Fiona's attention enough to make the woman respond.

"Nope. No. Won't help." She opened the nightstand drawer and dropped the phone into it before sliding it shut again.

If they're gonna keep jerking me around like this, they can't still expect me to be on call my entire senior year. If I actually have the job, it won't matter. Let it go.

Amanda closed her eyes and rested her head against the edge of the mattress, drawing deep breath after deep breath.

She hadn't intended to draw out her ghost-wolf, but apparently, her magic had plans of its own.

In an instant, she was padding forward across her room on four smoky white paws and passed instantly through the door into the hall.

What am I doing? Walking around like this in the middle of the day where anyone could see me? I can't just—

She stopped when a strange, icy tingle raced up her spine. Each hair of her ghost-wolf's hackles stood on end, and she felt every single one.

That's new.

Turning, she scanned the hallway and started to head for the back staircase before an incredibly strong scent overwhelmed her.

It was Matt Hardy's scent—definitely the smell of a shifter and definitely him, but with something else. Something that smelled a little like burning plastic and a lot like heavily concentrated magic.

No way is he in the girls' dorm right now. No way.

She sniffed the air and walked down the hall, trying to find the source of the scent and straining for any sound of movement in any of the rooms around or below her.

Everybody's still at lunch. Why do I smell—

The sudden and disorienting sensation of watching the walls, floors, and ceilings streak past her in a blur without the lurch in her gut that came with falling in a physical body was almost as nauseating. Amanda fully expected to be thrust right back into her body in her bedroom again, but she wasn't.

She and her ghost-wolf had fallen through two stories of the dorms and the round table in the first-floor common room directly below where she'd been upstairs. With no explanation.

Also new.

Lifting her snout, she sniffed the underside of the table, paused to make sure the common room was empty, then padded uneasily across the room toward the back door. Walking *through* the closed door wasn't any harder than usual, but the second her ghostly paws moved across the grass behind the dorm building, the scent she'd caught upstairs hit her with an overwhelming intensity.

Okay, so he's outside. What is *that?*

The burnt-plastic smell reeked now, and while it wouldn't be hard to follow the trail, Amanda still paused.

I guess there's a chance he could've gotten sprayed by a skunk. Kinda smells like that at first.

She sniffed the air again and stood perfectly still in the shadow of the building. Almost two hundred voices from the outdoor cafeteria echoed across the campus toward her, bouncing off the brick walls of the kitchens and both dorm buildings. Nobody screamed in disgust and agony, which would have been perfectly understandable if a skunk had sprayed them.

No other creatures stirred in the ferns and reeds at the water's edge, and if a critter that had gotten too close to a shifter boy had been racing across the open campus grounds to take cover, Amanda and her ghost-wolf definitely would have noticed.

Two blackbirds swooped low from the roof of the girls' dorm, their wings fluttering so close to her face she could *almost* feel the gusts of air left in their wake.

But I didn't. So how did I feel whatever that was upstairs?

Another intensely strong whiff of Matt-plus-plastic-magic hit with her full force. All thought of anything else—the students in the outdoor cafeteria, anyone else walking around campus, or even where her teachers were in the middle of the day—disappeared.

Her ghost-wolf sniffed diligently and broke into a trot across the grass, heading north across campus toward the boys' dorm. The weird smell only grew stronger, and by the time she passed the back of the building, Amanda was sure the stink would make her physical body physically sick. Even if it didn't blast her back into her room first.

Then a blaze of red light in the corner of her eye made her stop, and she turned to see the source of it.

Matt sat with his back against the side of the building, his knees drawn up toward him and his forearms resting on them. His hands were open and facing each other, and between them pulsed a flickering red glow of crackling magic. It swirled in a loosely round shape, passing back and forth between his palms and twisting down his wrists.

The smell of burning plastic was almost unbearable.

Amanda couldn't look away from the sight of another shifter—a boy she'd seen as a wolf and had gone for a run with two nights ago—casting real, non-shifter magic right in front of her.

It was surprising enough to have heard it from Calsgrave in the greenhouse. But seeing it somehow felt like a massive slap to the face, and she had no idea why.

Matt sniffed the air, then turned his head as if he expected to see someone walking on two legs around the back of the boys' dorm at any second. Instead, he saw a translucent wolf of shimmering white smoke standing there with her head lowered between her shoulders.

Amanda saw the same flare of red magic between the boy's hands now blazing behind his eyes too.

His lips curled into that crooked smile, and he cocked his head. "Whoa..."

The magic sputtered out between his palms, his eyes returned in an instant to their insanely bright blue, and he dropped his hands to the grass like he meant to get up. "How did you—"

Amanda gasped and fell over sideways on the floor beside her bed. It took her at least a minute to calm her breathing down again, and when she did, her arms shook as she pushed herself back up into a sitting position.

Matt was a shifter. He could do magic. That was the truth and accepted by everybody who knew about it, including the Academy faculty. Amanda herself could accept all those things too. After all, she'd been training with her magic since sophomore year and had gotten in with the shifter big leagues because of it.

But the *kind* of magic Matt had...

It was a type Amanda hadn't seen or heard anything about. Not from the grumbled tales of Johnny's exploits told around the dinner table. Not from Ralthorn's long and excruciatingly detailed accounts of Oriceran's magical races that had made their way to Earth so many hundreds of years ago. Not even in her top-secret work with the Coalition at the Canissphere and all the strange new variations of magic the divergent creature species possessed.

That kind of magic had made her ghost-wolf's hackles raise, and now it made the hair on the back of her human-form neck stand on end too.

"What the hell *is* he?"

Amanda scrambled to open the nightstand drawer and

fumbled inside until her fingers closed around the Coalition phone. After having to delete almost every single word because she'd spelled them all completely wrong the first time around, she finally finished the text to Fiona and practically stabbed the screen to send it.

Shifters with magic. Not the wolf kind. Red and burning plastic. Do you know?

It was a ridiculous text to send anybody. Knowing Fiona, the woman would most likely bring it up the next time they saw each other in person and ask if Amanda had been drunk or high when she'd sent it. It was all the shifter girl could manage to think of without completely losing her cool and diving into the dark tunnel of her thoughts that stretched deeper and darker by the second.

This can't be good. No way is this good. How could Glasket know what he can do and still let him come to school here?

She clenched the Coalition phone between both hands and stared at the floor in front of her.

Still, if a text like that didn't get Fiona's attention, nothing would.

That made her feel even worse because the only thing that made sense about what she'd seen and smelled of the boy's half-shifter magic—what she'd *felt* with her magic, and so far, it hadn't steered her wrong—was that Matt Hardy wasn't like the rest of the kids at the Academy. He was the only one here who'd shown up with an ability to cast dark magic, and that wasn't something the faculty taught here.

Which meant he'd learned it somewhere else, from someone else.

Like his parents.

For the rest of the day until dinner, Amanda sat in the same spot on the floor of her dorm room and waited for Fiona to send her *something*. Even a short, simple reply saying they'd talk about it later but not on the phone would have been better than what she got.

Absolutely nothing.

At 5:13 p.m., she gave up trying to will a message's magical appearance into her phone and chucked it back into the drawer before slamming it shut. Then she stood, smoothed her hair away from her face, and drew a deep breath. Her friends would worry if she didn't show up to eat.

Just play it cool. Don't freak out. There has to be an explanation for this.

Trying to convince herself was one more exercise in futility she could add to all the others under her belt.

"Stop." She vigorously shook her head to fling all the warring thoughts loose and stormed toward the door.

Glasket knows. Calsgrave knows. They wouldn't let him on campus grounds if they knew he used dark magic.

Her fingers closed around the doorknob, and her stomach sank into a dark pit somewhere in the vicinity of her toes.

Unless he cast light magic too and I'm the only one who caught him playing with something else.

Swallowing thickly, Amanda forced herself to leave her room and make her way down to the first floor. By the time she stepped outside into the muggy heat of mid-August, her breathing had at least slowed into something resembling calm normalcy. That didn't exactly mean her pulse shared the same agenda.

Crap. He'll hear that for sure. How does nobody know about this? Am I completely freaking out over nothing?

As she walked quickly toward the kitchen building and the outdoor cafeteria on the other side, she absently raised a hand to the back of her neck. The memory of feeling her ghost-wolf's hackles rising against a known threat—one her magic could identify all by itself, whether or not Amanda knew what it was—was almost more vivid than experiencing it the first time.

My magic doesn't lie. Not after everything I've been able to do over the last couple of years. What the hell am I supposed to do about it now?

The line in front of the banquet tables stretched toward the edge of the kitchens. The sound of the entire student body talking, laughing, joking around, and passing the time while they waited to plate their dinner made Amanda grit her teeth. Nobody knew. Nobody had any reason to suspect there was anything wrong on a campus that was supposed to be safe and completely secure.

"Coulier!" Jackson leaned out of the line and waved her forward. "Come on. We saved you a spot."

"Hey, no cutting."

The wizard frowned at the freshman half-elf standing behind him and pointed. "Normally, I'd say you're right. But don't tell *her* that. I mean, unless you're feeling super lucky today."

The freshman turned to look at Amanda, and one of his friends leaned toward him to whisper in his ear. His eyes widened, and he spun quickly back. "I'm good."

"Yeah, that's what I thought."

Amanda walked stiffly toward Jackson and her friends, all of whom stared at her as intensely as the gaggle of freshmen. Except the freshmen whispered to each other, repeating whatever ridiculous rumors they'd heard in the last few days about the Academy's first and only shifter student—until recently. Amanda's friends stared at her as if she'd walked out of the swamp covered in blood.

"Whoa." Jackson looked her up and down. "What happened?"

"I get it." Grace nodded and put a reassuring hand on the shifter girl's shoulder. "I feel the same way when a great idea turns out to be not so great. You'll figure it out."

Summer snorted. "Yeah. That's totally what happened." When

Amanda didn't say anything and stared blankly ahead at the kids in front of them, the witch's smile disappeared. "Seriously, though. You okay?"

"Sure." She couldn't look at any of her friends. "Just hungry."

"Yeah, but you get *hangry,*" Alex added. "Not herrified."

Grace frowned at him. "What?"

"Hungry and terrified. Obviously."

"I'm fine. Just... You know what? I'll feel better after I eat something." Finally, she tore her gaze away from the back of the junior boys' heads in front of her and turned toward her friends. "Promise."

When she grinned, all four of her friends let out matching cries of alarm and stepped away from her.

"Whoa, whoa, whoa." Jackson lifted both hands. "Take it easy."

"What?"

"Ha." Summer stepped toward her and started to reach out for Amanda's shoulder, then stopped and folded her arms instead. "You look like you're about to do one of those shifter things you told us about."

Grace took another sidestep away from the shifter girl and wouldn't stop sneaking quick, completely indiscreet glances.

"Yeah, like rip out somebody's throat," Alex whispered.

That wiped the attempted smile right off Amanda's face. "Maybe don't mention that kinda stuff right in the middle of the dinner line, huh?"

"Maybe don't show up looking like the dinner line *is* your dinner."

She rolled her shoulders back and darted glances at the kids walking away from the banquet tables to find their seats beneath the pavilion. So far, none of them were Matt.

"Sorry. I'm...distracted."

"Yeah, no shit." Summer scratched the side of her head and looked the shifter girl up and down before rolling her eyes. "You know, I'm kind of allergic to talking about someone else's issues.

Or anyone's issues. So I'm gonna say whatever this *distraction* is, you need to leave it somewhere else. Like, where the rest of us aren't."

"I said I'm sorry." Amanda pressed her lips together and met her best friend's gaze. "I'm trying."

"It's okay." Grace nodded vigorously and looked like she was trying hard to conjure a small smile. "Totally okay. We're all trying, right? You don't have to tell us anything if you don't want to. But if you do, we're here. Right, guys?" She looked at Summer and the guys, but none looked back at her or said a word. So she nudged Alex and Jackson in the shoulder because they were closest. "*Right?*"

"Yep." Alex nodded.

"She already knows that," Jackson added quickly. "We're always here. Whatever it is. As long you *never* smile at us like that again."

Grace stared at Summer and widened her eyes until the other witch jumped and pointed at herself. "We went over this. I'm allergic."

"Not to being a good friend."

"Okay, fine." Summer gestured toward Amanda. "You need to get something off your chest, yeah. I guess I'm down to hear it. If I'm around."

Grace closed her eyes and huffed out a frustrated grunt.

"Thanks, guys." Amanda nodded and couldn't look at her friends any longer than a few seconds at a time. "I appreciate it. I'm fine, okay? Nothing to talk about."

"Still." Grace shrugged. "Just in case."

"Yeah. Just in..." Amanda's gaze fell on Matt as he finally came into view, walking away from the banquet table. Her pulse shot up to a bajillion beats per second, and her mouth went suddenly dry. She didn't think it could get any worse until he stopped at the drink station to pour himself a glass of iced tea.

When he looked up, it was like he already knew where to

look. He met her gaze instantly, and his cheeks dimpled when he flashed her a smile and raised his chin. Only now, that smile and those dimples felt like incoming bombs instead of the noteworthy traits of a shifter boy she might have started to like.

"Case," Grace said.

"What?"

"Just in *case*. You never finished—what are you staring at?" The blonde witch looked over her shoulder and saw nothing but Academy students moving back and forth between the banquet tables and the covered pavilion. "Hey, maybe you should go see Nurse Aiken."

Summer narrowed her eyes. "Yeah, I don't think Nurse Aiken's got anything for what's wrong with her."

"Huh." Completely oblivious, Jackson scratched his head. "I had no idea that was a thing."

"What?"

"You know. Shifter-specific illness or whatever. Though you'd think a school nurse would've put two and two together by now and stocked up on stuff to handle that kind of... What? Why are you laughing at me like that?"

Grace's face contorted so much that she looked like she was in pain. Summer choked on a laugh, then they both burst out laughing.

"Okay, whatever." The wizard waved them off. "A guy can't think out loud anymore?"

Alex snickered. "Must be a real mess in your head, man."

"What did I say?"

"Pretty sure shifters don't get different diseases. Not a thing."

"Yeah, well, we can settle this right now, can't we? Who's right, Coulier? Hey. Amanda." Jackson's hand on her arm ripped her away from her frozen staring at Matt. He now sat at a table with Tommy and the other senior boys, looking happy and carefree and not threatening in any way.

"What?" she muttered and stepped away from the wizard.

"Who's right?"

"About..."

"Jeeze, you really *are* out of it."

"Jackson thinks shifters get different diseases than everyone else," Grace clarified.

"Where'd you hear that?" Amanda frowned at him and couldn't help a small smile. "That's pretty ridiculous."

"I... Summer said..." He grunted and tossed his arms in the air. "You know what? Forget it. I'm just the dumb guy with ridiculous ideas. It's fine."

"Hey, nobody said you were dumb."

"How would you know?" He made a face at her and let out a bitter laugh. "You didn't even hear what we were talking about."

"Fair point. Still, shifters aren't *that* different from everyone else." She forced herself not to look at Matt's table or him.

If we were, some weird shifter sickness might explain what I saw today. It doesn't.

CHAPTER FIFTEEN

Amanda spent the rest of that week doing everything she possibly could to avoid Matt. She didn't go for any runs. She sat at the end of a row of desks that already had somebody in the chair beside hers during History of Oriceran. Since that was the only class the seniors had to be in consistently this year, that was the only real obstacle.

The rest of the time, she made sure she was either with one of her friends, in her room studying and trying to come up with all these *lists* of things she needed for her classes, or at least somewhere in the common room. The boys weren't allowed in the girls' dorm.

The shifter boy didn't try to chase her down, but whenever she caught Matt staring at her, Amanda couldn't help but feel like he was laughing at her. It could have been because he was a teenage magical wielding dark magic and hiding it from an entire school—faculty included. Then again, it could have been because he'd seen what *she* could do with her magic and was curious to find out more.

Either way, Amanda poured her focus entirely into the lists of supplies her teachers had requested and in picking a bounty hunter from the strange list of names Ralthorn had given them. She didn't stop by the training building to watch the first two seniors duke it out one-on-one with Petrov, but no one else did, either.

Apparently, the rest of the class agreed with Annabelle that sparring with their Combat Training teacher was better off left as a private thing.

By the time the weekend rolled around, though, Amanda felt like she was about to lose her mind. She still hadn't gotten any form of response from Fiona, no calls or texts from the Coalition or Dr. Caniss' team of scientists, and she had way more free time on her hands than she'd imagined possible. All the seniors did.

If she weren't so busy trying to avoid Matt Hardy at all costs, she would have gone for a run out in the swamp every single day to run off the extra energy brought on by so much boredom. But she couldn't.

She didn't even act on the insanely strong urge to march right up to Glasket's office and ask the principal if she knew what the shifter boy could do. If Fiona didn't think it was a big enough deal to at least reply—and the shifter woman was more likely to teleport right to the school and whisk her mentee away if she were in any real danger—Amanda would keep her head down and focus on school.

And stay away from Matt.

That proved difficult to do the following week when the entire senior class crowded onto two airboats again to make their scheduled trip down to the kemana with LeFor. Because Matt had somehow squeezed his way through the other thirteen kids smashed onto the airboat Shep was steering and right up to Amanda's side.

She couldn't get away.

"Hey."

She stared out across the swamp, pretending to be intensely interested in the overhanging tree branches rushing past them.

Giving him the complete cold shoulder made her feel like a jerk, so she nodded quickly and muttered, "Hey."

He chuckled and lowered his head, but when he looked back up at her, she felt his gaze roaming all over her face as if he were touching her instead. "Is it just me, or does it feel like we're right back where we started last year?"

"I…don't really think we started anything."

"Come on. You look seriously angry every time you see me, and you've been avoiding me pretty much all the time. I thought we already…worked all that out."

"Nothing seems weird to me."

"Really?" A frown flickered across his eyebrows, but he smiled again and tried to play it all off as no big deal. Mostly. "I kinda thought you'd be out over the weekend. I waited for you."

Oh, man. He's really going there right now. I am so *glad nobody else can hear this conversation over the airboat fan.*

Amanda swallowed and quickly shook her head. "Yeah, I was busy. Lots of lists and figuring out problems for class, you know?"

"In the middle of the night?"

Crap.

She stared out at the water again and couldn't come up with a single thing to say.

"Okay, let me try again." Matt leaned toward her, his head barely inching over her shoulder as he lowered his voice. "About what happened the other day. When you saw me—"

"I don't know what you're talking about." Amanda tried to dip away from him, but there was nowhere else to go on the crowded airboat. "I didn't see anything."

"There's no way it was anyone else but you. And I'm pretty sure if anyone else had seen you sneaking around the boys' dorm like *that*, they'd probably say the same thing."

"I wasn't *sneaking*," she hissed.

"Okay. Sure. Not sneaking." Matt bit his lip and raised an

eyebrow. "Just walking around campus during lunch as a see-through wolf—"

"It's none of your business, all right?"

"I saw you. You saw me. Now you're back to pretending I don't exist as if you saw me...I don't know. Torturing small animals behind the dorm or something."

She turned her head slightly toward him and tried to take in his whole expression without making it ridiculously obvious that they were having this conversation. "Were you?"

Matt laughed and looked away before sighing. "I really hope that was a joke."

"Most people say stuff like that when they're trying to avoid answering the question."

"No, Amanda. I wasn't..." The airboat slowed as Shep turned down the fan's throttle, and Matt swallowed before lowering his voice again. "I wasn't torturing small animals. Look, I get that you weren't *trying* to find me, and you're weren't *trying* to be seen. But it happened. So I think we should talk about it. Later, obviously."

"I don't think that's—"

"Whoa, now, Mr. LeFor," Shep called from his post at the stern in front of the airboat's giant fan. "Watch out for the landin'. Pull it starboard. No, no, your *other* starboard. Toward you—"

A heavy *thump* came from the edge of the small island in the middle of the Everglades. The students on the airboat LeFor handled cried out in surprise and an effort to keep their footing. Summer and Brandon both leapt from the edge of the second airboat to land squarely on solid ground, and the rest of the seniors swayed and stumbled against each other.

Shep shook his head and let out a wheezing laugh. "Reckon that's one way to get'er done."

Amanda stared at the island as Shep pulled the second airboat in for a soft, smooth docking against the edge of the water.

It's been three years. How does LeFor not know how to steer an airboat yet?

"All right, now, seniors," the Academy's resident driver and groundskeeper called. "Y'all know the drill. Get on out and let's get down into the kemana."

The first line of students at the edge of the airboat surged around Amanda, laughing and making jokes at the expense of their Augmented Tech teacher. They teased the other half of the class stepping off the airboat and looking like they'd escaped a brush with death as well. She started to head after them, but feeling Matt's fingers brush against hers made her pause. Her first reaction was to jerk her hand away and finally turn to face him head-on. "What are you—"

"Friday night," he muttered, staring intently into her eyes. "It doesn't have to be a run, but we should at least go over what happened. Give each other a chance to explain."

"I don't know. That's probably not a good idea." She glanced at the island again, where the senior class converged around a weary-looking LeFor and found Summer staring at her with a smirk.

I'm not supposed to be talking to him. Dark magic, Amanda. Remember?

"We gotta go—"

Tommy brushed roughly past her and made her stumble forward off the airboat. She staggered onto dry land and scowled at the boy, but Tommy glanced over his shoulder with a mischievous smile and shrugged. "My bad."

"Amanda." Matt got caught in the rest of the class stepping off the boat. She turned halfway around to see him looking at her with more urgency than when he was hiding from every girl in the school. "Please?"

"I don't—"

"Coulier!" Jackson shouted.

Amanda was already facing forward again and heading

toward her friends as the other senior boys roughhoused with each other. Most of the girls walked carefully across the island, making sure they didn't step in anything gross.

That was almost really bad. I can't let myself get stuck with him like that again. No, we can't talk. I saw what I saw, and nothing he could say will change that.

When she reached Summer, the witch tossed her arm around Amanda's shoulders and grinned. "You're really in it now, huh?"

"You don't know what you're talking about."

"I know what I *saw*..."

"Stop." Amanda shrugged out from beneath her friend's arm and shook her head. "It's nothing."

"Uh-huh. Sure."

"What happened?" Jackson asked, looking way too eager to be in on the conversation.

"Shifter girl was just—"

"Saying we should hurry up and get to the entrance." Amanda nodded toward the rest of the class trekking past the outhouse in the center of the island. "Let's go."

Jackson opened his mouth to say something, but a thick ball of mud exploded against the back of his head and made him stumble forward. He whirled around and balled his fists. "Hey!"

Evan and Jack burst out laughing at the edge of the island, where they packed more mud balls between their hands and searched for new targets.

"Oh, yeah?" Jackson raced to the water's edge beside the airboats and stooped to grab a handful of mud for himself. "You want war, Brunsen? I'll give you war!"

The wizard spun and launched a mud ball at his friends as LeFor stepped in front of them to take his place at the kemana's entrance. If it weren't for the teacher's quick reflexes and a burst of yellow light striking the projectile away from him, he would have gotten Jackson's mud ball to the face.

Instead, it exploded and splattered all over Evan and Jack behind him.

"Mr. Pris!" LeFor roared. "This isn't—" At the sound of the boys' groans, the teacher spun and scowled at them before snapping his fingers. "Drop it."

"He started it."

LeFor slapped Jack's hand, and the newest mud ball hit the ground with a wet *thud*. "I finished it. This is why we don't bring freshmen to the kemana."

Evan snorted. "We're seniors."

"Oh, really? I couldn't tell. Cut it out."

Shep tried to keep a straight face as he ushered the rest of the senior class toward the edge of the island and the magical entrance that would take them straight down beneath the swamp and into the kemana. "All right now. All y'all who came in on Mr. LeFor's airboat gather 'round him now. He'll take y'all in first, and the rest of y'all're with me."

LeFor nodded at the wizard driver, his scowl unchanged, and waited for his half of the students to crowd around him in the invisible circle on the ground. "If I see another mud fight or any other fight while we're here, nobody's getting a passing grade this semester."

A collective groan rose from both groups of students. Half of it cut off abruptly when LeFor grabbed the crooked tree branch hanging beside his head, pulled, and the entire group disappeared within the circle of yellow light glowing briefly on the ground.

"Y'all heard your teacher," Shep called as he stepped into the circle to take his place for the second drop underground. "No fights. I ain't fixin' to drag students back to school with broken bones 'n smashed faces." He flashed them all a gap-toothed grin. "Don't mean there ain't other ways to have yourselves some good fun down here today, ya hear? Come on, now. Let's get movin'."

Amanda crowded into the circle with the rest of the class, and in an effort to get as far away from Matt as possible, she squeezed between Jasmine and Annabelle to put herself at the edge of the circle beside Shep.

He looked down at her with a knowing smile. "Everythin' all right, Miss Coulier?"

"What? Yeah." She shrugged. "I like being at the back."

The wizard barked out a laugh. "Me too, girl. Me too. Here we go."

That was all the warning he gave before the ground dropped away beneath them in a blaze of yellow light. Somebody screamed the entire three-second trip as they plummeted underground and into the kemana. When they stopped, the scream lasted another second. Then the kids who weren't already racing away down the stairs off the landing platform and down the stairs burst out laughing.

Shep chuckled. "You all right, Miss Porter?"

Grace stood stock still as the platform emptied, her eyes wide and her chest heaving. "I'm fine. I'm *fine*. I just...wasn't ready."

"Uh-huh. Best head on with the rest of your class, now. Y'all got lotsa shoppin' to do."

"Come on." Pressing her lips together, Amanda grabbed Grace's hand and pulled her off the platform toward the stairs.

Only when they reached the bottom of the massive cavern stretching out before them farther than they could see did the witch finally pull her hand out of Amanda's. "I'm fine."

"Okay. You looked a little shell-shocked."

"I'm not—"

Summer's wild cackle burst through the cavern, causing a brief lull in the droning background noise of a bustling kemana before it picked right back up again. She pointed at Grace. "I didn't know you could *scream* like that!"

"Well, it's not something I do all the time," the other witch snapped.

"Ha! What, did you think we got on some amusement park ride or something?"

"Shut up." Grace shoved the girl playfully in the shoulder and huffed out a laugh. "I've never been to an amusement park, anyway."

"Wait, *what*?" Summer gawked after her. "Holy shit. You tunnel kids really missed out on *everything* good, didn't you?"

"I wouldn't say *that*," Jackson said as they all followed LeFor and Shep across the kemana's stone floors toward the one and only Worlen & Carp where they'd been buying their supplies for the last two years. "Having no adults around was pretty great. No one to stop us from throwing mud. I'll tell you that much."

Summer snorted. "Yeah. No parents sounds like freakin' paradise."

Amanda and the rest of her friends all turned to look at the rainbow-haired witch with various expressions of discomfort.

She stared blankly back at them, then clicked her tongue. "Oh. Damn. I meant...hypothetically."

"Not really hypothetical when only one of us actually *has* parents, right?"

The tension between the two witches thickened by the second.

Crap. They're really gonna have it out with each other down here, aren't they? This was supposed to be a fun *trip.*

But Summer surprised them all and shrugged as she sighed. "You're right. My bad, Blondie. But *I'm* not the one who has parents. Even if I knew where they were, they'd be dead to me anyway."

Jackson cocked his head. "What?"

"Doesn't matter." Summer smacked Amanda's shoulder with the back of a hand. "Shifter girl's the only one of us with *real* parents. I'd pick them any day of the week."

Amanda's eyes widened as she leaned away from the other girl. "Wait, what?"

"Hypothetically." Summer glanced at each of them, then rolled her eyes. "Jesus, you guys seriously need to lighten up. And quit being all sappy. I'm getting itchy. Come on."

She stalked forward and stormed between Jackson and Alex, who both stepped away at the last second to let her pass and turned to stare after her.

"What just happened?" Grace muttered.

Amanda grinned. "I guess Summer Flannerty's been working on her issues."

Jackson wrinkled his nose. "I thought she was allergic."

Alex snorted out a laugh and shoved the wizard forward as they hurried after the rest of the class.

Grace blinked furiously. "She said I was *right*."

"Because you are." Amanda waved the girl forward. "Most of the time."

"*Most* of the time?"

"And everybody knows it. Come on."

The blonde witch finally started walking, but she squinted at Amanda as a slow smile crept across her lips. "What did you *do* to her over the summer?"

"Absolutely nothing." The shifter girl shrugged. "I think that was the point."

"*Please* take her home with you for Christmas break. Maybe she'll come back next semester with more than half a soul."

CHAPTER SIXTEEN

The owner of Worlen & Carp didn't look nearly as overwhelmed by a class of twenty-six students from the Academy of Necessary Magic as he had the first time they'd stepped into his shop sophomore year. He didn't exactly smile, but he nodded at LeFor standing outside the entrance before the first group of kids stepped inside to peruse his inventory and grab everything on their lists for their required "work kits."

He was only willing to allow six in at a time. Max.

Amanda didn't make it into the first group, but she wasn't in a hurry. Instead, her attention was only halfway on listening to her friends point out the crazy pixie selling yellow snow cones or the gnome on a bicycle hawking "the planet's most intuitive underwear with smart-magic technology" as he swerved between pedestrian groups.

Summer fell into another fit of laughter. "I mean, how stupid do you have to *be* to think anyone's gonna buy that crap?"

Alex shook his head. "Not even humans are dumb enough to buy yellow snow cones."

"Ha. You sure?"

The other half of Amanda's attention, though, was on trying

to find Matt Hardy so she could make sure she stayed as far away from him as possible. Since he was constantly moving around with the other senior boys and hadn't yet gone into Worlen & Carp himself, keeping an eye on him took some serious effort.

"Hey. *Hello*?" Summer snapped her fingers in front of Amanda's face. "Earth to shifter girl..."

"What?"

"You coming?" The witch gestured toward Grace and the guys, who were now heading into the tech shop. LeFor did a quick headcount inside the store, then nodded for them to go inside. "I mean, unless you don't *want* to buy a bunch of useless crap we'll probably never use but won't get out of this hellhole without."

Amanda snorted. "Yeah, okay. I'm coming."

They hurried toward the shop, and Summer marched inside with a grin as she stared at the shelves of electrical components and the kind of magically enhanced tech impossible to find aboveground.

"Hold on, Miss Coulier," LeFor said, bringing his hand down in front of her to stop her. "That was six."

"Aw, really?"

He looked down at her and raised an eyebrow. "I'm sure you're not *that* disappointed. As soon as someone comes out, you can go in."

"All right." She shrugged and backed away before turning to scan the kemana again. It was nearly impossible to pick out any faces among the crowds of magicals strolling back and forth, talking and laughing, haggling prices, or hurrying across the giant cavern with important business of their own.

Who am I kidding? I'm not looking for his face. I'm looking for his magic. Red, sparking, dark magic that shouldn't be allowed in our school.

Though after Matt had practically begged her to talk to him about what she'd seen—about what they'd *both* seen of each other

—Amanda's conviction that the shifter boy was a dark magical in wolf's clothing had lost a lot of its strength.

He wasn't angry. Someone with dark magic would've been pissed someone figured them out, right? Wouldn't he have tried to kill me or something?

The new wave of thoughts made her dizzy, and she battled with trying to pick a side. How did she *really* feel about Matt Hardy?

Was she even clear-headed enough to make that kind of decision about a shifter boy she maybe liked and had already gone for a run with in the swamp? Her home?

Right when she started to feel like she had to get some fresh air before she completely lost her mind, a shout came from inside Worlen & Carp.

"Are you freaking *kidding* me?"

It was Summer.

"No, no. Hold on. I *know* it works. Try again."

LeFor scowled and marched into the shop.

"I said try it again!"

"That's enough, Miss Flannerty. What's the problem?"

Amanda headed toward the shop's open door and peered through at the cashier's desk along the righthand side.

The owner spread his arms and shook his head. "Kid's card was deactivated. Nothing I can do."

Summer pointed at him. "That's bullshit. I—"

"I said *enough*." LeFor glared down at her and pointed at the door. "Step outside. Cool off. Then we'll figure out how to move forward."

With a frustrated grunt, Summer spun away from the counter and stormed outside.

Amanda glanced at LeFor talking with the shop owner, then hurried after her friend. "What happened?"

"The usual. Jesus Christ, I should've expected this. That bitch already took everything else away, so why wouldn't she take this?"

"Whoa, hold on. Who?"

"Fucking Marianne," Summer snarled, pacing back and forth in front of the Oriceran bead shop on the other side of the dark alley beside the tech shop.

The dwarf woman handling the register inside stared at Summer, then hurried toward the door, closed it, and turned the lock with a quick metallic *thunk*.

Amanda grimaced but ignored the store owner's wariness. "Summer. What did she do?"

"Fuck!" The young witch dropped onto a stack of crates and buried her face in her hands. "This is it. I'm so done."

"Hey." Sitting beside her friend, Amanda clasped her hands in her lap and waited for Summer to say more. The other girl's shoulders shook, but she didn't make a sound with her face covered and her obvious attempts to slow her heavy breathing. "Maybe I can help."

"You can't." Summer dropped her hands into her lap and craned her neck to stare at the kemana's roughhewn ceiling. "I meant what I said back there. That my parents are already dead to me."

"Okay."

The witch scoffed. "But dead parents can't drain your entire bank account and close it all without saying a damn thing about it."

Amanda's eyes widened. "*That's* what she did?"

"It wasn't a fucking ghost, Amanda. I know that much." Gritting her teeth, Summer shook her head. "That was *my* money. I worked for it. I saved it. She told me when I got kicked out of SoNM that she wasn't paying for anything anymore. So I got jobs. And I'm not eighteen, so she just..."

"She could still do whatever she wanted with your money."

"That's all I have." Summer heaved a sigh. "Like, literally. That and one stupid backpack. I can't even buy the dumb tools for class, and they don't *budget* for kids with parents."

"I'm so sorry."

"Don't." The witch leaned away from her. "I don't need pity, okay? I'll figure it out. Jesus, I mean, I thought she went far enough when she left all my crap out in the yard and disappeared. But she had to come back and do *this*? A year later? I can't..."

Tears shimmered in Summer's eyes, and she looked away, grimacing to hold them back.

"Okay. Hold on." Amanda stood from the crate, glanced around the kemana, and stepped back into the alley.

"What are you doing?"

"Just checking something."

"Don't tell me you're gonna try to *steal* my kit gear while LeFor's standing right there."

Amanda spun and laughed. "No, that's something *you'd* do. I'll be right back. Just...make sure nobody follows me, okay?"

"Whatever."

She slipped her backpack off her shoulders as she headed toward the kemana wall in the alley. Then she crouched in the corner beside the wall of Worlen & Carp and unzipped the front pocket to pull out her Coalition phone.

Not supposed to have this down here either, but I know Johnny leaves way more in my account than I need. Maybe I have enough for both of us.

When she turned on the screen, and it flashed from black to bright white, she wasn't expecting two stacked notifications of incoming texts. From Fiona.

Crap. She waited a whole week *to answer. No way can I get in trouble for not seeing this.*

She signed into her phone and pulled up the texts. The first was short and made absolutely no sense.

Come on, kid. I thought that last one would at least butter you up a little. You still pissed at me?

She'd sent it this morning at 6:54 a.m., which would have been right as Amanda was heading across campus with the rest of the seniors to get on the airboats. The second text, which had come in Sunday morning at 1:37 a.m., made her pause.

I know. You're fine. Melody says hi, so check to make sure you got what she sent you. Might hold you over 'til you're back in the lab.

What she sent me? Amanda snorted. *I didn't get anything from Dr. Caniss.*

Then the rest of the message sank in.

Fiona knows. About shifters with Matt's kind of magic. And I'm...fine?

A mixture of relief and rage flooded through her all at once—relief that at the very least Fiona didn't think shifters like Matt were an actual threat. Rage because her mentor had let her stew for an entire week over how she was supposed to handle the shifter boy who'd seen her ghost-wolf and who might or might not still be too dangerous.

I should've told her he was at the Academy.

She closed out her texts and opened her email account to search for whatever Dr. Caniss had apparently sent. The only two unread emails were a spam ad for new-home financing and an alert from her bank that her account statement was ready to view, and that was from last month.

"Your little huddle back there's starting to creep me out," Summer called over her shoulder. "And you're taking forever."

"Sorry. One sec."

Amanda closed her email, opened the bank app, and signed into her account.

Don't get distracted by cryptic messages and mail you never got from a psycho scientist, Amanda. You can handle all that later.

It was amazing that her Coalition phone even worked down here in the kemana. Then again, it was more advanced than any other phone out there and probably didn't use a regular service network. Still, the home page of her online banking dashboard took a few seconds to load, and when the information finally appeared, Amanda choked.

"What the fuck?"

"Sounds like we're both having a bad day," Summer grumbled.

Amanda ignored her and opened her checking account to view the transactions.

No way. This is definitely a mistake. Johnny would never do this.

The first transaction on the list loaded and made it clear that Johnny had not added more to her account than the regular thousand dollars per semester. Because the statement name for the newest deposit read 'Omega Industries.'

A deposit for fifteen thousand dollars.

What is happening?

"Hey!" Summer spun on the crate and hopped off the other side to head toward her friend. "You're screwing with me, aren't you?"

"Ha!" Amanda slapped a hand to her head and couldn't stop staring at the phone. "I don't... This... *What?*"

"Guess I was wrong. *I'm* the only one having a shitty day, and you..." Summer paused halfway down the alley and cocked her head. "You look like you just won the lottery or something."

With another sharp laugh, Amanda spun toward the witch with her phone outstretched in one hand. "I just got— Crap." She whisked the phone behind her back and crouched beside her backpack again.

"Please. Like anyone cares what we're doing back here. And I've seen your phone."

"Yeah." Swallowing, Amanda turned off the phone's screen

and shoved it back into her backpack. "I know."

"So what are you freaking out about? Did the shifter mob send you a love letter or something?"

The zipper whisked sharply shut, then the shifter girl lugged her backpack over her shoulder and grinned. "Something like that, yeah."

Summer scoffed and looked her friend up and down. "Jesus. Blondie's the worst liar I know, but you're still at the top of the list. Spill it."

Amanda hurried down the alley and roughly grabbed Summer's arm before hauling her along too. The witch let out a nervous laugh but didn't complain. They stopped in front of Worlen & Carp, and Amanda drew a deep breath. "This is a one-time thing, okay?"

"Not really. You do weird shit all the time."

"You have to sit down and talk to Glasket after this. Let her know what your mom—"

"My *dead* mom."

"—did to your account. She'll figure out a way to help you."

Summer folded her arms. "Now I'm confused *and* pissed off. You're all happy-slappy after your secret phone huddle, and you just told me to give Glasket a sob story so she'll help me. What's *wrong* with you?"

"Nothing." Amanda bit back a laugh. "Right now, absolutely nothing."

"You're so full of—"

"Summer." She looked at her friend and raised her eyebrows, her cheeks already sore from grinning, and she couldn't help it. "Get your list."

"That's it. I'm outta here." The witch started to turn away, but Amanda grabbed her hand and pulled her back.

"I'm serious. Get it out. We're going in that shop together."

Summer frowned. "Because…"

"Because I got my first paycheck."

CHAPTER SEVENTEEN

Mr. LeFor tried to argue that students were responsible for themselves, but that line of reasoning didn't hold up when Amanda reminded him of the Academy's budget for student stipends. No one else asked for an explanation after that when she dropped two plastic bins of both her and Summer's supplies for Augmented Tech on the counter and pulled her wallet from her backpack.

The shop owner frowned and hesitated to take her card. "You sure you can cover this, kid?"

She slapped her card down on the counter and slid it toward him. "I'm sure."

He glanced at LeFor standing outside the door again, then at a grinning Summer standing beside her friend. "I don't want any more trouble in here again. If *your* card's no good—"

"Trust me. It's good. Just ring me up."

The dwarf grunted and ran her card, and without any other reaction whatsoever, he slid her card back and proceeded to box up the girls' purchased supplies.

"Thank you very much." Amanda grabbed her box and nodded at the guy before turning swiftly to head for the door.

"Yeah." Summer eyed the dwarf up and down, then tucked her box under her arm and snorted. "Thanks."

He shook his head and let out a heavy sigh as the girls left his store and LeFor ushered two more inside to take their places.

"Miss Coulier." The teacher waved her back toward him, folding his arms and dipping his head when she backtracked. "I'll talk to Glasket about a reimbursement—"

"Why?"

He blinked quickly behind his thick, black-rimmed glasses. "Because that's not your responsibility."

"No, I wanted to. Besides, you don't want Summer to fail your class because a crappy magical did a really crappy thing, right?"

LeFor glanced at Summer, who talked to Alex and Jackson with wild hand gestures, half of which pointed back at Amanda.

"I don't want any of you to fail my class," he said. "Even Miss Flannerty."

"Cool. Then we're good. How much longer do we have?"

LeFor looked at his watch, then silently counted the senior students milling around against those who still hadn't made it into the store. "An hour."

"Great. See you at the platform." She spun and marched happily toward her friends.

Jackson and Alex stared at her, the Wood Elf's eyes narrowed and the wizard's wide in confusion. "How much was it?"

Amanda tried to scowl at Summer, but her ecstatic grin wouldn't obey. "You told them?"

"Hey, you didn't say it was a secret. It's not like they don't already know you work for the shifter mafia—"

"Stop saying that. And I'm not telling you, so quit asking."

"Hey, it's not a big deal, Coulier." Jackson shrugged. "I mean, first paychecks after an internship aren't *supposed* to be huge, right?"

"What?"

Alex shoved his hands into his pockets. "Trust me. Even fifty bucks is a lot to *us*."

"Um..." She laughed again and scanned the kemana.

I am not *talking about my giant paycheck. To anyone. They won't believe me anyway.*

"We only have another hour, so let's go do something fun."

"*Super* fun lugging these dumb boxes all over the place," Summer muttered.

"And you're avoiding the question," Jackson added.

"Yep. Come on." Amanda headed down the wide avenue, searching for the storefront of SweetPops and already coming up with a list of exactly what she wanted to get there. "Where's Grace?"

Alex jerked his thumb out toward the row of brightly colored storefronts with window displays of gaudy outfits that would have stuck out in any century on Earth. "She's with Annabelle. Something about the last Homecoming dance."

Jackson rolled his eyes. "I don't get it. It's not like they're gonna *buy* something."

With a shrug, Amanda headed for the candy store, weaving her way through the other pedestrians and the enchanted ads and random objects flying through the air. Summer and the guys wouldn't stop asking her what was going on as they tried to keep up, but she ignored them. She wouldn't answer their questions anyway.

For now, at least, this was *her* secret.

I finally have a secret that doesn't make me feel like crap and won't get me busted.

When she reached the front of SweetPops, though, she stopped short. Her smile faded.

Inside, Tommy and Evan clowned around with the samples of firecracker gum. Beside them, Matt picked up a package of self-whistling candy straws and laughed. Then he paused and turned to meet Amanda's gaze.

Her heartbeat pounded in her ears, and the box of tech supplies almost slipped right out of her instantly clammy hands.

The shifter boy kept smiling at her and raised an eyebrow like he wasn't quite sure where she stood on their interrupted conversation about another conversation he wanted to have.

Amanda wasn't quite sure, either.

Fiona didn't freak out over my text. Matt doesn't exactly look like someone who wants to kill me for what I know. Screw it. I'm not letting anything stop me today.

"You okay?" Summer asked.

Blinking quickly, Amanda nodded and headed into the store. "Totally. Hey, what do you guys want? It's on me."

Jackson stopped and looked like she'd just slapped his face. "Seriously?"

"Yeah, but if you spend the next hour standing there trying to decide if I'm lying, you'll miss out."

Alex passed the wizard and thumped his friend on the chest. "Must've been more than fifty bucks."

"A hundred?"

"Who cares, man? It's all on her."

The rest of that week practically flew by. Despite hearing absolutely nothing else from the Coalition, Dr. Caniss, or Fiona, Amanda was on top of the world. She'd replied to her mentor's text asking if she was still pissed with a simple "Nope" and called it good. Apparently, so had Fiona. Even the ridiculous amount of free time the seniors had this year to focus on their self-directed assignments had lost its restless effect.

Amanda had a job.

That had to be what this was because nobody paid a fifteen-year-old shifter girl fifteen thousand dollars just for fun. Not even the Coalition of Shifters.

Now she only had to wait for them to get in touch and tell her when she'd be going back to work.

Matt didn't try to approach her again that week either, but she felt him looking at her during class and caught his crooked smile from his picnic table during meals. She still hadn't decided if she'd let herself talk to him about their weird magical discoveries of each other, but it no longer seemed like the horrible idea she'd first thought it was. She'd figure out that part later.

Although Jackson and Alex seemed oblivious to all of it, Grace and Summer questioned Amanda almost every chance they got when the guys weren't around.

"What is going *on* between you two?"

"You're not fooling anybody, shifter girl."

"Except for maybe yourself. You should go talk to him."

"Maybe she already has."

It got worse when Summer got a kick out of trying to guess how much Amanda's first paycheck was. The witch was relentless. Amanda finally had to put an end to it when Summer raced across the central field before lunch that Friday, wearing her insane grin and waving a paper in the air. "I got it! Holy shit, I figured it out!"

Turning from the lunch line, Amanda shook her head and stepped back before the witch could run right into her. "Summer, this is seriously the last time I'm telling you this, and I mean it."

"Okay, cool. Whatever. But I know—"

"I'm not giving you a number, and I won't even tell you if you somehow guess it."

"Great. So listen—"

"And no. Nothing happened with..." Amanda glanced across the outdoor cafeteria. "Nothing's going on. Stop asking. Stop guessing. Because I'm *this* close to throwing you across the field."

"Who cares about *you,* shifter girl? I picked my bounty hunter!" Summer waved the paper in her friend's face and laughed maniacally. "I can't *believe* it took me this long to figure out!"

Grace folded her arms. "My guess it's because you haven't done any work on *any* of our projects until now."

"Well, yeah. But I should've put two and two together. Sooner. It was a given for the shifter girl, but then it hit me. I know him *too*."

The blonde witch scoffed. "Did you blow something up again? You did, didn't you? *And* you hit your head."

"Ha. I wish."

Amanda's eyes widened when she saw the list of famous bounty hunters in Summer's hand. "Really?"

"Yeah. *Oh*, yeah. I'm doing my report on Johnny Walker the pissed-off dwarf."

Jackson and Alex burst out laughing. "That's what you're freaking out about?"

"You know what, Romeo? This has nothing to do with you. Back off."

"Okay, well... Cool, I guess." Amanda pressed her lips together. "Have fun."

"Oh, it's gonna be fun, shifter girl. 'Cause I'm gonna pick your brain for every single tiny detail."

"Nope." Amanda shook her head. "No, you're not."

"That would be considered cheating," Grace added.

"You and your cheating, Blondie. Jesus." Summer rolled her eyes. "It's not cheating. It's called interviewing sources, okay? Jesus, lighten up."

"You should start with the library or at least looking up articles online."

Summer ignored the other witch and squeezed into the lunch line beside Amanda. "So. What can you tell me about him?"

"Nothing." Amanda could hardly keep herself from laughing in her friend's face. "This is *your* assignment."

"You're the best resource for figuring this shit out, shifter girl."

"*Or* I could set you up with an interview."

Jackson and Alex snickered.

Summer shot her a deadpan stare. "Please. You're not *that* good."

"You're right. He hates interviews."

"See? That's what I mean." Summer clapped a hand on Amanda's shoulder and shook the other girl vigorously. "I'm not gonna find this kinda stuff in a *library book*."

"Okay, stop." Flinging the witch's hand away from her shoulder, Amanda couldn't help but laugh. "I'm not doing your report on Johnny Walker, okay?"

"Nobody asked you to. Just answer my questions. Like, is he *really* a drunk, or do dwarves have a super high tolerance? Oh! And who taught him how to build all that crazy stuff at his house? How come he lives in a dinky little cabin in the swamp when he could probably buy up all the Everglades and build a castle on it instead?"

"Where'd you find how much money he has?"

"I didn't." Summer grinned. "But you just told me it's enough to buy the Everglades—"

"No, *you* said that."

Summer spun away from their friends and stalked up the line. "This is gonna be awesome."

"What is she doing?" Grace asked.

Alex leaned sideways to get a better view of the banquet tables. He raised his eyebrows and flatly replied, "Cutting the line and shoving everyone out of the way."

"What?"

"Hey, we were here first."

"Get in line, Summer."

"Come on. That's not how this works!"

"Oh my God." Grace closed her eyes. "She's gone full psycho."

Five seconds later, Summer spun away from the tables with a loaded plate in hand, caught Amanda's gaze, and grinned before hurrying to the table and dropping onto the bench to start stuffing her face.

"I mean, at least she's finally excited about *something*," Amanda muttered.

"I'm not sure that's something we should be happy about. You know, as her friends. Who do everything with her. And the rest of the school knows..."

Alex's lips barely parted as he smiled, which was almost as creepy as when he'd lost his mind over Petrov's angry outburst last year. "I like it."

Jackson snorted and punched the Wood Elf in the arm. "You would."

"I just said I do."

Grace shook her head. "I seriously hope she burns out about this. Before the end of the day would be nice."

"No way to tell." Amanda watched Summer pull a pen out of her back pocket, flip the paper over on the table, and scribble down notes with one hand while she stuffed her face with the other.

She's either honestly excited about a report on Johnny, or the whole thing with her bank account sent her way off the deep end.

CHAPTER EIGHTEEN

That night, Amanda lay awake in her bed, all but watching the time tick away on the alarm clock beside her bed. Matt had asked her to come out and talk with him tonight. They didn't have to go for a run, but he wanted a chance to explain. For them *both* to explain.

That part made her hesitate the most.

Why do I have to explain anything to him? I have the same kind of magic every other shifter has. I just know how to use it.

Maybe that was the point. Maybe Matt had absolutely no idea because his parents were as private and closed-up as hers had been.

Amanda wanted to trust the shifter boy, but she couldn't bring herself to leave her dorm room and head down to the open grounds behind the buildings. And she knew without a doubt he was down there waiting for her.

Thankfully, he didn't bring it up at all again that week, which was a good thing. Amanda didn't think she could handle trying to navigate a cute boy with potentially deadly magic when she had her first sparring session with Petrov that week.

The Combat Training teacher looked disappointed to see her that Wednesday morning as she stepped into the training building and kicked off her shoes to set them off the edge of the mat.

In here alone to fight Petrov for class credit. This is so freaking weird.

"It's about time, Coulier." The teacher already had his shoes off, his bare toes digging into the plastic mat covering as he stretched his neck from side to side. "I can finally get a good exercise out of these sessions."

She raised her eyebrows and tried not to look at him as she joined him in the center of the room. "Not sure what that's supposed to mean."

"It means I expect you to give me everything you got. Because we both know you're already better than ninety-eight percent of your class."

Amanda rolled her shoulders back and couldn't help a small smile. "I'm guessing that the other two percent is Blake, right?"

"Lively's scheduled for next week. So maybe. Maybe not."

"Okay. So." She flexed her hands and wiggled her fingers, her shifter senses intensely sharpened now that she stood in the training room that was never this quiet or this empty. "How do we—"

Petrov lunged toward her, grabbed her wrist, and spun her around before kicking one foot out from under her. His other hand on her opposite shoulder forced her to one knee, and then he had her in a pitiful excuse for an armlock. "We start by expecting our opponent to make their move at any second. You're slow today. Get up."

Amanda tried to stand and grunted out a sigh when he didn't release her arm or her shoulder. "Like this?"

"If you can."

He really likes screwing with me, doesn't he? Fine. I'm gonna nail this session.

Grimacing against the slight pain in her shoulder but hoping it looked worse than it actually was, she puffed out another breath and glanced slightly over her shoulder to see the very edge of Petrov's bald head gleaming under the lights. "You really don't want me to hold back? Like, at all?"

"That's the point, Coulier. If you can't get over your—"

She ducked beneath his grip on her shoulder and rolled onto her hip, spinning out of the armlock and grabbing his hand, still gripping her wrist. Petrov released her and tried to pull back, but she jerked him toward her and lifted her feet. He tried to block one leg from connecting with the side of his head, but by the time he'd raised his free arm to do so, she hooked her other leg under his other and rolled again.

Amanda was small, but her shifter strength more than made up for it. Petrov landed on the mat with a *thud,* his free arm now pinned beneath him and his other arm twisted up behind him. And he had the shifter girl's knee in his back, pinning him down but still leaving a little room for him to get out of the hold.

If he could.

Petrov grunted. "Now you're paying attention."

"Are you?"

He huffed out a laugh. "I am now."

A flash of yellow light flared from his hand pinned under his chest, and a hot, brief pain raced through Amanda's ribs, loosening her hold. She rolled off her teacher and grabbed her side with a snarl. "What—"

"We're sparring, Coulier. Not dancing. It's all fair game when you're in a real fight. Including magic."

"You really want me to use my magic?"

That made him widen his eyes where he now crouched on the mat after rolling off his stomach. "Now *that* I'd like to see. Last year at this school, Coulier. Better make it count."

Her upper lip twitched as she snarled, and as the tingle of her shifter magic flooded through her, she knew Petrov saw her eyes flash silver. Then she charged him and did exactly what he told her to.

She didn't hold back.

The seniors were used to seeing one of their classmates stumble across campus after their sparring sessions looking sore, a little bruised, and run ragged. They'd joked about it for the last few weeks, giving whoever it was a good-natured ribbing while knowing their turn was coming up. Nobody laughed or called jokes at Amanda as she limped across the central field five minutes after the bell for the start of the next class had already blared across campus.

They just stared.

"Whoa, whoa, whoa." Summer nudged Alex in the arm and pointed. "Dead shifter walking. Am I right?"

"You guys are awful," Grace chided. "Look at her."

Jackson's mouth popped open. "Can he *do* that?"

"I don't think so." The blonde witch took off across the field and skidded to a stop in front of Amanda. "Oh my God. *Amanda*. You should go see Nurse Aiken. Like, right now."

"What?" The shifter girl snorted, then immediately grimaced and gripped her side. A small laugh escaped her. "I'm fine."

"No, you're not. You're *bleeding*."

"Just a little."

"What did he do to you?"

Amanda swiped her sweat-sticky hair away from her face and walked past Grace. "Trust me. Nothing worse than what I did to him."

Summer threw her head back and cackled. "No way!"

"Hey, if you have a broken rib or something," Grace continued, hurrying after her friend, "that could—"

"Heal pretty quickly all on its own? Grace, I don't need to see the nurse. I can handle it."

"Then I'm going to Glasket right now to tell her what happened. He's a teacher. You're a student. This isn't okay." The blonde witch stormed toward the center building, but the look of utter shock on Alex's face made her stop.

"Dude, dude, dude!" The Wood Elf slapped Jackson's shoulder repeatedly until the wizard shoved him away.

"Hey, we don't have to spar *each other*—"

"Look."

Amanda and all her friends turned to see Petrov in the doorway of the training building. He stood hunched over, one arm wrapped around his midsection and one side of his face already so swollen and purple, his features were indistinguishable. And he scowled across the field at the shifter girl who'd bested him on his mat.

"Oh, shit…" Summer tried to laugh again, but her shock made it come out as a stuttering, high-pitched giggle instead.

Petrov growled, his exposed teeth on the un-swollen side of his mouth flashing in the sunlight like his shiny bald head before he reached around the corner to grab the door. Then he pulled it shut and disappeared inside the training building with a loud *bang*.

"Damn." Jackson laughed in surprise and rubbed the back of his neck. "Grace, I think *he* needs Nurse Aiken more than Coulier does."

"You know what?" The witch cocked her head and swallowed. "I think you're right."

News spread over the next few days about what had happened during Amanda's sparring session, and the other classes of students who normally would have had Combat Training class on Thursday enjoyed a surprise and uncharacteristic day off. No one saw Petrov, so the speculation and the rumors only launched even further into absurdity.

A small group of freshmen thought Amanda had killed their Combat teacher.

She didn't have any broken bones, and her shifter's ability to heal a lot more quickly than anyone else sealed up her cuts in twenty-four hours until they were nothing but raw, red, itchy lines. Her quickly fading black eye was the only visible proof that she'd sparred at all.

Petrov didn't do a thing to correct the misconceptions flooding around the school, but by that Friday, the door to the training building was open again first thing in the morning for the next senior to step inside and face him one-on-one.

Amanda gave herself the rest of the weekend to recover, making sure to check her Coalition phone as frequently as she could. Instead of going down to the kemana with her friends or sitting in to watch the Louper match that week, or pacing back and forth in her dorm room, she spent her free time in the greenhouse.

The uncharacteristically bland list of seeds she'd ordered the first week of the semester had come in surprisingly quickly. She'd stopped by the greenhouse multiple times a day to see how the new plants were progressing. Brown Amalath, BloodSun, and Flowering Arrowberry were innocuous even without comparing them to the volatile, deadly magical species she'd cultivated over the last three years.

She hadn't found anything remotely exciting in *Orion's Plant Emporium: Fifth Edition*, so the best thing she could come up with was to grow more plants with magically medicinal properties and help Nurse Aiken out a little more.

Amanda had a strong feeling Matt was still waiting for her on Friday and Saturday nights, but she kept a tight hold on her magic to make sure her ghost-wolf didn't slip out on its own when she was trying to get to sleep. Any day now, she expected another message or call on her Coalition phone, and the last thing she wanted was to get caught up in running through the swamp with a shifter boy who "just wanted to talk."

Waiting to be called back to her job—her real, secret, very *well-paying* job—was a twenty-four-hour endeavor all on its own. Somehow, Amanda was still able to listen to her friends brainstorming about their various solo projects and focus on her work when she was alone without the distractions.

Then Homecoming snuck up on her faster than she expected, and the entire student body filled with that buzzing energy she still didn't understand. As expected, the girls at the Academy—practically all of them except for Amanda and Summer, which wasn't a surprise—got aggressive quickly.

Mostly when it came to Matt Hardy and which one of them was *finally* going to get the dreamy boy with the blue eyes to go to Homecoming with them, let alone any school dance at all. That part wasn't surprising at all, but what caught Amanda off guard was the fact that she felt sorry for him.

That doesn't mean I'm gonna ask him to go to the dance with me. Or hang out during the dance. Or talk to him at all.

The Wednesday night before Homecoming, Amanda finished writing out her final plan for Mrs. Zimmer's "manufactured scenario" assignment at almost 11:00 p.m. She read it over one more time, wrinkled her nose, and slipped the notebook into her backpack.

It's good enough, I guess. If it's not, I'll have to start over from scratch. Awesome.

Stretching out her back from having hunched over her work for so long, she headed for her dresser to start changing into her pajamas and stopped.

A red light flickered softly at the base of her dorm room window, and the smell of intense magic and burning plastic made her nostrils flare. "No."

She launched herself at her bed and scooted forward on her knees to peer through the closed blinds.

Yes, it was Matt.

He stood at the base of the girls' dorm, his arm outstretched to the side as he wiggled his fingers. The crackling red magic twisting around his wrist and his hands was bright enough to light up his face, and he was grinning right up at Amanda's window.

She jerked away and scrambled backward off the bed.

What is he doing? How the heck does he know where my room even is?

That thought would have made her laugh if she wasn't so pissed off about being interrupted on a Wednesday night with the red light and that *smell.*

Of course, he knows where my room is. Same way I could find his *window if I tried hard enough.*

For another two minutes, she paced back and forth across her room, her readiness to get to bed and enjoy a decent night of sleep gone now.

He thinks he can show up, play a little dark-magic trick, and get me to talk. He's crazy.

Amanda had no intention of going downstairs to meet with him, but that changed the instant the red light snuffed out, and there was nothing but darkness outside her window. Then a knot tightened in her stomach, and she slowed her pacing.

I shouldn't feel bad about this. Not my problem. I don't owe him anything.

She stopped to listen for movement coming from outside,

sniffing the air to double-check that yes, the burnt-plastic smell was fading. Now, she could no longer pretend she was avoiding him and assume he was out there waiting for her as he'd said. Amanda had seen him beside the building, and knowing how well shifters saw in the dark, there was no way he hadn't seen her looking at him too.

Then Fiona's vague text came to mind. *"I know. You're fine."*

Amanda growled softly and gritted her teeth.

Screw it. If I can put Petrov out of commission for a day, I can handle one shifter boy.

She stalked out of her room and remembered at the last second not to slam the door shut behind her and wake up the entire school.

If anyone else sees him doing his little magic trick, the whole school's gonna start panicking. Oh, yeah. We're gonna talk, all right.

CHAPTER NINETEEN

Even when she was on a mission to talk some sense into a boy who was starting to drive her crazy—and not in a good way—Amanda's habit of leaving the girls' dorm in the middle of the night through the back door was still hard to break. She shoved the door open and stormed out into the muggy air, although it was a lot cooler now at the end of September.

Crickets chirped, and cicadas droned all around her. An owl hooted. The three-quarter moon was bright enough to light up everything across the campus that didn't fall beneath the shadow of the buildings, and Matt Hardy was nowhere in sight.

Nope. He can't light up my window like that and not expect me to come after him.

A gentle breeze picked up from the north, and with it came the scent she was single-mindedly trying to find.

Clenching her fists, she stalked toward the boys' dorm, scanning the grounds in case someone else decided to pop up and mess with her too, just for fun. Nothing moved except the rustling tree branches and swaying reeds at the river's edge. Then she reached the back corner of the boys' dorm, fully expecting Matt to be on the other side of the building.

She almost ran head-first into him at the back of the building instead.

Matt sucked in a sharp breath and stepped back. Amanda stayed where she was and glared at him. "This has to—"

"I *knew* that would finally get your attention." He chuckled and spread his arms. "Honestly, I haven't had to work this hard to get someone to notice me in…maybe ever, actually."

Amanda blinked furiously and leaned away from him. "What?"

"I mean, I told you I'd be waiting weeks ago. You didn't show up one time, fine. I figured maybe you needed some time to figure out what you wanted to say."

"What *I* wanted to say? You're the one who—"

"Then you didn't show up the next weekend, or the next, and I started to think I'd done something wrong. Again. Which doesn't make sense, 'cause it's kinda hard to screw up when you won't talk to me."

"I…" She wrinkled her nose. "What do you mean, again?"

Matt's eyes crinkled at the corners when he grinned, his dimples popping up as always, and he slipped his hands into his pockets. "So we *are* gonna have this talk."

"No. I came out here because you were flashing your weird light outside my window."

"Yeah. That was…kind of the point. You wouldn't meet me out here on your own, and I *know* you haven't gone for a run since the last time. We both know how much that sucks. So I figured maybe you needed a good reason to get out here, and I could finally apologize."

All the frustration spilled right out of Amanda and deflated into complete bafflement. "You want to apologize."

He glanced at the swamp and shrugged. "That's what I said."

"For what?"

Swallowing, Matt nodded toward the water's edge and the

open grounds along the campus' northeastern front. "Maybe we should take a walk? I mean, we're standing right under—"

"Corey's room. I know. It's hard *not* to smell him." She hadn't meant it as a joke at all, but the shifter boy laughed.

"You have no idea what a relief it is to be around someone else who knows what that's like. Come on." He took off toward the edge of the swamp and only turned once to flash her the same crooked, almost self-deprecating smile.

He wants to apologize? If it's for practicing dark magic on school grounds and getting caught doing it, he's gonna have to try a lot harder than an apology.

With a growl of frustration, Amanda took off away from the boys' dorm and forced herself not to run after him to keep up. The shifter boy slowed a little until she reached his side, then they were on yet another nighttime stroll along the edge of the river with no one else around to see them.

"Okay." Matt sighed. "That's way better. I think I was starting to—"

"Apologize for what?" Amanda muttered, staring brazenly at him as they walked.

That made him a lot more nervous than when they'd made this outing before, and neither one of them could look at each other for longer than a few seconds. He wrinkled his nose and stuffed his hands deeper into his pockets. "Getting right down to it, huh?"

"You said you wanted to explain. Now you're saying you want to apologize. So which one is it? 'Cause those are two completely different things."

Matt glanced at her sidelong glance with a confused frown. "They don't have to be."

"Well, pick one and start talking. It's Wednesday."

He laughed sharply. "We don't have to *be* in class in the morning. Unless there's some kind of shifter rule I don't know about against talking on Wednesdays. Or Fridays. Or Saturdays..."

Amanda rolled her eyes and turned. "I shouldn't have come out here—"

"Amanda, wait."

When he grabbed her hand, she wanted to jerk it back and punch him in the face. But her body wouldn't catch up with her racing mind, and she stood there, half-turned toward the dorm buildings, and stared at him with wide eyes.

Matt stepped closer and gently released her hand. "Sorry. I make bad jokes when I'm nervous. Full disclosure… I've never done this before. So it's weird. Bear with me, okay?"

"You've never done what before?"

"This. Figuring out how to talk to you about what happened." He glanced at the star-studded sky and grimaced. "You know, *I'm* normally the one keeping secrets about where I come from and what I can do. Not the other way around."

"I'm not keeping secrets." She said it with a completely straight face, but the smile threatening to break through the shifter boy's tightly pressed lips made her clench her jaw.

Yes, that's a lie. He can totally smell it.

"Trust me. I'm not trying to make this weird, but I know it already happened. So here's my apology."

Amanda folded her arms and frowned. "Okay."

"I'm sorry I freaked you out. Don't say I didn't, because obviously, that's what happened. Fine." Matt drew a deep breath, widened his eyes like he couldn't breathe, then let out the rest of it in a long string of words mashed together and a single breath.

"I shouldn't have tried to ask you about your magic when I saw it, and I shouldn't have come on as strong as I did trying to talk to you about it, but I've *never* seen anybody do that, and I really, really, *really* hope you'll tell me how you did it so I can stop driving myself crazy trying to figure it out on my own and coming up with nothing."

He inhaled deeply when all the words finally stopped spilling out of him, then let it out again in a heavy sigh. "There."

She stared at him, and her arms went completely slack before unfolding themselves and dropping at her sides.

Is he for real? That's what this is about? My *magic?*

Matt ran a hand through his hair and looked at the ground, a nervous smile twitching at the corner of his mouth. "This is the part where you say something. Like...anything, because I—"

"You want *me* to explain," Amanda muttered. "Because *my* magic freaked *you* out."

"Um...yeah?"

"You thought I was avoiding you because *I* didn't want to talk about what *you* saw?"

He opened his mouth, paused, and sighed. "I'm doing it again, huh? Coming on way too strong about it. I'm sorry. You just... I mean, I didn't even know a shifter could *do* that—"

"Hold on. Just...back up." Frowning, she pointed at him. "What were *you* doing that day behind the dorm?"

"Practicing. I guess." Matt's crooked smile tightened. "Why?"

"Because this whole time, I thought you wanted to talk about *you*. Try to explain what you were doing so I wouldn't, like, go to Glasket and tell her what you are."

Matt bit his lip but failed to hide his smile. "You don't know what I am."

"Yeah, obviously. But...I mean, *that's* why I've been avoiding you." Amanda shook her head and stared at the ground. "You wouldn't tell me, and your dad seems like a creepy guy already. Then I saw you doing magic I *know* other shifters aren't supposed to be able to do. Because I can already *do* what the rest of the world thinks is impossible for us, and it sure as hell isn't the magic I saw you playing with that day."

Her voice echoed over the water, and a bird took off from its perch in the shadow-darkened trees before swooping low over the river.

Okay, I guess we both had a lot to get off our chests.

Matt pointed at the ground. "You forgot your shoes."

"What?" Amanda dropped her gaze to her bare feet and blinked. "Oh. I didn't even think about shoes."

"Because you were ready to come out here and teach me a lesson about trying to scare you with magic I'm not supposed to have?"

She let out a wry laugh. "You picked up on that, huh?"

"Okay." He stepped out of his shoes, peeled off his socks to stuff them inside, then stood again with both sneakers in one hand and nodded toward the north end of the campus. "So...if I tell you why I'm not some criminal you need to tell Glasket about, will you tell me how you can walk around the school as a wolf made of smoke?"

Looking up from his shoes, Amanda smirked. "If you think you can handle it."

CHAPTER TWENTY

They walked in silence for a while, but Amanda didn't have a problem giving Matt a little more time to think about what he wanted to say. If he needed it.

So this isn't what either of us expected. Fine. At least we can get it all out in the open and quit trying to ignore it. I *can stop trying to ignore it.*

The moonlight rippled across the water as a lizard scurried down the bank at their approach. Matt walked with one hand thrust into his pocket and kept opening his mouth to say something before changing his mind.

Finally, Amanda couldn't help but try to give him a little nudge along. "Why don't you start with telling me about your dad."

He let out a long, slow exhale. "That's what I'm trying to do."

"Okay. You said your mom's a shifter, right? And that your dad isn't. So..."

"Yeah, that's not as straightforward an answer as it sounds like." Matt bit his lip and scowled at the dark sky. "He's...kind of a shifter too."

"You said he wasn't."

"I know. See? It's *that* complicated." Running a hand through his hair again, he sucked in a breath through his clenched teeth and closed his eyes. "Do you know what a Lorikor is?"

"Um...I don't think so." Amanda tried to smile. "Unless I'm walking next to one right now."

"Kind of. My dad's a Lorikor. Or he used to be. Or he used to be *only* that and not anything else, but now he's a shifter too, and I'm... Yeah, I don't know what the hell I am."

Nodding, she stared at the ground passing beneath them and tried to put all that together in a way that made even a little sense. She couldn't. "How did he *become* a shifter?"

"He doesn't talk about that part," Matt muttered. "Trust me, I've tried to get the whole story, but opening up isn't exactly one of his strengths. I don't know if anyone can crack him, honestly. From what I've figured out on my own, I think...I think someone *made* him a shifter."

"Like they experimented on him, or..."

"No clue. So that's fun." He glanced at her sidelong. "I told you it was weird."

"Trust me. It's not any weirder than some of the stuff I've seen in the last three years. I promise."

"I'll try to believe that." He scuffed his feet in the grass as they reached the illusion on the edge of campus that hid the entrance to the Academy's dock.

"So what's a Lorikor, then?"

"Right. They're basically...well, the reason I can't go to school dances."

"With girls."

"I mean, I wouldn't go with a dude."

Amanda snorted. "That's why all the girls here are so...weird about you, right? Because you're half Lorikor?"

"Yeah." He drew another sharp breath. "I wouldn't be telling you any of this if you weren't a shifter. I couldn't. It's like telling somebody their entire life is a hallucination."

"So you hypnotize teenage girls."

Matt let out a fully unrestrained laugh at that and shook his head. "I don't even have to *do* anything. It's the magic I was born with, I guess."

She nodded. "The creepy red stuff."

"Not exactly. That's from my dad's extra shifter-ness. Okay, look, a Lorikor is basically an incubus. Only real, Oriceran, and there's not a whole lot of work that goes into… affecting certain people. Or magicals."

"Oh. Okay, yeah." Amanda nodded quickly. Then it morphed into shaking her head. "I have no idea what you just said."

"Uh… You know how male dogs go completely psycho when a female's in heat?"

She barked out a laugh and quickly slapped a hand over her mouth. "Yeah, I have two dogs at home. And they're already a little psycho to begin with."

"Right. It's like that. Except the psycho dogs are teenage girls, and…this is *really* weird to say out loud."

Amanda's mouth dropped open, her gaze darted around the swamp, and she held her breath as the pieces finally slid into place. "*Oh…*"

"Go ahead and take a minute if you need to—"

"And you can't do anything about it?"

His pursed lips twitched toward the side of his mouth, and he shook his head.

"Wow."

That's not even close to what I expected. I think it's worse.

"So that's where my dad's serious need for privacy comes in. Obviously."

"Obviously." She met his gaze and spread her arms. "Why wouldn't you tell me if I wasn't a shifter?"

Matt shrugged. "Doesn't work on shifters. I guess my parents figured that out when they met, and that pretty much sealed the deal for them. Now I get the best of both worlds."

"Okay. It's getting way easier to be glad I'm a shifter and not anything else."

"You're not *anything* else?" A frown flickered across his eyebrows, and he shrugged. "Because I had no idea shifters who are regular shifters could do…whatever you were doing."

With a nervous laugh, she stepped through the illusion of tall reeds and disappeared. "I'm definitely not anything else. And yeah, I'm sure."

He hurried after her, and they made their way down the dirt path toward the long dock stretching out into the swamp. "So then how did you do that? Wolf magic or whatever."

"Honestly, after everything you just said, I'm pretty sure you'll be disappointed."

"Nah. I don't think you could disappoint me if you tried." When he stepped closer beside her, his fingers brushed hers, and Amanda almost stopped walking. Somehow, her legs kept moving all on their own. "I mean, unless you keep avoiding me after this 'cause I totally freaked you out."

She pressed her lips together and shook her head. "Nope. It takes a lot to freak me out. Like, a lot. But I would *definitely* be freaked out if I wasn't a shifter, and you told me my whole life's a hallucination because you're half-Lorikor."

They both laughed and slowed as they reached the edge of the school dock and the two airboats moored on either side.

"I'm glad you're not anything else." Matt's fingers brushed against hers as they stood at the water's edge, and when he laced their fingers together to hold her hand, she didn't pull away.

This is insane. Bad idea. Stop.

"Yeah." She looked up at him with a small smile. "Me too."

Amanda told him everything she could about shifter magic, about Oriceran shifters' connection to the Saithe who helped them access that magic, and about what she'd had to do under Fiona's supervision to do the same thing for herself. Of course, she left out the incriminating details about the hidden cellar in the greenhouse. Nor did she mention how illegal Fatethistle was on Earth. Or that she was one of the few shifters on the planet who could use their magic the way she could—including moving physical objects and having telepathic conversations with the divergent mermaids underwater.

She also didn't mention anything about her work with the Coalition and Dr. Caniss or her promotion from intern to active fifteen-year-old employee who received massive paychecks.

He was already nervous, and I really don't need to make his brain explode right now.

At some point during her story, they sat on the dock to dangle their legs over the edge and into the water. Half of her mind was focused solely on the fact that they'd been holding hands the whole time. It should have been weird. It wasn't.

When she finished, it took Matt a lot longer to say something.

Maybe I did make his brain explode, and now he'll be avoiding me.

Finally, the shifter boy drew a deep breath and lowered his head. "I have one question."

"Oh. Okay."

He turned to look at her, and his crooked smile returned without any of the self-consciousness or embarrassment he'd been wearing all night. "What do I have to do for you to help me with shifter magic?"

Amanda's mouth popped open, and her surprised laugh bounced across the water and into the trees. "That's your only question?"

"Yeah. 'Cause that is *so* freaking cool. What else would I wanna know?"

"I don't know. I'm not the one asking me questions."

His smile widened into a flashing grin, and he looked down at their interlaced fingers resting on the dock between them. "Just think about it. And don't tell me I only have to say please or something. If you went through all that to be able to use your magic, I should at least have to work for it a *little*."

"Oh, yeah. Believe me. I'm not giving away all the secrets for free."

"I didn't think so."

When he looked up at her, Amanda felt like her stomach was either about to sink through her legs and out her bare feet or surge up and out of her throat.

We were doing this last year too. I have no idea what this is. Or what I'm doing. Or why this should be the worst idea in the world but doesn't feel like it. Shit.

"I'm really glad I annoyed you so much outside your window that you finally came out to talk to me again."

She choked back a laugh. "Yeah, I was pretty sure this was gonna turn out a lot differently."

"Sorry."

"No, you're not." She bumped her shoulder against his, but instead of letting her knock him away, Matt leaned closer.

He was staring at her lips.

Get up and run away! What's wrong with you?

The corner of his mouth twitched in and out of a smile. "Do you think we—"

Amanda jolted when her Coalition phone buzzed in her back pocket.

No. No, no, no.

"Whoa." Matt chuckled and leaned slightly away. "What's that?"

"Nothing." She plastered a tight, unconvincing smile onto her face and shook her head. "Definitely nothing."

"It sounded like a phone."

"It's not."

He pressed his lips together and raised his eyebrows. "Okay."

Seriously, who texts a kid in school at midnight on a Wednesday?

"What you were gonna say?" she asked.

"Uh... Well, it's kinda weird now."

"Not even a little. I'm listening."

Matt lowered his head again. "I wonder if there's—"

Her phone buzzed again and again, and Amanda could only sit there trying to ignore what was obviously a ringing phone for so long. "Oh, come on!"

Laughing, Matt released her hand and grabbed the edge of the dock with both hands instead. "Go ahead. I won't tell anybody."

"I'm sorry. This stupid..." She ripped the phone out of her back pocket and saw the unsaved number she recognized as the Canissphere's weird all-inclusive hotline. "Sorry." She took the call and slapped the phone to her ear. "What?"

"Huh. You *are* awake. It's Rick."

"Uh-huh..." Her gaze drifted toward Matt, but she instantly forced herself to look at the water instead.

"You got what we sent you, right?"

"Yep."

What's the point of trying to be vague? Matt can hear this entire conversation.

"Good. You can expect something else from us in the next few days. To help you get back out here on your own. When it's there, Dr. Caniss wants you to report in person within two hours. Got it?"

"Yep. Sounds great. I gotta go bye..." Amanda ended the call and froze, not seeing the moonlight sparkling on the water or the shadows of the trees dancing across it. She felt like her body was picking itself up and shipping out somewhere far, far away from the dock.

Where she'd just blown open a lot more secrets she hadn't been ready to share because *Dr. Caniss* wanted her to *report*.

"So." Swallowing thickly, she lowered the phone into her lap. "I guess you heard all that."

Matt cleared his throat. "Yep."

"And you probably have a few more questions."

"Nope." He smiled at her and shrugged. "If you wanted me to know, you would've told me with everything else. You spent most of last semester somewhere else, so it's not a surprise."

"Oh. Okay."

"Plus, we were only out here to talk about our weird magic, right?" With a soft chuckle, he picked himself up off the dock and offered her a hand. "So I'll show up outside your window with some red lights when I wanna talk about whatever that phone call was."

Playfully rolling her eyes, she took his hand and let him haul her up. He didn't let go.

"Or you could send your ghost-wolf out to get me. That would be cool."

She snorted and turned away to head down the dock, which made him finally release her hand. "I'm not going anywhere near the inside of a boys' dorm. Not even with my *magic.* Hard no."

Grabbing his shoes, Matt hurried to catch up with her. "Yeah, I don't blame you."

CHAPTER TWENTY-ONE

After everything she'd learned that night and shared her secrets with Matt, Amanda had no idea how to feel about any of it the next day. Or the next. Knowing what the shifter boy was and how he could do what he did, explained the reactions he'd been getting since he'd shown up halfway through last year.

It didn't explain Amanda's reaction at all.

Mainly the fact that she couldn't stop thinking about him or their conversation or how much she wanted to go for another run with another shifter but couldn't.

She hated it.

Grace and Summer noticed right away that something was different, but Amanda wasn't ready to spill the shifter beans on that one yet. It didn't help that the entire school had caught the contagious excitement of the Homecoming Louper match that Friday and the ensuing dance on Saturday.

So she locked herself up in the greenhouse during her free time—which was most of the day every day—and poured herself into growing the very safe, very boring plants she'd ordered. That still left her plenty of time to work on her reports, write-ups, and projects for each of her senior year classes.

Amanda wasn't interested in watching the Louper match, but she went out to the central field that Friday night anyway to spend time with her friends. Since Matt didn't generally show up with the rest of the school when it wasn't required—to avoid being swarmed by the girls in every class, especially this close to the dance—it felt safe enough. She had no idea how she was supposed to feel about him now.

A Lorikor's powers didn't work on shifters.

So if I can't stop thinking about him, that means I'm screwed.

The day of Homecoming was as busy with excitement as every other year. Grace and Annabelle had somehow managed to buy completely new dresses from one of those ridiculous shops in the kemana. They went crazy with painting their faces and using whatever they could find on campus to decorate their Homecoming outfits.

"Costumes," Summer said as the girls' dorm quickly emptied to head for the dance in the central field. "You guys bought costumes for Homecoming. Come on, Blondie. Halloween's next month."

Grace glared at her from beneath the layers of glitter and sequins painted and stuck onto her face. "At least I'm dressing up. You're not even trying."

"To do what? Blind everybody?"

Rolling her eyes, Grace laughed and pulled Annabelle along with her by the hand. "Come on. I wanna be first through the archway." She paused briefly to look Amanda up and down. "You're not dressing up either?"

The shifter girl shrugged. "I'm not that into dressing up, Grace. I thought you would've figured that out by now."

"It's our *last Homecoming.*"

"Yep."

"Okay, whatever. See you guys out there."

All the other girls who'd dressed up for the occasion hurried down the stairwell and across the common room to spill outside onto the lawn. Amanda and Summer took their time. Small groups of freshmen girls with their hair and makeup stations set up in the common room took their time helping each other finish getting ready too, but they were stalling more out of nerves than anything else.

"So what's really going on, shifter girl?" Summer bumped her shoulder against Amanda's and smirked. "You're acting weird."

"Because I didn't dress up for the dance and don't wanna rush out to be the first through the archway? That's what I've been doing for the last three years."

The witch scoffed. "You know what I mean. All the looks and the dreamy staring at the wolf-boy."

Amanda gave her a warning glance and turned to gauge the reactions of the other girls still in the common room.

At least she didn't say his name out loud. I have no idea who else even knows Matt's a shifter.

"It's a shifter thing, okay?"

"Duh. Two shifters in the same school. Twenty bucks says I can nail exactly what that *shifter thing* is on the very first try."

"Don't." Amanda pushed open the front door of the dorm, and the growing noise of girls fawning over each other's dresses and boys shouting and roughhousing each other filled the air. The student body had gathered in front of the archway and the magical veil separating the central field from the rest of the school.

Everyone was way too excited. Amanda couldn't focus on any of it.

"So you guys *haven't* been sneaking out in the middle of the night to do your *shifter thing* together?" Summer asked, waggling her eyebrows.

"No. Stop asking. There's nothing to tell."

"Your loss." The witch shrugged and nudged her friend again. "I'm gonna go stuff my face with snacks the second they open this thing up. See you there."

Then Summer took off into the crowd, shouting for the underclassmen to get out of the way so she could get a spot right in front of the veil. "Seniors first, kids! We earned it."

Amanda shook her head and searched for the rest of her friends. Grace and Annabelle had joined Jasmine and Blake, all of them looking like they were at some kind of magical-elite ball instead of a dance to celebrate the Louper team and school spirit. Jackson and Alex clowned around with Tommy, Evan, and some of the braver junior boys before a game of magical-light hacky sack started.

Maybe it won't be so bad this time. Matt's obviously not coming, and I don't have to hide to answer the stupid Coalition phone at the last minute. Hopefully.

She reached absently toward her back pocket and the phone she refused to leave back in her room after missing Fiona's rare and unexpected texts.

I can have a little fun tonight. No problem.

A tingle of excitement mixed with dread washed over her when she caught the familiar scent in the air. Two seconds later, half the noise of the students waiting expectantly for the veil beneath the archway to lift hushed to tense silence. The boys kept shouting and shoving each other around, but all the girls had stopped squealing over dresses and hair and makeup to whisper to each other instead.

They were all staring at Amanda.

No, no, no. Not right now. Please.

"Figured I should stop trying to hide all the time," Matt said behind her. "I'm starting to think maybe that wasn't such a good idea."

She turned with wide eyes and found him smiling sheepishly at her. The first thing that popped into her head came flying out of her mouth. "I thought you didn't go to dances."

He chuckled nervously. "That was kinda the impression I had about you too."

Amanda's senses intensified ten times, and the other girls whispering to each other sounded as loud as if they were standing right beside her and talking to *her* instead.

"I don't get it. Why her?"

"She's been ignoring him since he got here."

"I asked him three times to go to Homecoming with me, and he said he didn't go to dances."

"What's so special about Amanda?"

"She didn't even dress up."

Amanda swallowed and tried to smile.

If I can hear them, so can he. This sucks so much right now.

"I mean, it's the last Homecoming dance we'll ever have," she muttered, trying to focus on his blue eyes instead of the constant surge of petty, judgmental comments. "How many have you been to?"

Matt rubbed the back of his neck and shrugged. "None. I'm pretty sure you can tell why right about now."

"Honestly, this isn't the first time I've had to ignore a bunch of rumors about me."

He let out another nervous chuckle, and a knot of apprehension and guilt tightened even more in her gut.

He's never been to a school dance. Ever. And I'm worried about what everyone else is gonna think of me*?*

"Okay, listen." Amanda forced herself not to turn around and snarl at all the girls she could feel glaring daggers into her back. "It's senior year. This is part of high school, right?"

"Maybe for everyone else." Matt grimaced and started to turn. "Sorry. I shouldn't have even come out here. I'll just—"

"Wanna go with me?" she blurted.

He stopped, swallowed, and cast a wary glance at the students behind her—the boys still roughhousing on the grounds in front of the archway, and the girls oscillating back and forth between batting their eyelashes at the Lorikor-shifter boy and shooting dirty looks at the back of the shifter girl's head.

"To the dance, I mean," she clarified. "We can...you know. Be stared at together, I guess."

Matt shook his head. "You don't have to do this."

"I don't do crazy things I probably shouldn't because I *have* to, Matt."

He cracked a smile and lowered his head. "Are you sure?"

"Yeah. If you want to. I totally get it if you don't."

They stared at each other for a moment, and she quickly wiped her once more clammy hands on her jean pedal-pushers before swallowing thickly.

If he says yes, there's no way to hide this anymore. Why don't I want him to say no?

The boy bit his lip and nodded once. "Okay."

"Okay?"

"Yeah." Matt's carefree, crooked smile returned, and he shrugged. "I mean, we're the only two shifters here, right? We gotta stick together somehow."

Butterflies exploded in Amanda's stomach, and she wiped her hands on her pants again.

Now I'm gonna be sick.

"You don't have to—"

"I want to." He nodded and awkwardly held out his hand. "If you can show up to dances for three years by yourself, I can handle one with someone who knows who I am."

She stared at his open hand between them.

"And it makes it a lot easier when it's someone I like," he added.

Her throat closed up.

Crap. I really am *gonna puke right here.*

"Yeah," she whispered, her mouth moving in complete opposition to all her instincts telling her to slap his hand away and take off running into the swamp. "That makes it a lot easier."

Despite the hair on the back of her neck standing on end and the prickling sensation of so many stares boring into her from behind, Amanda took his hand like they were about to shake. Matt laughed and reached down to take her other hand instead before lacing his fingers through hers. "Just because we didn't shake on it doesn't mean I don't owe you one."

"Ha. Right." She turned and stared straight ahead at the shimmering veil of light blocking off the archway.

He leaned toward her and muttered, "Thank you."

A sharp laugh of surprise burst out of her. "You owe me one now, so be ready for a shifter girl to call in a favor."

"I can handle favors." He grinned and pulled her gently forward with him toward the rest of the students. "It's the dance I'm worried about. I don't even know if I *can* dance."

"Trust me, nobody here can either."

They both laughed at that and headed forward toward the crowd of students waiting for the Homecoming dance to begin. The girls had all stopped whispering and making flirty faces at Matt Hardy. Now they were completely silent, and they all glared at Amanda Coulier, holding hands with the crush of every teenage girl in the school.

Except for her friends. Grace stood perfectly still in her shimmering dress and sequined makeup, her mouth hanging open and her eyes bulging. There was no animosity in *her* stare, just complete and utter shock.

Summer grinned and smacked the blonde witch's bare arm with the back of a hand. "Holy shit! I *knew* it!"

"Yeah right," Grace muttered. "Nobody knew this would happen. She's not... She didn't even dress up."

"Looks like you did all that work for nothing, huh, Blondie?"

"Shut up. I look amazing."

A bright light flashed across the veil inside the archway, and the magic blocking the students from the central field and the dance lost its opaqueness. Bright lights were barely visible around the dancefloor behind it, and Summer laughed before pointing at the veil. "Time to party!"

The students closest to the archway surged forward through the veil, the boys shoving each other through and the girls dejectedly turning to enter the dance they'd been hoping to go to with Matt Hardy.

"Hardy!" Tommy shouted. "Hey, guys. Check it out. He actually showed."

His group of friends turned to see Matt and Amanda at the edge of students filing into the dance.

"Yes!" Evan punched his friend in the shoulder. "Dude, you owe me two bottles of Juicy Tune. Pay up."

"I don't have it *on me*."

Amanda's smile had been growing all on its own since the second Matt had taken her hand in front of the entire school. It faded when she saw Jackson turning around in the group of senior boys to see her and the Academy's newest senior walking into the dance together. The wizard's eyes widened as he glanced back and forth from Matt's self-conscious smile to the shifter boy's hand holding Amanda's. In two seconds, his entire face bloomed with one of his darkest flushes yet, and he didn't respond when Jack shoved him toward the veil.

"Come on, dude. The food's the best part. Let's go."

Jackson's gaze flickered toward Amanda's once, and when he realized she was looking at him, he spun and hurried after his buddies to disappear behind the veil.

Oh, man. I didn't even think about Jackson. What kind of friend does that make me?

She and Matt stepped through the archway with the last of the students. Amanda didn't register the dancefloor decorated this year in a checkered pattern in Academy green and gold, or the green and yellow lights bobbing around the central field to act as a ceiling. Or the life-sized statues set around the perimeter of the field and made to look like giant chess pieces. If she'd looked close enough, she would have seen each chess-piece statue was a humanoid alligator dressed as kings, queens, pawns, knights, bishops, and rooks.

The only thing she could focus on was how insanely guilty she felt in the moment.

For the crushed look on Jackson's deeply flushed face.

For asking Matt to the dance when his hand was as clammy as hers and betrayed he was just as uncomfortable.

For being the one girl in the entire school Matt Hardy wanted to talk to because she was a shifter immune to his Lorikor magic and wasn't doing anything to make him like her.

And yes, even for thinking she liked him back, as weird as the whole thing was.

The kind of friend who doesn't care about anyone else's feelings. That's what this makes me.

Still, Amanda had been to a dance with Jackson. Not officially, of course, but they'd at least danced together. For as weird as that had been, it had made him ridiculously happy. Everyone at the Academy knew how Jackson Pris felt about the school's token shifter girl. Now everyone at the Academy knew Amanda was at the dance with Matt instead. Holding his hand.

But I don't like Jackson. Not that way...

She gritted her teeth and was barely aware now of even the dirty looks the other girls threw her way. The quick beat of whatever music the faculty and staff had chosen for the night thudded in her ears with her heartbeat and only halfway drowned out the noise of an entire school on the dancefloor to have a good time for Homecoming.

Only half of them were having a good time now. Maybe more than half, now that Jackson stood at the refreshments table covered in green-and-gold-decorated cookies and brownies and cakes, stuffing his face with whatever happened to be right in front of him and scowling.

"You okay?" Matt asked.

"What?" Amanda glanced up at him, and her stomach lurched when his blue-eyed gaze fixed on hers, and the dimples in his cheeks wouldn't let up.

"If you changed your mind, I totally get it—"

"No." She surprised herself by gently squeezing his hand and smiling back. "You were right."

"About what?"

"About not trying to hide all the time." Drawing a deep breath, she nodded. "You're not the only one who's been doing that."

Matt's crooked smile widened. "Two shifter kids blazing a trail, huh?"

"Something like that."

"How about this? If either of us wants to leave, we say it, okay? No hard feelings. I mean, walking around the swamp last year wasn't anywhere near as scary as this, right?"

Amanda bit her lip through a small smile. "I've been through some seriously scary stuff. Like, the deadly kind of things that would probably make most adults run away screaming. Is it weird that school dances are still at the top of the list?"

Matt laughed and shook his head. "You know, I think that's kind of the point."

"Of dances?"

"Yeah, to scare us all straight so we focus on school again afterward."

Her cheeks hurt already from smiling so much, and the knot of guilt in her stomach softened a little. "Okay. Deal. If either of us wants to leave, we say it."

"Cool. Do you…wanna leave?"

Amanda could have sworn Matt and every other kid on the central field heard her gulp down the dry lump in her throat. "No. Do you?"

"I mean, maybe after the dancing starts and you see how bad I am. Right now? No. I can't believe I'm saying this, but I think this might work."

"Finally being at a dance?"

"With you? Yeah."

He wouldn't stop staring at her, and when he leaned slightly toward her, she looked away and scanned the dancefloor. "Me too."

Matt squeezed her hand, and she broke into a wide grin despite the weirdness of how close he stood beside her and what she thought he'd almost tried to do.

Yeah, if he kisses me right here in front of everybody, we might have to leave the dance. With an angry mob of teenage girls chasing me with magical pitchforks.

The music died, and Matt sniffed gently before pointing at the refreshments table. "Do the pixies set out a spread like that for every dance?"

"Yep." She couldn't look at the banquet tables where Jackson still stuffed his face with desserts, and Alex had stopped eating to eye the wizard up and down with a concerned frown.

"Wow. I had no idea what I was missing." Matt chuckled. "Should we go check it out?"

"Um...I don't know if—"

The music quickly faded, and on the stage, Glasket cleared her throat into the enchanted microphone bobbing around her head. "Welcome, students, to your Homecoming dance this year."

The susurrus of students talking and laughing and commenting on the decorations dwindled to an impatient drone, although everyone looked up at the stage to hear what their principal had to say.

The woman had dressed up in a glittering golden dress trimmed in Florida-Gator green. She'd slicked her hair back away from her face to make room for the sequin-covered head-dress—the top of an alligator's head, sharp teeth protruding from the underside and glittering in the light.

"Is it me, or does Glasket look like she's getting eaten by a gator?" Matt muttered.

Amanda barked out a laugh and forced herself not to glare back at the girls closest to them, who turned and shot her even more dirty looks. "It's not you."

"Cool."

"For most of you, this is only the beginning," Glasket continued. "For this year's senior class, I'm sure tonight comes with a bittersweet edge. Your last Homecoming dance at the Academy of Necessary Magic. We will *always* encourage fun and adventure on this campus in addition to hard work and dedication to your studies. However, I want to remind this year's senior class, especially our Louper players who brought back an incredible victory in last night's game, how much you all have taught *us* at this school over the last three years. The rest of you have some big shoes to fill. Yes, even the Louper team."

"Go Gators!" Patrick shouted.

The more avid fans of the game pumped their fists in the air and echoed the cry.

"Thank you, Mr. Jules." Glasket grinned and nodded. "This school has come a long way in proving itself as both a valuable and extremely resilient institution within the circle of magical academia. And yes, most certainly as a school who can give the other teams a run for their money during every single match."

"Start the dance!" Tommy shouted.

"Too bad Pete's not here to DJ," Evan added, and students burst out laughing.

"Yes, we all miss Mr. Cross'...antics." Glasket's smile tightened briefly. "We'll get to the dance in a second. First, I'd like you all to give Mr. LeFor—Coach LeFor, to the Louper team—another brief moment of your attention before the rest of the night is yours."

Somewhere on Amanda's left, Summer's load groan split through the murmurs of the other students. "Does it never end? We just wanna party!"

Amanda pressed her lips together and didn't dare try to look at her friend, shouting for the freedom of the night to begin finally.

At least Summer's enjoying herself at her last Homecoming too. I guess this is as good a time as any for her to be obnoxious and get away with it.

CHAPTER TWENTY-TWO

Glasket gestured toward the side of the stage, where Mr. LeFor nodded before climbing the stairs. The redhead teacher was decked out in green and gold too. Only he looked like he'd dressed for a competitive Louper match played by a professional adult team instead of a school dance.

The Louper team obnoxiously cheered when he took the stage and *thumped* a hand against his green and gold jersey with an alligator's open jaws plastered across the front. Then he raised a hand, and the noise decreased only slightly. "I'll make this quick. Just a little boost to school spirit tonight. Because this is the first year the Florida Gators have held the top of the scoreboard for the season since our very first match, and *we're gonna keep it*! Championship, here we come!"

The Louper team roared in approval and quickly started up a chant.

"Ga-*tors*! Ga-*tors*! Ga-*tors*!"

The rest of the student body picked it up quickly, and LeFor stuck his hands on his hips, smirking and looking as proud as if he'd already won the championship singlehandedly.

"Yes." He cleared his throat. "We deserve a little celebrating. But that doesn't mean we can just—"

An obnoxiously high-pitched *beep* echoed across the grounds from the end of the gravel drive beyond the entrance gates.

LeFor frowned but kept going. "It doesn't mean we can just—"

The horn *beeped* again three times, and two tiny white headlights flashed on the drive.

The Louper coach turned to scowl at the source of the interruption. "We can't just—"

Whoever was beeping the horn laid into it one more time and sent one long, drawn-out tone across the campus for a full five seconds.

LeFor growled in frustration, and the students burst out laughing.

"Speech! Speech!" Tommy shouted, pumping his fist in the air.

"Watch it, Brunse," LeFor warned.

"Please continue," Glasket told him. "I'll go see what this is about."

She picked up the skirt of her glittering gown and strode briskly away from the bright lights of the central field toward the headlights on the gravel drive, her silhouette darkening until she was barely visible racing across the grass.

"Looks like someone else has a problem with school dances too," Matt muttered.

Amanda chuckled. "Interrupting school dances is kind of an Academy tradition at this point."

"Oh, yeah?"

"I told you about the time we were attacked by wild boars, right?"

LeFor ruffled his straight red hair in frustration, then leaned toward the floating mic. "Anyway, we're gonna have a great rest of the season, and if we don't bring home the championship this year... Well, that's impossible."

The Louper team roared and took up their chant again.

"Have a good dance." LeFor spun away from the mic and stomped down the stage, glaring at Petrov when the Combat Training teacher snorted and shot him a thumbs-up.

The music turned back up to full volume—some new pop song Amanda hadn't heard before but seemed ridiculously popular with everyone else—and the dancefloor broke into dancing, cheering, and jumping around.

"This is…weird," Matt muttered.

She looked up at him with a playful frown. "The music?"

"*Yeah.*" He swept his other hand toward the dancing kids around them. "I've never heard this stuff."

"I don't know any of the music, either. Maybe it's a shifter thing."

Matt's loud, unabashed laugh drew several more dirty looks from the girls around them before they ended up pulled away from their friends. Through no fault of their own, the two shifter kids at the Academy remained at the far end of the field inside the archway with a wide circle of space around them.

Amanda shrugged. "Just checking in. If you wanna leave *now…*"

"I said we'd wait 'til you see exactly how much I can't dance. Then we'll check in again."

"Okay. Go ahead—"

"Nope. You're coming with me."

She shouted in surprise when he tugged her behind him toward the sea of bodies spinning wildly to the music, and the music pumping from the giant speakers beside the stage drowned out her laughter.

Matt spun to take her other hand and grinned. "If you run away now, I'll *know* I'm terrible."

"It's not like I have anything to compare it to—"

The music cut off instantly, and a collective groan rose from the students.

"Are you *kidding* me right now?" Summer shouted.

Glasket hurried up the steps to the stage and said quickly into the mic, "I promise this is the last interruption. Miss Coulier, can you please meet me behind the stage?"

Amanda's stomach sank lower than it ever had. The fact that most of the students who'd just launched into their enjoyment of the Homecoming dance started booing made it even worse. So did the continued booing when the music picked back up again and only a few students went back to their dancing.

"Crap."

Matt frowned as Glasket hurried off the stage. "That was a shitty way to get your attention. You didn't do anything."

"I know. Apparently, I don't have to." She pulled her hand out of his and headed toward the side of the dancefloor beside the entrance arch. She didn't want to walk through a crowd of kids glaring at her and voicing their disapproval.

"Amanda, wait." He took off after her, but she didn't bother to turn around or slow.

I knew this was a bad idea. Coming to a dance with Matt. Getting death-glares from all the girls. And now I'm *the reason the dance gets interrupted. Again.*

"Amanda!"

Her cheeks burned, and her gut squirmed as she slipped around the edge of the dancefloor.

"Shut up!" Summer barked. "Everybody quit—hey!"

A stream of silver light darted from Summer's hand and leapt straight up into the sky. Three large bursts of green erupted at the top and sent a cascade of magical fireworks around the dancefloor. The music kept going, but now the students focused on Summer Flannerty and her famous light show.

"We're at a dance, you morons," she shouted. "So cut the shit and let's party!"

A cheer arose, and the other kids crowded around her with renewed excitement before the dancing picked up again.

Leave it to Summer to make herself the center of attention. I'll have to thank her for it this time.

Amanda finally reached the edge of the central field and the stage, where the teachers were huddled in a group and talking in low voices.

"Miss Coulier." Glasket nodded at her. "I'm sorry to have called attention to you like that, but this seems like something of a time-sensitive matter."

"Yeah, so was trying to get away from the *entire school* booing at me."

"Again, I apologize. Perhaps I should have chosen a more discreet method."

"No kidding."

"Hey." Matt jogged toward them and slowed, his eyes wide with concern. "What's going on?"

"This is a private conversation, Mr. Hardy." Glasket pointed at the dancefloor. "Please return to—"

"Maybe I can help."

"That's very thoughtful of you, but I don't think that's appropriate. Go enjoy yourself at the dance, Mr. Hardy."

"It's okay," Amanda blurted. "He can stay."

Glasket and the other teachers stared at her. "I wasn't aware anyone had cleared your...extracurricular engagements for sharing with other students, Miss Coulier."

"Matt's a shifter. He already knows about the Coalition." Amanda folded her arms. "And I'm pretty sure neither one of us would last very long if we went back to the dance."

The principal blinked quickly, looking thoroughly berated by that one simple statement with more than one meaning.

Yeah, she knows what he is too.

"Very well. I have to inform you, Mr. Hardy, that when Miss Coulier takes her leave, you are still required to remain on campus."

Matt frowned. "Where is she going?"

"I'll let her explain that one however she likes. Follow me, please." Glasket took off across the edge of the field toward the gravel drive and the two small, bright headlights glowing in the darkness.

Amanda glanced at Matt before heading after their principal. "Sorry about this."

"If anyone should be sorry, it's *her*." He nodded toward Glasket. "She interrupted the whole dance and basically said it was your fault."

"Yeah, I know. She doesn't exactly handle this kinda thing very well."

"What kinda thing?"

"It's complicated."

"Hey." Matt grabbed her hand again and held her back. Amanda tried as hard as she could to keep her gaze focused on the headlights waiting for her at the entrance to the school grounds, but it was impossible when he muttered, "Look at me."

With a sigh, she met his gaze, and the butterflies returned. Only now they were heavy and made of rocks instead of light and fluttery.

"You can tell me what's going on," he said gently. "If you want to. I get it if you don't. It's just... If Glasket's this freaked out, it doesn't look like something you can brush off."

"Miss Coulier," Glasket called, stopping halfway toward the gravel drive to turn around and wave them forward. "Please do hurry up."

Amanda pulled Matt forward by the hand and leaned toward him as they walked quickly to catch up with the principal. "Okay, I don't have a lot of time, so here's the basic explanation that's gonna be super confusing and I won't be able to clear up until I get back."

"Get back from where?"

"I work for the Coalition of Shifters, Matt. I'm one of only a few shifters who can do what I do with my magic, and I had an internship with this lab out in Colorado before they actually... you know. Hired me for real. That's where I was last semester. I was working. They have a deal with Glasket that whenever they need me, I have to pack up and leave campus."

"You work for... Wait. So she doesn't care about you skipping school?"

"Trust me. I don't skip anything. I just do it all at the Canis-sphere between jobs."

"The what?"

"The lab." Amanda swallowed thickly. "That's who called me the other night when we were at the dock."

"You already have a job."

"Yeah."

Matt let out an unconvincing chuckle. "Doing what?"

She stopped, looked up at him, and wrinkled her nose. "Capturing and identifying divergent species of magical Oriceran creatures who've evolved on Earth. Hopefully, before they end up causing a bunch of problems for everyone because nobody knows what they are, what they can do, or how to stop them."

He blinked quickly. "So you're...what? A teenage scientist?"

"No, I work with scientists. I'm basically their on-call monster hunter."

"*What?*"

"Miss Coulier!"

"Shit." Amanda nervously licked her lips. "You really don't have to come with me for this. But I'll probably be gone for a while."

"There's no way in hell you can say something like that and expect me to walk away *now*." He squeezed her hand again and nodded toward the glowing headlights. "Come on."

They hurried toward the gravel drive and a very impatient Principal Glasket waiting there with her arms folded and a confused scowl darkening her features. Amanda couldn't help the grin threatening to split apart her entire face.

He doesn't care. He's not even freaked out. So...what? He thinks it's cool*? Or maybe he wants to make sure I'm not lying about the whole thing just to get rid of him. Jeeze, Caniss really picked the worst night for all of this.*

"Next time, Miss Coulier, I would very much appreciate a little more haste on your part," Glasket snapped.

"Next time, Dean Glasket, I would very much appreciate you not calling me out in front of the whole school."

The woman opened her mouth, shut it quickly again, and drew a deep breath. "Fair enough. Mr. Crowley, she's ready. Wherever you are, you can come out now." Glasket spun in a slow circle, stumbling a little on the gravel in her high heels. "Mr. Crowley?"

"Whoever he is," Matt said, "I'm guessing he's the one who showed up on the scooter, right?"

Amanda finally took a moment to look at the source of the small, bright headlights that had flashed across the campus. Yes, it was a motorized scooter—probably blue, but it was impossible to tell in the darkness out here—with a matching helmet dangling from one of the handlebars.

"That's an accurate guess, Mr. Hardy," Glasket muttered. "It seems the envoy who arrived to collect Miss Coulier has...left the premises."

"What did he say?" Amanda asked.

"That Dr. Caniss gave her apologies for such late notice, but it was time for you to use what they gave you and return to your post. That's all."

"Oh, jeeze..." Amanda rolled her eyes.

That's what Rick said. I'd be getting something else, and they'd be reaching out in a few days. Of course, he couldn't have told me it would be today.

"It's for me."

"I'm sorry?" Glasket looked like she'd stumbled into an invisible wall.

"The scooter."

"Why in the world would a shifter from the Coalition show up on this vehicle with news like that and simply leave it here for *you?*"

"I think they're fed up with sending someone to escort me." Amanda spread her arms. "And I don't have a car. Or a license."

"I..." The principal frowned. "Hmm."

"Hey, does that look like a note?" Matt pointed at the scooter's seat, and Amanda released his hand to go check it out.

Sure enough, whoever had driven her new ride onto campus and interrupted LeFor's Homecoming speech with an obnoxious scooter horn had left Amanda a note. She snatched it up and quickly scanned the brief contents. "Yeah. I have to go."

"Right now?" Matt looked back and forth between the shifter girl and their principal.

Glasket shrugged. "If they're confident enough in your ability to make the journey on your own, Miss Coulier, so am I. Although I do think—"

Another rapid blast of fireworks shot up into the air above the dancefloor and exploded in fiery sparks. The students screamed and cheered and burst out laughing.

"If Miss Flannerty ends up setting the campus on fire with that volatile display, I don't care *what* her test scores are." Glasket headed back toward the dance, then turned halfway around. "Be safe, Miss Coulier. Mr. Hardy, I'm sure I don't have to inform you everything you've seen or heard tonight remains between you, Miss Coulier, and myself. Correct?"

He shrugged. "Who am I gonna tell?"

"That's precisely—" More fireworks and cheers cut her off, and she spun again. "You two can figure it out."

Then she stalked away toward the dance and left Amanda and Matt alone with the scooter's softly idling engine.

He glanced at the note dangling from her hand. "Any chance I can get the CliffsNotes version of that too?"

Amanda shrugged and handed it to him. "Go ahead."

While Matt read her summons from Omega Industries, she walked around the scooter toward the built-in compartment that was as much like a trunk as this thing was likely to get. She turned the note over in her mind—short, sweet, and clear to *her,* if not everyone else.

The standard chauffeur is now below your paygrade. Any maintenance, repairs, or upgrades come out of your pocket. You'll find what you need in the trunk. Two hours.

She fully expected to find some kind of toolkit or a write-up of the next job tucked away in the scooter's rear compartment. Instead, Amanda discovered her backpack squashed down into the box, complete with her pre-packed clothes and materials for school.

Wow. The messenger went into my room. Good thing I already had my stuff ready to go, or this would've been a complete waste of time.

Right on top of her backpack was a small black device with a red button in the center. Above the button, someone had used a label maker to write out yet another short, vague set of instructions and had taped it to the device: *Property of Omega Industries. Press to Enter.*

"Two hours?" Matt handed the note back as Amanda closed the trunk again. "As in..."

"As in, my boss will blow a fuse if I don't show up when she expects me to." When the shifter boy frowned, Amanda added flippantly, "She's basically a robot."

"Your boss is a robot?"

"I know. It's weird, right?" She smirked and stuffed the note into her pocket. "I have a *boss.*"

"Okay, I'm way more lost than I thought I'd be." Matt chuckled. "Don't get me wrong. All this is...actually pretty cool. But I still don't get what's going on."

"Join the club, Matt." Amanda approached him and gazed up into his wide eyes. "I'm really sorry. I wanted to be able to stay at the dance with you. You know, this whole thing started as an internship because they needed somebody who could do the job without breaking everything or blowing it up or shooting at the wrong target because they had no idea what they were—"

He cut off her nervous rambling with the last thing in the world Amanda expected right now.

Matt kissed her.

Then all the words left her head faster than they'd been tumbling out of her mouth, and she gave herself all of three seconds to enjoy it and take in his scent overwhelming her. After that, her brain went back to scrambling itself at full power because she *didn't* have the time to enjoy it.

She didn't have the time *not* to enjoy it, either.

Finally, Matt pulled away and gently settled his hands on her hips to pull her a little closer. "Sorry."

"What?" Amanda blinked and tried not to sound like she could barely remember what words were.

"I know you have to go. I just... That was really cool."

A halting, breathless laugh escaped her. "Me rambling about my job?"

"Yeah. This whole thing." His crooked smile returned, and he lowered his head toward her. "And you. I didn't want you to leave without knowing that."

"I..." She pressed her lips together to hold back the grin threatening to break through. It didn't work. "Thanks."

Matt bit his lip and backed away. "Any idea when you'll be back?"

"No. Trust me, I wish I had an answer for that. Now more than ever." Amanda playfully rolled her eyes and wished she'd stop saying stuff.

Now more than ever? What is wrong *with me? Now he's gonna think I'm totally desperate.*

"It'll be, like, before winter break, right?" Matt ran a hand through his hair and sighed. "I mean, so I have an idea of how long I'll be running around the swamp and getting snacks with the pixies as the only shifter here."

She barked out a laugh. "I can say I'll *probably* be back before break. But, um..." Amanda stepped backward toward the scooter. "If you wanna stay updated, ask Summer. You know, if you're not afraid of maybe getting punched in the face first."

Matt chuckled warily. "Is she a monster hunter too?"

"Nope. Just my best friend."

She'll probably punch me *in the face for making her the messenger without asking first. She might even if I* had *asked.*

"I really gotta go."

"Yeah." He shoved his hands into his pockets and kept smiling at her as she grabbed the helmet off the scooter's handlebar and strapped it on.

Then she climbed up into the seat and studied the simple controls.

Should've had Johnny teach me how to ride one of these things instead of trying to drive Sheila. That thought made her laugh out loud. *Right. Johnny Walker wouldn't touch a scooter with a ten-foot pole.*

"Do you know how to work that thing?" Matt asked.

"Not really. Can't be that hard, though. I'll figure it out."

"Good luck."

Amanda grinned at him and realized she was still wasting time by falling for a shifter boy she really didn't want to drive away from on a Coalition-provided scooter. "See ya."

Grabbing the handlebars, she searched for the gas and brake pedals before realizing it was all part of the handlebars instead. So she twisted the throttle a little and lurched around the drive with a spray of gravel before turning to face the long road off the Academy grounds. The scooter fishtailed a little on the drive, but she corrected it instantly and looked over her shoulder to see Matt walking backward away from her. He laughed and raised a hand in farewell. Amanda nodded, then forced herself to drive away.

The scooter's engine hummed beneath her. The shouting, laughing, and cheering of every other student at the Academy of Necessary Magic enjoying their Homecoming dance faded away, and the party went on without her.

No big deal. I get to drive away from my school in the Everglades to get to my work at a shifter lab in Colorado. In two hours. After being kissed for the first time by a boy I think I like...

The scooter wobbled beneath her hands and started to skid. With a sharp breath, Amanda corrected it instantly again and blinked quickly before staring straight ahead at the road lit up by the headlights.

Focus, Amanda. You won't keep *this job if you crash this thing on the first ride.*

She did focus. Still, her grin and the butterflies battling in her stomach stayed where they were.

CHAPTER TWENTY-THREE

Fortunately, the Starbucks in Everglades City was still open. The barista who greeted Amanda tried to smile even though the small, fifteen-year-old girl entered the store *with* her motorized scooter instead of leaving it outside where all the normal customers left their vehicles.

The girl couldn't have graduated from high school all that long ago herself, and she seemed more amused than anything else as the shifter girl tried to sneak her new ride through an empty Starbucks at almost 9:00 p.m.

"Nice scooter."

Amanda wrinkled her nose. "Thanks. I'm just, um...taking it—"

"With you on the train, right?"

"What?" Amanda froze, her eyes wide.

"It's totally cool. That's why I work the late shift." The barista chuckled. "After dark is when all the weird stuff happens. Trust me, a girl walking her scooter through the store isn't anywhere close to the weirdest thing I've seen."

"Oh." Swallowing thickly, Amanda tried to sniff the air subtly. *She doesn't smell like a magical.*

"Are you..."

"Nope. I'm totally normal. All human." The barista gestured at herself and grinned. "Sometimes I wish I wasn't."

"Ha. Yeah, I get that."

"Well, I'm not gonna try to stop you. So have a good trip."

Amanda paused, glanced at the menu on the wall behind the other girl who had to be a few years older than her and smirked. "You're still serving coffee, right? Like, you're not just hanging out behind the counter so magicals can bring weird stuff onto the train?"

The barista laughed. "What do you want?"

The shifter girl opened the scooter's storage compartment to grab her wallet out of her backpack. "Whatever has the most caffeine. And a buttload of sugar."

"You got it. Give me a sec."

Amanda approached the counter and pulled out her bank card.

Now, this *is the kinda thing Glasket should be teaching us in that stupid Life Skills class. If this is what being an adult with a job and getting around on my own is actually like, it's way better than I thought.*

The one unexpected downside was that her new scooter barely fit in the Employees Only supply closet at the back of the Starbucks. It took Amanda a whole five minutes to maneuver the thing inside before she realized she could sit on the scooter and fit them both. Holding her sugary, highly caffeinated venti frappuccino in one hand and happily sipping away, she reached toward the brass lever with the other. This time, she didn't care that the drop into the Starbucks train station still made her sick.

Drinking more frappuccino helped.

The train was completely empty when she awkwardly walked

her ride out of the closet elevator and into the open car waiting for her. Apparently, it was waiting for someone else too, because she spent the next fifteen minutes sitting on the train with no indication the thing was about to take off.

Her thoughts went back to Matt as she sucked on her straw and crunched overly sweetened ice chunks.

He kissed me. Because he thinks the craziness of my life is cool. *That's...a lot to live up to.*

It still didn't wipe the smile off her face, but she almost dropped her drink when the car doors *hissed* shut behind her and the robotic female voice she knew so well carried through the car's overhead speakers.

"This train is now departing."

"Wait, what?"

"Please remain seated until you arrive at your destination. Thank you."

"Crap. What happened to the two-minute warning?" Struggling to swing her leg over the seat of the scooter, Amanda hissed when her foot caught on the rear compartment, and she was already on her way down when the Starbucks train lurched forward and sent her crashing onto the red velvet cushion of the car's seat.

Somehow, she managed to land with her arm stretched out in front of her and her late-night frappuccino cushioned against the back of the seat without spilling a drop.

I hate this train. I hate this train. I hate this train!

She made it to the station beneath downtown Denver forty minutes later—after readjusting herself at the first stop and scrambling to prop the scooter sturdily enough so it wouldn't crush her during the next leg of the train's route. When the doors opened, Amanda had to straddle her ride again and walk the thing backward through the sliding doors and into the long dark hallway beyond. The hallway, of course, was too narrow to turn the scooter around and face forward, but it didn't matter at this point.

I've always teleported from here. Guess that's what the big red button's for, right?

She grabbed the device from the back compartment and gave herself another five minutes of sitting in the empty train station hallway and enjoying the rest of her drink. It was hard to tell whether her racing heartbeat and intense alertness came from the hyper-caffeinated treat or from almost being crushed by the scooter on the speed-defying Starbucks train. Either way, she was wide awake now and probably would be for quite some time.

They wanted me to show up and work. So I'm showing up, ready to work.

When she finished her drink—slurping down every last bit and taking off the lid to scrape out all the whipped cream with the straw—Amanda sighed and looked down at the black device with the giant red button.

Here goes nothing.

She glanced over her shoulder at the still-empty hallway, then gripped one of the scooter's handlebars tightly in one hand before thumping the red button with the other.

Her stomach lurched. All the air squeezed out of her lungs, and her legs turned to Jell-O. An agonizing jolt raced up her fingers around the scooter's handlebar, and it felt like the transition would yank her entire arm from its socket and rip it clean off before the nauseating spin of being pulled through space ended.

Amanda fully expected it never to end.

Then it did.

She gasped at the disorienting shock of every particle of her body slamming back together in one place. The frigid air of nighttime at the end of September in the Rocky Mountains—

especially compared to the same in the Everglades—was almost as jolting, and she tipped sideways before she remembered she was sitting on a scooter in the valley and couldn't move her legs fast enough.

Amanda and the scooter crashed sideways into the soft dirt and grass of the valley floor, and the empty frappuccino cup flew from her hand. She groaned, clenched her eyes shut, then opened them to stare at the sky with a hundred pounds of motorized scooter crushing her leg.

Wow. The stars are so much brighter *out here...*

With a snort, she shook her head and forced the scooter back up to its rightful position. Now her arm, the opposite leg, and her *head* pounded fiercely, and all the excitement she'd carried with her into this solo venture from school to work was gone.

Just a learning curve. It's fine. Now I know exactly how to handle this next time.

Brushing off the aches in her limbs, Amanda stepped onto the scooter again, sat, and revved the engine. A plume of exhaust puffed out behind her, and she bounced across the cold grass toward the invisible but still very real outer wall of the Canissphere.

Good thing I've been here enough times to know exactly where I'm going. Or I'd be crashing this thing into a wall instead of driving it right into the open tunnel...

Despite her familiarity with the valley, a sudden pit of dread filled her stomach at the thought of riding blindly into anything but the lab's entrance. At the last second, she clenched her eyes shut and squeezed the handbrake. The scooter skidded to a halt with a squeak of rubber tires on tile, and the low purr of the engine echoed all around her.

Oh, man. Okay. I made it.

Amanda opened one eye and found herself in the very same entrance tunnel she'd used countless times before—only with an escort. With a small smile of victory, she turned off the scooter's engine and got off to walk the vehicle down the long hall toward the Canissphere's main dome.

The lab was quiet and calm this late at night, with only a handful of Dr. Caniss' employed shifters sitting at the circular tables and studying printed reports or holding muttered conversations with their associates. Among them were Dr. Caniss, her assistant Lucy, and Fiona Damascus.

Fiona saw the shifter girl first and grinned. "Well, look who the wolf dragged in. With a Vespa."

As always, Dr. Caniss stood over the table although Lucy and Fiona had obviously been sitting for a while. The biologist jerked her head up from the report she'd been going over and didn't look Amanda in the eye. Instead, she took in a sweeping glance of the scooter, then looked at her watch. "You're late."

"Seriously?" Amanda blew stray strands of hair away from her eyes and sighed. "What time is it?"

"Nine sixteen."

"Okay, I didn't even leave school until seven-thirty. Technically, I still have another fifteen minutes. Most people would call that being early."

"Fourteen minutes. If we were running on your *personal* timeline, Amanda."

"What?"

"Rick left your new vehicle on the premises at precisely seven-fifteen, as instructed." Caniss returned her attention to the report on the table. "Which makes you one minute late."

Amanda's mouth popped open, and she widened her eyes at Fiona, looking for any form of support whatsoever. The redhead woman folded her arms and kept grinning. "Okay, nobody told me the clock started when he dropped the scooter off before I was even there to see it."

Caniss glanced up, completely expressionless. "I was told you received a call from him Wednesday night."

"Well, yeah. But—"

"And that his instructions were clear. Once he delivered the vehicle, I expected you to arrive here within two hours. I'm hardly inclined to believe Rick minced words with my instructions."

Amanda heaved a massive sigh. "Fine. So I'm one minute late. I think that's still pretty good."

"*Pretty good* doesn't keep this facility running as tightly and efficiently as it does, Amanda. If you can't make the necessary accommodations in your schedule to meet deadlines and arrive at your post *on time,* you will become the wrench in our machine. Is this your intention?"

"No." Amanda stared at the woman. "No, I intend to be here and do my job—"

"Well, so far, I'm unconvinced. Feel free to change my mind while you're here." With a curt nod, Caniss looked down at her report again and stabbed the paper with a finger, lowering her head to address her assistant. "I want this cross-referenced with the variant frequencies from Analysis. It's not a large anomaly, and I want to ensure it stays that way."

"Yes, Doctor." Lucy closed the report folder and cradled it to her chest as she stood. "Anything else?"

Caniss glanced from the folder to Amanda, then finally to Fiona. "That's all for tonight, Lucy. Ms. Damascus can handle the rest."

Fiona raised an eyebrow. "Oh, I can, can I?"

"You're perfectly capable. I don't have the time or the patience to coddle your team leader into the next stage of her responsibilities. You have both. And experience." Caniss spun smartly on her heels and marched off across the main dome toward one of the other branching tunnels across the room. She didn't offer a word of farewell or any indication she was glad to see her newest and youngest employee at the lab.

Lucy nodded at Amanda, then hurried off in a different direction to finish her boss' tasks for the night.

Amanda blinked. "Team leader?"

"That's your title." Fiona stroked her chin. "Working title, obviously. Sure, I follow your lead in the field. When I'm in the field with *you*. Until that happens again, I think I'll stick to calling you my protégé."

The girl snorted. "Thanks."

"Anytime, kid." Fiona studied the scooter and chuckled. "You know, I bet you would've been at least one minute *early* if you'd left that thing in the parking lot."

"What parking lot?"

"The Starbucks, kid. Trust me. They're not gonna tow it. One time, I left a mail truck out there for two weeks, and nobody said a word. United States Postal Service, to be exact."

Amanda opened her mouth and for a minute couldn't figure out what to say. So she went with, "You stole a mail truck?"

"I borrowed it. That's pretty irrelevant at this point. It was a long time ago." The woman dismissed it all with a flippant wave. "I'm just saying, kid. You kinda took yourself through more trouble than that thing's worth. I mean, how much did that thing cost? Couldn't have been more than a thousand bucks."

"I..." The girl clenched her jaw and tried not to lose it right there in the empty central dome. "I didn't think I could just *leave* it in the parking lot."

Fiona burst out laughing. "Why wouldn't you? That thing's supposed to get you from A to B. Then you took B to C at breakneck speed and C to D at the push of a button. Hell of an entrance riding your scooter right in the lab, though, I gotta say."

"You know what would be awesome? If somebody told me all this stuff before leaving me to figure it out all on my own, then making fun of me for it. Like, anyone. Ever."

Fiona's chair *screeched* loudly across the tile floor when she stood, and she didn't bother to push it back in beneath the table as Lucy had. "Don't sweat it, kid. You did great for your first time. And you know Melody's incapable of showing actual emotion. She has the worst case of chronic resting bitch face I've ever seen, but we both know she's glad you're here. Or you wouldn't *be* here."

Amanda finally managed to crack a small smile. "Is that what you tell yourself too? That she's glad *you're* here?"

"Ha. Are you kidding? That robot in shifter's clothing *hates* me." Fiona waggled her eyebrows. "But I've made myself invaluable, and she can't get over how much she hates that too. Come on. I'll show you to your room."

The girl frowned. "I already know where my room is."

"Not this one, you don't." The woman approached her and clapped a hand on her mentee's shoulder. "You got an upgrade, kid. At least in this place, that means all-inclusive."

"*Please* tell me I don't have to sleep in a spaceship cubby in the wall anymore."

Fiona's smile faltered. "Sorry. The room's an upgrade. Just not the bed. Okay, fine. The doc's a robot *and* a sadist. But hey. You'll have plenty of room for your *sweet new ride*."

Amanda rolled her eyes. "I get it. I'll leave it at the Starbucks next time."

"Eh, only if you want. It's a great conversation starter." Chuckling, Fiona headed toward the tunnel branching from the central dome that led to the lab's residential area. Amanda shook her head and walked the scooter across the dome after her. "I'm sure you have a ton of questions. As usual. So I'll drop you off, you can get a good night's sleep, and we'll get cracking at the whole shebang in the morning—"

"Sleep?"

At the surprise in Amanda's voice, her mentor turned and looked her up and down. "Don't tell me you're the only teenager in the world who doesn't like sleep."

"If I was supposed to show up here only to sleep, why does it matter what time I got here?"

"Really? You're asking *me* why the doc does anything?"

Amanda sighed. "Good point."

"I know. So that's the plan. A good night's sleep, and one hell of a headache in the morning. Which is pretty much your jam, right?"

"It's gonna be worse than that," the girl muttered.

"Ha. You're funny."

"Right. Super funny. Especially when there's no *way* I'm going to sleep right now."

"Too excited, huh? Hey, I get it. It's been a while."

Amanda tightened her grip on the scooter's handlebars. "More like I chugged a gigantic frappuccino on the way here."

Fiona spun with wide eyes and searched her mentee's face. "*Really*… Well, then, I guess we can do all our catching up *before* you get to work tomorrow."

"Don't you have to sleep?"

"Please. When you get to be my age, kid, sleep is like a fly buzzing around your head. Most of the time, it's just annoying. Sometimes you catch it, but it takes a hell of a lot more effort than ignoring it altogether."

Amanda fought back a laugh. "Right. When exactly will I get to be your age?"

"Ha. Nice try. You know, for a girl who downed the legal limit of caffeine and sugar, you're moving pretty slow. Pick it up or get on your ride, kid. We got a lot to cover."

CHAPTER TWENTY-FOUR

Amanda's new room at the Canissphere was quite an upgrade. At least three times bigger than her last room "for interns," this one had a full walk-in closet, a toilet and shower with an actual door to separate them from the rest of the space, a mini-fridge, and a desk twice as big as the last one. Plus, it wasn't built into the wall this time.

There was a stiff-looking armchair across from the bed, but at least it was something else to sit on besides the cheap office chair behind the desk. The bed, however, was still a recessed hole in the wall with barely any headroom and another twin-sized mattress.

"See?" Fiona gestured toward the bed and chuckled. "Even the doc thinks sleep is a waste of time. You know, honestly, I don't think she sleeps more than a few hours a week."

"Seriously?"

"Yeah. Like, maybe two." The woman glanced at the ceiling. "And a half."

Amanda parked her scooter along the left-hand wall opposite the private bathroom, then nodded at Fiona standing in the doorway. "Thanks for the check-in. Should we go somewhere else to—"

"Nah, the rest of this place is boring as hell. Especially at night. This is way cozier, huh?" The woman grabbed the rolling desk chair and swung it toward her before plopping down into the seat. Then she reached behind her and slapped the panel on the wall to close the hydraulic sliding door. "Go ahead. Take a seat. Trust me. I'm not gonna steal the Vespa out from under you."

"Can't we go for a walk or something?"

"Because you have the jitters? Ha. Nope. First rule of being an adult with responsibilities, kid. No caffeine after three p.m. Unless you're trying to pull an all-nighter, and unfortunately for you, that's probably not gonna be tonight."

Rolling her eyes, Amanda headed for the uncomfortable-looking armchair and dropped into it. It was as stiff and unwelcoming as it looked. She shifted around a few times, trying to find a better position, and finally gave up.

Fiona leaned forward and propped her forearms on her thighs before clapping her hands together and staring at her mentee. "So."

"So?" The girl raised her eyebrows. "You said we have a lot to talk about?"

"Yeah, but I've been waiting this whole time for you to bring it up. So let's hear it."

"I have no idea what you're talking about."

"Oh, come *on*. The one suggestion you made that had a practical application—"

"Hey."

"For specific use at the *lab*, if you'll let me finish." Fiona lurched upright in the chair and spread her arms. "And you aren't even gonna bring it up?"

"Uh…I probably *would* if I knew what—"

"The teleport, kid! Jesus, how much coffee did you *drink*?"

"Oh." Amanda let herself smile and glanced at the scooter's rear compartment where she'd returned the device. "Yeah, that was a nice touch."

"All part of the plan." Fiona rubbed her hands together. "You know, getting a fifteen-year-old employee out on base when she can't drive, doesn't have a license, and isn't one of the shifters who can teleport is a *lot* harder than it looks."

"Oh, really?" The girl folded her arms. "I hadn't noticed."

"I mean on my end, kid. Not everything's about you." Shaking her thick red curls back over her shoulder, Fiona grinned. "Yes. *I* found a way to get you from C to D. I'm glad it worked because I didn't exactly have the time to test it out beforehand. Or a willing subject, come to think of it..."

"Wow. Good thing you're confident in a teleportation device you've never actually *used* before."

"I know, right? Good thing you didn't decide to bring a buddy. It only works for shifters at this point. So you can tell that pain-in-the-ass-witch friend of yours the lab is *still* off-limits. Unless she wants to blow herself apart into a million pieces halfway between Denver and the mountains." Fiona snickered. "Which, honestly, I wouldn't put it past her to at least try."

Amanda drew a deep breath and paused.

All summer and a few months of school without hearing from Fiona, and I forgot how insane she is.

"Summer's not trying to get into the lab, so you don't have to worry about that."

"Great. How was it? The jump, I mean."

Amanda grimaced. "It sucked. Thanks for asking."

Her mentor kicked herself back in the office chair and howled with laughter. It didn't stop even when the back of the chair crashed into the side of the desk. "But it—Whew! It got you here in one piece. That's the best test-run I've ever had."

"Glad I could be your guinea pig and not die," the girl replied flatly.

"Yeah, me too. Ha! Okay." Fiona slapped her thigh. "Let's get down to it, then. First things first, tell me about the shifter."

Amanda's mouth ran instantly dry, and she pressed herself against the back of the armchair. "What?"

"Come on, kid. You sent me a pretty cryptic message the other night, but I got the message loud and clear. Looks like I taught you well. So tell me about it."

"Fiona, that was a *month* ago."

"Yeah. And I told you that you had nothing to worry about."

"No, you said, 'You're fine.' Which didn't help me *at all.*" Amanda folded her arms. "I had to figure it out on my own."

"Good. That's how this works. We all gotta buckle up and figure it out on our own. Otherwise, we're just wasting space." Fiona snorted. "Some of us still do, but that's a different conversation. I'm interested in *this* one."

The girl stared at her mentor and pressed her lips together.

She didn't give me a helpful answer when I texted her, and I had to go crazy for weeks before I figured out what Matt is. And that was basically an accident.

Amanda didn't particularly want to get into a conversation about Matt Hardy with her mentor. Still, now that Fiona had brought it up, the girl's growing curiosity was impossible to ignore. "Okay, fine. He goes to my school—"

"Wait, wait, wait. Hold up." Fiona lifted a hand to stop her. "If a shifter like this was able to run up onto the school grounds willy-nilly, you guys have a serious breach in security."

"I didn't say—"

"Which means Glasket's getting lazy. Huh. And here I was, thinking the witch had her priorities straight. I should call her."

"It's not like—"

"Yeah, I'm gonna call her." Fiona pulled her Coalition phone from her back pocket and turned on the screen. "Damnit. It's way too late. Hey, kid. How much do you think your principal *actually* sleeps in that school with all those kids running around at all hours—"

"Fiona!" Amanda's shout echoed around the room and made the shifter woman pause with her finger aimed at her phone in mid-point.

"Yeah?"

Amanda huffed out a sigh. "How much coffee did *you* drink?"

"I thought I told you nothing after three p.m. Didn't I?"

"Okay, never mind. Just listen to me."

"Yep. Sure. I'm all ears." Fiona chuckled and slipped her phone back into her pocket. "What's up?"

Oh, man. She's really lost her mind this time.

"The shifter I texted you about."

"Uh-huh. You found him and gave him a run for his money, right? I bet you did. Any scumbag who tries sneaking into a school like that deserves to—"

"He didn't *sneak* into the school, Fiona. He's a student. Another senior."

"Another..." Fiona smirked. "Okay, what's your game, kid?"

"No game. I'm serious."

"Huh." Crossing one leg over the other, the redhead tapped her fingers against her lips. "So I guess Glasket already knows, then."

"Well yeah. He transferred to the Academy halfway through last year, and I—"

"And *you're* not the only shifter kid at school anymore." Fiona's grin was dangerously predatory. "Bet that rubbed your fur in all the wrong ways, huh?"

Amanda drew a deep breath. "Yeah. At first."

"Oh? Now that you got sending me a panic text out of the way, you're suddenly feeling better about *that* kinda shifter at school with you?"

"I mean..." She couldn't help but think about having asked Matt to go to the Homecoming dance with her—however last-minute—and the little bit of fun they'd had for all of ten minutes before Glasket ripped it open with a poorly thought-out announcement. And getting kissed…

Fiona snorted. "Yeah, you got over it, all right. Way over it. On the other side of the fence. You wanna tell me what you're smiling about over there in your little dreamland?"

Amanda looked sharply up at her mentor. "No."

"Uh-huh. So what happened, then? Did this shifter boy tell you what he is, or was he too scared to own up to what he has no control over whatsoever?"

"What?"

"I'm guessing it was the first one."

"Wait, how did *you* know?"

"Please, kid. I've been around the block way too many times to count, and I don't even wanna try. What did you call it? 'Shifters with magic. Not the wolf kind. Red and burning plastic.' It's one of the easiest things to spot if you know what you're looking for. Not like the transformed make a habit out of showing off anyway. Most of them." Fiona nodded. "So how'd you get him to spill the beans?"

"I accidentally snuck up on him…practicing."

"What do you mean *practicing*? What is that? Some kinda euphemism?"

Amanda rolled her eyes. "No. I mean practicing with that red magic that smells like burning plastic. The whole reason I texted you."

"Oh. Well, that's interesting."

"But Matt said it wasn't Lorikor magic. That it came from a different—"

"Hold up, kid." Fiona pointed at her and raised her eyebrows. "Who said anything about Lorikor magic?"

Amanda folded her arms. "I just did."

"No wonder you freaked out and texted me. Now *I'm* confused. What are we talking about here?"

"Matt Hardy. The shifter boy at my school who uses weird red magic and not shifter magic. What part of this is confusing?"

"The part you haven't explained yet. Where exactly does this talk about Lorikor magic come into play?"

"Um..." Frowning, Amanda wiped her hands on her thighs and stared at the floor. "Because that's what his dad is. Or was. I don't know. He couldn't tell much more about that part, but I thought—"

"You thought you'd bring it up with me because *surely* Fiona would know what the hell this kid is, right?" She barked a laugh and slapped a hand against her head. "Sorry to disappoint, kid, but I'm gonna tell you right now I have *never* seen a half-Lorikor, half-transformed shifter. Didn't even know that was a thing. But now that you bring it up, it makes sense."

"Okay, what's that?" Amanda pointed right back at her mentor. "You said transformed before. What does that even mean?"

"Ah." Fiona's smile widened, and she glanced at the ceiling to collect her thoughts. "Wow. We're identifying new breeds *and* getting a history lesson tonight, huh? Definitely up there in the top, oh...twenty most unexpected conversations, but okay. Let's roll with it."

"Fiona."

"Yeah."

The girl licked her lips and shrugged. "Can you focus and tell me what's going on?"

The woman looked her up and down. "Look who's telling who to focus. Ha. All right. Transformed shifters, kid.

"About...thirty-five years ago, give or take, some Dark Families did some Dark-Family shit with a random pool of the population on Earth. Magical and non-magical. They didn't discriminate, which in most cases I'd say is an admirable quality, but this is the exception. They tried to make their own army. Of shifters. Yes, when I say *make,* that's exactly what I mean."

"They…turned people into shifters? With dark magic?"

"People and magicals, kid. Didn't matter. If you haven't already learned in your history class what happened to the Dark Families after that, ask your teacher. This is as deep as I go."

Amanda studied the floor and tried to put the pieces together in a way that made sense. "So Matt's dad is a *transformed* shifter. And that makes him—"

"Second-generation, yeah. Born with it and everything. He's lucky he didn't have to figure it out on his own without anyone to show him what was up. Because believe me, even trying to train some of the other second-generation shifters was a serious pain in my ass. Your friend is a hell of a hybrid. Which one of his folks gave him the Lorikor part?"

"Um…his dad."

"Damn. *Two* of 'em. In the same family! That's like one in a bazillion chance, don't you think? And the kid's mom?"

"A shifter? I think."

"Whew. That's some kinda—" Fiona froze, then barked out a laugh and leaned forward toward her mentee. "It's perfect. We could care less about a Lorikor because their fancy little obsession tricks don't mean a thing to us."

"Yeah." Amanda ran a hand through her hair and tried not to scowl. "I noticed."

"Of course you did. Poor kid's been running around high school with every single girl trying to catch him by the tail, and you're the only one who… Oh, *wow*."

"What?"

"Aw, come on, Amanda. He told you all this stuff himself?"

The girl swallowed. "Yeah."

"Yeah. I bet the two of you have been spending a *lot* of time together."

"We—" Amanda blinked furiously. "I mean, we have all our classes together—"

"Ha! Don't bullshit a bullshitter, kid. Everything about your face right now tells me I'm right. And everything *I* know about teenage shifters tells me you have a boyfriend."

"What? No."

Fiona chuckled and sat back in the office chair, clearly pleased with herself. "Yeah, yeah. Deny it all you want."

"He's *definitely* not my boyfriend. I don't have a boyfriend. I don't want a boyfriend. I'm not... That's ridiculous."

"Right. Total denial. That's fine. You're young." Fiona grinned. "The denial part only gives up a *little* anyway. You enjoy yourself while it lasts, kid."

"You're putting words in my mouth."

"Oh, yeah? You go on a run with him yet? Yeah, it would have to be all by yourselves because you're the only ones."

Amanda froze.

How does she know all this? There's no way going for a run with Matt falls under 'not everything at the Academy is a secret.'

The woman pointed at her. "That's a hard yes."

"No, I—"

"You're in it deep, kid. Has he made a move?"

"Fiona!"

"He *did*. A-ha! Look at that!"

Amanda stood from her chair and pointed at the door. "Time for you to go?"

"What? Come on. We're having a little chat. Me and you. Experienced adult to...somewhat-proficient novice. You don't have to bottle it all up, kid. I get it. Might make things a little hard for *you,* seeing as you have an army of slobbering adolescent girls plotting your downfall at every waking moment. At least while he's there on campus..."

"Stop. Please." Amanda lowered her arm with a sigh. "I don't wanna talk about this anymore."

For a moment, her new room at the Canissphere fell entirely silent but for the low, barely audible hum of the power generated through the entire facility and keeping Caniss' *machine* running tightly and efficiently.

Then Fiona's smile disappeared, and she nodded. "All right. Maybe I took the ribbing a little too far. Sorry, kid. I thought you could handle it."

"I can handle it." Sitting stiffly in the armchair again, Amanda shook her head. "I just don't wanna handle it *here* while I'm supposed to be at work. Okay?"

"Ah… Keeping your personal and professional baggage separate. I like it."

Despite how hot her cheeks were and how much she really, *really* didn't want to talk about Matt when it came to anything other than what he was, Amanda let herself smile a little at the underhanded praise from her mentor. "Great. So should we focus on why I'm here? Because nobody's told me what's going on yet."

"Yeah, you'll get a briefing in the morning. It won't surprise you to hear there's another creature out there we need somebody to handle. Obviously, that somebody's you."

"Is that seriously all you can give me right now?"

Fiona dropped her forearms onto the armrests and swiveled the office chair back and forth. "Pretty much."

"Awesome."

"Don't sweat it, kid. After that last…whatever the heck that crazy thing was with all the wings and hooved and scales and crap, this one'll be a piece of cake. I can feel it." They stared at each other. Then the woman cleared her throat. "Anything else you wanna ask me?"

Amanda glanced around the room and finally got hold of enough courage again to meet Fiona's gaze.

How does she know what I'm thinking like that? She can't, right? It's gotta be a bunch of serious lucky guesses. Over and over.

"Oh, come on, kid. I can see the gears turning. Spit it out."

"Yeah. I have a question." Amanda's mind spun with all the weird facts she'd gotten from her crash-course lesson in shifter history. "About the transformed."

"Uh-huh. Everybody does. Shoot."

Drawing a deep breath, the girl grimaced. "They were...made by the Dark Families."

"That's what I said."

"Okay, so does that mean their magic is... You know."

Fiona smirked. "Dark?"

"Yeah."

"You tell me, kid. You're the one with a transformed Lorikor bo—" She cleared her throat. "Friend."

Amanda nodded. "I mean, I thought so at first. When I felt his magic. It didn't...feel right. Then my ghost-wolf kinda went haywire on the whole thing and took over."

"All on its own?"

"I think so."

"Huh." Fiona didn't give any other indication she even had an opinion at this point. "Keep going."

"That's how I found him. I didn't *know* it was him, but then I saw him casting that weird magic that smelled like nothing else. I mean, it stinks. Then he saw my wolf, and..."

The redhead nodded again with a slow, sympathetic smile. "Let me guess. You freaked out and thought he was some kind of spy sent into your school to tear it apart from the inside out. And this other kid couldn't believe he saw *your* magic. Giant misunderstanding and you had to figure out how to clear the whole mess up all on your own. The two of you."

"Oh my God, you really *can* read my mind."

"Ha. No. I'm just acutely aware. And I like you, kid. Trust me. I don't spend my time figuring somebody out if it's not worth every second." Fiona rubbed her hands together, then gestured. "So you tell me. Is your friend using dark magic or not?"

"I..." Amanda's mind flashed with the memories of the brief moments she'd spent with Matt so far, all of which felt like they'd lasted forever. "No. I don't think so."

"Great. Problem solved."

"I didn't ask if he was *using* dark magic." Amanda pulled her legs up onto the armchair and crossed them beneath her. "I asked if the transformed *have* dark magic. Because that's what made them, right?"

"Sure. But you're asking the wrong question." Fiona chuckled at her mentee's confused scowl. "Listen, kid. It's not the magic that decides who we are. Whether we're 'dark' or 'light'. If we make good choices or really, *really* crappy ones. It's the other way around. Always has been, always will be. Understand?"

Drawing a deep breath, Amanda tried to smile but was too focused on all the pent-up anxiety finally draining out of her when she exhaled. "Yeah. I get it."

"Good." Fiona slapped her thighs, then pushed herself off the office chair. "And *that*, my curious friend, is how you end a conversation on a high note. We're switching gears tomorrow, so think out whatever you need to think out tonight and leave the rest in this room. That briefing with the doc's at five. So you have..." She glanced at her watch. "Little less than seven hours. That's plenty of sleep if you can force yourself. I highly recommend forcing yourself. Big day."

"Right." Amanda nodded as her mentor smashed a hand against the panel beside the door and somehow managed to hit the right button. "Big day."

"Which, as you know, means a big payday when everything's said and done."

The girl snorted and shook her head.

"'Night, kid."

"Good night."

When the door *hissed* and slid shut again, Fiona's low chuckle cut off halfway as the shifter woman headed down the hall.

Amanda dropped her head back against the armchair's cushion and puffed out a breath through loose lips.

That was worse than getting her to tell me about shifter magic. Or why I even want *to use it and be a bounty hunter in the first place. But now I know.*

For now, at least, her racing heartbeat after so much caffeine and sugar had subsided into something more like normal levels, but she had no idea how long it would last. At the very least, though, she had more or less concrete answers about Matt and what he was and that she didn't have to worry about him using transformed-shifter magic Fiona didn't seem all that worried about.

Even after having to drill it out of her mentor, the reassurance was a huge relief.

She stood and crossed the room to pull her backpack from the scooter's rear compartment.

Might as well try *to get some sleep. There's nothing else I can do tonight.*

When she rifled through her things for a tank top and a pair of shorts for the night, she remembered that wasn't entirely true. So she pulled out her Coalition phone and opened a new text to mark off the last thing on her very short list of to-dos for the night.

Got called back to work. New job. No idea how long this time. Tell everybody I'm sorry I didn't get to say bye. Also, if Matt asks you about me, tell him. He already knows.

That last part made her grimace, but she sent the text anyway. Most likely, Summer wouldn't see it on the other cell phone stashed somewhere in her room until tomorrow, and Amanda didn't really expect a reply.

Or if I do get one, it'll probably be a string of cursing me out for making her play Witch-in-the-Middle. Nothing I can't handle, I guess.

Then she realized what she'd left out of the text and sent another one she hoped would make Summer a little less likely to blow up at her after all this was said and done.

Nice fireworks, by the way. Thanks for the backup.

With that, Amanda changed into her pajamas, set the phone on the floor beside the bed, and took two full laps of her new room before realizing there wasn't a single light switch. It took her another five minutes to find the new app someone had remotely installed in her Coalition phone that controlled the room's lighting and thermostat.

Oh, yeah. Right. Makes perfect sense to put a remote-controlled light-switch app in the Health and Fitness collection. Does no one here know how smartphones work?

With a snort, she dimmed the lights as far as they would go and crawled under the sheets before making sure to set an alarm for 4:20 a.m. Somehow, even after her impulsive caffeine consumption, Amanda's eyelids drooped as she lay in the bed and stared at the ceiling of the sleeping nook curving not even two feet above her.

Okay. Maybe I'm crashing.

That was perfectly understandable, but she still spent at least another half hour trying to push the memory of Matt kissing her out of her mind so she could sleep.

CHAPTER TWENTY-FIVE

Six hours of unconsciousness was more than enough to get Amanda up and out of bed with plenty of energy to start her first official morning of being an employee of the Coalition of Shifters and working directly under Dr. Melody Caniss. At least, it was her first official day of actually *knowing* she had a real job.

After a quick shower, a change of clothes, and a brief stop in the central dome for a plate of eggs and bacon from a smiling Dominique, Amanda made her way toward what she now thought of as the War Room. Beyond getting an upgraded room, nothing else had changed. The scientists and research analysts who knew her and had no problem with a fifteen-year-old girl working for Omega Industries smiled when they saw her and greeted her with a "Morning, Amanda," or a "Welcome back. Good to see you."

Everyone else, though—and there were plenty of shifters at the lab who'd spent years building up their careers only to be shown up by the same fifteen-year-old girl—avoided Amanda's gaze and grumbled when she passed.

Great. Good to know having a job is like high school. With adults.

She reached the War Room at 4:55 a.m., ready to show Caniss

she meant business by being a whole five minutes early, but the door was shut. And it wouldn't open even with Amanda's keycard.

"Oh, come on..."

"Hey. There you are." Bill walked swiftly down the corridor, dressed in his usual thick canvas overalls and beaming at her. "Heard you got in last night. On a scooter."

Amanda playfully rolled her eyes. "Yeah. There's supposed to be a briefing this morning, right?"

"Jeeze. She's really running you through the gauntlet, isn't she?"

"Who?"

"Dr. Caniss." Bill chuckled and waved her after him. "We're not in there today. The briefing's down in one of the exam rooms."

"Seriously?" With a heavy sigh, Amanda shoved her keycard into her back pocket and shook her head. "The exam rooms are on the complete opposite side of the dome."

"Uh-huh. Which she should've told you. Then I remembered Dr. Caniss doesn't really ever do anything she *should* if it's not a direct and immediate convenience for *her*, so I figured I'd find you here and take you back with me."

"Aw, man." Amanda grimaced and took off down the hall to join Bill and match his quick but still calmly urgent pace. "I was trying to be early."

"I'm pretty sure she realized that."

"She already gave me a lecture for being *one* minute late last night."

Bill ran a hand through his light-brown hair and shrugged. "Well, she likes her lectures too. Don't worry, kid. She's not gonna can you for not being given a brief before your brief. Look on the bright side."

"What bright side?" Amanda muttered.

"We'll *both* be late." He grinned. "There's no way in hell Caniss has enough bandwidth to lecture us both."

She laughed and felt a little better about having at least one friend at the lab who wasn't emotionally stunted, completely insane, or thought Amanda Coulier couldn't do her job because she was only fifteen.

Bill was, however, wrong about Dr. Caniss' capacity for chewing them both a new one when they arrived at the designated exam room.

"That's eight minutes this morning." Caniss glanced at her watch, then turned to scroll through something on a tablet someone had left out on the closest stainless-steel workstation. "I was under the impression you *wanted* this position."

Amanda folded her arms. "I was under the impression briefings for a new job would be in the same room as every other briefing."

Bill snorted and immediately cleared his throat to try covering it up.

Caniss glanced up at Amanda and blinked. "I was speaking to Mr. Farrow. But apparently, you're eager to take the blame for both of you."

"The blame?" Amanda scoffed. "Nobody told me we were meeting *here* this morning."

The biologist's gaze flickered toward Bill. "Well, evidently, *someone* did."

"And now we're all here," Bill added quickly, nodding once. "Or...most of us, at least."

"*Most* is not an acceptable ratio, Mr. Farrow. And its lack of precision is completely useless for—"

The door to the exam room burst open, the hydraulic hinges working overtime to keep the glass from cracking against the wall before the frame hit with a soft *thump*. Fiona hurried into the exam room, her wild red curls sticking up in a messy, unruly halo around her head. "What did I miss?"

"It certainly wasn't your love of the spotlight, Ms. Damascus."

"Yes, good morning, Melody. You're looking cheery today."

Amanda and Bill shared a look and tried not to laugh. Fiona glanced at her mentee and winked.

"Mr. Farrow." Caniss strolled across the exam room and stopped beside one of the cages holding a neon-green creature that looked like a platypus, tortoise, and porcupine all rolled into one. "Since this aligns with your area of expertise, I imagine you're more qualified to give us an accurate assessment of the situation."

"Sure." Bill cleared his throat, and Fiona and Amanda headed after him toward the cage. "This is UM-57204, brought in last week. I've been calling her Spike."

"Please refrain from deviating away from *facts*, Mr. Farrow."

"Right. Habit. Sorry."

Fiona snorted. "You named a female…thing Spike?"

"It fits." Amanda squatted in front of the cage to get a better look at the creature. Its neon-orange bill gave it the platypus look, and the hundreds of hard, bone-like spikes protruding from the dark-green shell on its back accounted for the tortoise and porcupine aspects.

Each spike was a glistening black until the very tip, and as far as she could tell, every single point that had to be more shell than quill was a completely different color. Dull-yellow feathers protruded from the creature's ankles above the feet armed with two-inch claws colored the same as the bone spikes. "She's beautiful."

"Yeah, I think so too."

Spike turned her head to meet Amanda's gaze, and a flash of yellow light swam around the creature's completely black eyes before fading again.

That's not good.

She carefully lifted both hands and rose to her feet again before backing away.

"What's up?" Fiona asked.

Amanda grabbed her mentor's arm and gently pulled the woman back with her. "She's pissed."

"You can tell all that by hunkering down outside the cage?"

Bill nodded and shot Amanda another knowing look. "You've gotten good at that, kid. Like...eerily good."

She shrugged. "Yeah, I had a good teacher."

He smirked. "Thanks. But Amanda's right. Spike hasn't been in a very...cooperative mood since we brought her in."

Caniss scowled. "I'll ignore your reference to the subject's nonexistent emotional state if you move past the subjective drivel and summarize the variables for us, Mr. Farrow."

"Right." He rubbed his chin. "UM-57204 is a divergent erksil. The origin species is much more dully colored, and the feathers on UM-57204's extremities are entirely new. It took me a week to figure out why she...exhibited so many aggressive traits."

Bill glanced at Caniss, but the doctor was busy tapping away on yet another tablet she'd picked up from a different table. "With this particular divergent species, the differences are easy to spot, but their purpose was way harder to pinpoint than most of the others we've brought in so far."

Fiona raised an eyebrow. "Such as?"

"Well, the feathers, for instance. Behind each tuft is a sort of pouch, I guess you could call it. Like what we see in kangaroos or male Emperor penguins."

"For hatching eggs?" Amanda asked.

"Well, at first, I thought that was it." Bill scratched his head. "Honestly, I still don't know whether these specific young hatched or birthed live. I mean, the platypus is one of only two mammals on Earth that lay eggs, so I'm leaning more toward that. Then again, if the leg-pouches aren't incubators, it's also possible they could be individual amniotic sacks that opened... well, during live birth."

Fiona wrinkled her nose. "You're saying this thing had babies out of its legs?"

"*Her* legs." Bill shrugged. "But yeah. It's possible."

"And the babies are..."

"Yeah, that's the problem." When the lab's resident zookeeper and newly appointed operative under Amanda's leadership looked at the shifter girl, his grimace said it all.

"Crap."

Caniss stopped her constant scrolling and tapping on the tablet to look up at them. "I don't see why this is such an issue for any of you."

Spike let out a low hiss and took one agonizingly slow step across the cage floor toward the biologist.

Amanda stepped slightly back as well. "Um...Dr. Caniss? You might wanna lower your—"

"The three of you completed a successful operation after it was botched entirely by the previous team. With whom I've ceased to engage in a number of what I considered to be previously effective contracts." She tossed the tablet onto the closest stainless-steel workstation, and Spike hissed again. This time with another flash of yellow light around her all-black eyes.

"Doctor." Bill cleared his throat. "I think we should step into the—"

"I don't care what you *think*, Mr. Farrow." Caniss was shouting now. "I care about what you *know*. Now the three of you are standing around in this exam room looking like you've never seen a divergent creature of any kind whatsoever. Am I missing a certain insight the rest of you share?"

The whole time, Spike shuffled in a slow circle until her back —and the points of every bone-hard spike—faced the biologist. Then she let out another warning hiss.

"This needs a little more...finesse," Bill muttered, raising his arm toward Caniss but not looking away from the creature in the cage. "Right now, that includes—"

"Will you stop blabbering?" Caniss shouted. "This shouldn't be anything new to any of you! How hard can it be to find a few helpless, harmless divergent offspring? Hmm?"

A low, rumbling growl came from Spike, who pawed at the cage floor with deadly sharp claws that raked off ribbons of steel in their wake.

"What is that obnoxious screeching? Say something!"

"Get down!" Bill leapt toward the doctor and knocked her to the floor before a spray of glowing green mist erupted from each of the hundred spikes on the divergent creature's back. The air filled with the scent of sulfur and rotting meat before Spike's attack struck the far wall of the exam room and blasted a hundred holes through the surface.

Someone in the next room over shouted in surprise. Then an alarm blared through the speaker system in the ceiling. Bill scrambled off his employer to grab a fire extinguisher resting on the closest workstation—only it was lime-green and clearly labeled in haste with "UM-57204" along the side.

He sprayed the contents on the wall, which elicited a thick *whump* in the air, and coated the hundred tiny holes in a growing green foam that plugged the holes and eradicated the stench almost instantly. Then he raced toward a panel on the wall, hit a button that cut off the alarm, keyed the intercom, and muttered, "UM-57204 excretion contained in Exam Room 4. Everybody okay in there?"

The intercom crackled with static before someone else's heavy breathing came through first. "Contained in Exam Room 3. I swear, if you guys don't figure out how to calm her down, I'm transferring down the hall. It missed the divergent tamaris cage by a foot this time."

"Yeah, we're on it, Mike. Sorry."

There was no reply, but Bill turned and gently set the UM-

57204-labeled extinguisher on the workstation beside him. With a heavy sigh, he almost leaned back against the wall still oozing green foam before he remembered what was there and lurched sideways to a safer location. "That, Dr. Caniss, is what makes it so hard to find a few divergent offspring."

Caniss had picked herself up off the floor and now stared at the holes in the wall with no expression whatsoever.

"And no," Bill added, his eyes wide, "I don't expect them to be hapless *or* helpless."

"Clearly." The biologist turned to face the rest of her small team and straightened the front of her white lab coat. "I believe this demonstration has made the parameters of your next objective clear. Feel free to use the strategy room and whatever available programs might help you with this…egg-hunt. I expect a full write-up on my desk by tomorrow morning."

With that, Caniss walked briskly across the room, completely ignoring the final warning *hiss* Spike sent her way before she jerked open the glass door to the exam room. Through the glass wall, Amanda, Fiona, and Bill watched the biologist march down the hall. Even after she'd disappeared down another branching corridor, no one said a word.

Finally, Amanda swallowed and pointed at the door. "Should we talk about this somewhere else?"

"Definitely." Bill reached into his pocket, pulled out a brown nugget of compacted food that smelled like the rotting meat from the creature's bone-spike spray, and tossed it through the bars of the cage. Spike's duck-bill snapped open and shut to catch the treat out of the air, then she let out another *hiss* and settled her belly onto the floor of the cage.

Bill gestured toward the door, and everyone got out as quickly and quietly as possible.

This is gonna be rough.

CHAPTER TWENTY-SIX

Fiona leaned back in her chair bolted to the floor of the strategy room and gave Bill a pert look. "When, exactly, did you realize there were a bunch of little acid-spraying platypines running around out there?"

Bill smirked. "Platypines. Hey, that's a pretty good one."

"Nobody's going to care what you *call* them if we have to contain who knows how many attacks on civilians and wildlife. Probably only civilians, because even Earth's animals are smart enough to stay the hell away from one of *those* things."

The zookeeper's smile disappeared. "Yeah, you're right. I get excited when I land on a good name for a divergent species. Sorry."

Amanda gripped the edge of the circular table in the center of the room doubling as a control center and one giant computer with multiple workstations. "Her question is pretty important, though. How many are there?"

Bill shrugged. "That's hard to say."

"Well, try, Bill." Fiona widened her eyes. "Try to say."

"Right. Well, the original erksil we're pretty sure Spike diverged from only births in litters of four. Without the leg-pouches, obviously. Still, she only has four of *those,* so I'm guessing it's the same number."

"How big are they?" Amanda asked.

"Uh...about the size of a nickel, give or take a few centimeters. That's if they gestated *inside* the pouches and were born from there that way. Probably three-quarters that size if the leg-pouches were only to incubate the eggs."

"So not big," Fiona said flatly.

"No. Not big."

"Great." Amanda shook her head. "What is it with the shifters here and not paying attention to where a mama creature's eggs are? Or babies. Or whatever happened."

"Yeah..." Bill scratched his head again. "I sent out a memo already."

"A *memo*?" Fiona snorted. "Did you remember to add, 'Hey, by the way, there are four tiny acid-spewing platy-babies small enough to fit in your pocket, so if your clothes start to melt onto your body, that's one of our targets?'"

He glared at her. "No."

"Oh, okay. Hey, go ahead and send a follow-up memo, then. That'll take care of the problem."

"Listen, when the retrieval team brought her in, we had no idea she'd just given birth. Or hatched her eggs." Bill shook his head. "There was zero indication of any young. By the time I found the leg-pouches and realized what they were for, she'd already been here for three days. You're welcome to read the report yourself."

"No thanks." The woman folded her arms. "I'll read your memo."

"Hey." Amanda stared at her mentor until Fiona finally spun toward her with a scowl. "If they're not here at the lab, that means we have to go out and find them."

"Needle in a haystack, kid. They could be anywhere."

"Probably not." Bill typed away on the keyboard in front of

him, then swiped the screen on the console, and the holographic projector opened at the center of the table before casting a blue light in the air.

Fiona scanned the image. "What are we looking at?"

"Norfolk Beach."

"Jesus Christ, Bill."

"Where's that?" Amanda asked.

"Virginia." He cleared his throat. "One of the most populated coastal regions in the state and a pretty great vacation spot, from what I hear. When there aren't baby platypines running around. Obviously."

Amanda sigh. "Okay, so how do we find them?"

"I…don't know."

Fiona lurched out of her chair and tossed her hands up. "So we're running out onto a beach completely blind and *hoping* those baby bombs don't explode while a few hundred people are trying to work on their tan? Which morons brought her in?"

"Erik and Boyd."

She grimaced. "Boyd with the scar or Boyd with the bad mustache?"

Bill cocked his head. "With the scar."

"Damn. Okay, he's actually pretty good."

"How did they find Spike in the first place?" Amanda asked. "I mean, that's what all the magical-frequency radars or whatever are for, right?"

The zookeeper cracked a smile. "Listen to you. You know, I bet you don't even need me anymore—"

"Oh, no." Fiona snapped her fingers and pointed at him. "You're not getting out of this one *that* easily."

"I'm complimenting the kid, Fiona. Relax. Besides, I can't bow out unless *our* team leader gives the go-ahead. So cool it."

"Sure. I'll go down a canister of that green foam you made for *Spike*! Because we have no way to *find* the mini death-turtles—"

"Guys!" Amanda spun in her chair toward them. "Seriously. Quit yelling at each other, okay? That doesn't help us."

Fiona snarled and gave her mentee a scathing glare. "You realize how annoying it is when you're the one who makes sense, right?"

"Sure. Be annoyed with me making sense, Fiona. Sounds good. Just let him answer, okay?"

Rolling her eyes, Fiona slumped back into the chair she'd evacuated and leaned toward Bill with a grimace.

Amanda forced herself not to smile.

Now I'm starting to get why everybody says teenagers are the worst. Probably not as bad as a grown shifter acting like one, but whatever.

"You said it." Bill nodded. "We picked up her magical signature from our satellite feed, but Spike's a fully matured…specimen. The original erksils don't manifest any kind of magic until they're mature enough to procreate, and these can't be older than a few weeks."

"Well, why didn't you lead with *that*?" Fiona spat. "We don't have anything to worry about until they're all grown up."

"No, the acidic secretion is already fully formed in the young. Defense mechanism. Magic didn't fuel Spike's attack on Dr. Caniss."

"Never mind."

"So the baby Spikes can't use creature magic we can track." Amanda ran a hand over her hair and grimaced. "But they can already do serious damage, and we have no way to find four of them the size of a nickel."

Bill nodded. "Or smaller."

A bitter laugh burst out of the shifter girl. "This feels harder than the thing that stole the mermaid egg."

"Yep." Fiona still glared at Bill. "How about that, huh?"

He ignored her. "It's a little trickier, sure. That's why Caniss called you in."

"There's no way we'll have a write-up for an operation ready to go by the morning." Amanda couldn't help a small smirk. "She's not gonna fire us for being late on *that* either, right?"

Both adults stared at her, then burst out laughing at the same time.

Fiona slapped the control table and shook her head. "Damn, kid. Whew! Keeping your cool and cracking jokes while we run around chasing our tails. Okay. I'm convinced. You belong here."

Bill wiped a tear from the corner of his eye. "Man. Okay, so we won't have a write-up in the morning. Maybe you can get a better look at Spike before then. You know, without risking your *actual* body under another spray attack."

"Yeah. I can handle that."

"Excellent." Fiona stood and gave them both a goofy salute. "I don't think we need to write up *that* part of the plan. Go do your thing, kid."

"Where are you going?"

"To go do *my* thing. Which might include a few drinks because I am *not* prepared to hear about how many beach-goers got their arms blasted off by a couple of divergent turtles too small to see. Even by us. Let me know when you figure something out."

The redhead walked quickly out of the strategy room without another word.

Bill sighed. "It's feeding time in the biodomes. I should probably..."

"Yeah, it's fine. Go ahead." Amanda scratched her head. "I'll let you know if I find anything."

"Sounds good. Just, uh...try not to get Spike riled up enough that she tries to spray again, okay? We relocated all the other creatures from that exam room, and there won't be any staff there to, you know..."

"Put out the acid-fire?" She smirked. "Yeah, I get it."

"Cool. Let me know if you need anything." Bill gave her an awkward nod and stood before leaving the room.

When his echoing footsteps faded down the hall, Amanda dropped her face into both hands and sighed.

Okay. No biggie. Just a day of me and my ghost-wolf hanging out with a seriously deadly turtle that has babies out of its legs. Another regular, normal day at the Canissphere.

She pushed herself out of the chair and stared at the holographic display of Norfolk Beach.

I better hole up by the exam room in case Spike feels like trying to melt me anyway.

Amanda spent the rest of the day doing just that. Fortunately, Dr. Blane was working in Exam Room 5 that day and agreed to let Amanda get comfy in a chair in the corner while she worked. "If you piss that thing off, you're the one who has to go spray down the room."

"Got it. Thanks."

It was a little hard at first to focus on drawing out her magic with all the squawking, growling, hissing, and general scuffling of the other newly collected creatures hanging out in the exam room. The scientists studied them for their first few weeks here before releasing them into one of the biodomes. Eventually, Amanda managed to drown out all the noise and focus on going full ghost-wolf.

Setting herself up in the room next door saved at least a little time getting back into Exam Room 4. She only had one wall to walk through instead of half the lab.

Spike hardly seemed to notice the girl's shifter magic in the room with her. For four hours straight, Amanda and her ghost-wolf sat quietly outside the creature's cage, occasionally pacing back and forth to see if she could get the thing's attention. Spike wasn't interested in visitors without a physical body.

After a quick break for lunch and grabbing three extra

protein bars from the basket in the central dome, Amanda went back to work doing the same thing. She learned absolutely nothing.

Even when she padded through the bars of Spike's cage to get a closer look at the creature, the angry mama platypine only stared at her blankly and didn't move.

I can't even tell if she can see *me. If she won't respond to this, there's no way I'm getting the attention of four baby Spikes swimming around on the beach. Or buried in the sand. Or walking around aimlessly down some street in Virginia waiting for someone to step on them...*

By dinnertime, she was mentally exhausted and physically aching from sitting in the chair in the same position for hours on end while she and her magic tried everything under the sun to get Spike to respond. Without any results.

Amanda grabbed a sandwich at Dominique's open window, thanked the woman with a weak smile, and shuffled down the tunnel into the residential quarters. Only when she swiped her keycard on the panel outside her door did she realize she'd been moving on autopilot. The tiny room on the other side of that door wasn't hers anymore.

With a growl, she stalked down the hall to find her newly upgraded room and nearly smashed the panel in when she slapped her keycard against it. She flopped down into the insanely uncomfortable armchair before the hydraulic door had finished sliding back into place.

She tossed the wrapped sandwich into her lap and ran her hands down both cheeks with a groan. "Why?"

Of course, there was nobody there to reply, and nobody had the answer in the first place.

Just me. Except I haven't found it yet, and somebody's gonna get their body blown apart by a hundred tiny acid sprays if I don't figure out how the heck to find these things...

So she decided to devour the sandwich instead, and once she finished, she grabbed her Coalition phone and performed a little due diligence of her own. Mostly, it was in fear that she was taking too long at a job nobody else could do, but there weren't any articles or breaking news reports of happy vacationers losing their limbs in a spray of green mist around the Norfolk Beach area.

Then her phone vibrated with an incoming text from her other number.

Why the hell couldn't you have told me that sooner? I'm not fucking Cupid, shifter girl. He won't *shut up* about you. It's like Romeo all over again, but with a guy who thinks he has a shot. You should buy him a stupid phone. How's it going?

Amanda snorted and typed her reply.

You know, just trying to save a few cities from death and destruction by a bunch of babies nobody knows how to find. Same old, same old.

Summer's next text was instantaneous.

Wtf?

Yeah, that one's gonna be hard to explain.

Amanda laughed and finished the conversation so she could focus on getting back to work.

Baby creatures. I'll tell you later. Try not to hurt him too much. Gotta go.

She dropped the phone into her lap and closed her eyes. Apparently, Summer had to have the last word even through texts.

Trust me. He can take a hit almost as much as you can. You're totally screwed.

The message ended with a grinning smiley face and a thumbs-up, and Amanda barked a laugh before getting up to pace around her much larger room.

Great. I have to find acid-bomb turtles, and hopefully, I get back to school before my best friend blows up my—

Her what?

With another snort, Amanda shook her head.

Focus, Amanda. You're not getting paid to think about Matt.

That didn't exactly make it any easier *not* to think about Matt.

It was impossible to get to sleep that night, even though Amanda was exhausted from a day spent using her magic and getting absolutely nothing out of it. She tossed and turned on her tiny bed and almost cracked her head on the low ceiling more than once.

This is ridiculous. If I'm not sleeping, I might as well try to do something useful.

So she closed her eyes, drew a deep breath, and slipped into her ghost-wolf again to go for a late-night stroll through the Canissphere. At this point, anywhere would have been more interesting than going back to Exam Room 4, but she had to try.

As soon as she passed through the wall of the last corridor, she knew something was different.

A low, mewling sound echoed down the hallway, and a green glow came from the exam room before it gradually morphed into a deep red, then bright orange, then a more subdued yellow.

Yes. Finally. Something new.

Amanda raced forward on silent, ghostly paws and stopped

outside the room, only because she hadn't expected to see anything like this.

Spike stood in her cage, though now the creature had gained another foot in height at least. Instead of the short, stubby legs on which she'd crawled around the cage, her legs had either elongated or unfolded, and the flaps of green skin behind the tufts of yellow feathers on each of her legs fluttered rapidly with a low buzz. The creature swayed from side to side, her colors changing with the glow emanating from her and casting a shimmering reflection against the glass. It sounded a lot like the animal was singing.

For her young. Holy crap. That's it!

Amanda gasped and sat bolt upright in her bed. Her head cracked against the low ceiling of the sleeping nook. "Damnit! Ow."

She furiously rubbed her head, then tossed off the covers and rolled onto the floor before snatching up her phone. Then she sent a group text to Fiona and Bill.

Night. That's how we find them. Spike's glowing and singing. We need to record it and play it back at the beach.

Before she sent the message, though, she racked her brain for any memory of where her very small but highly efficient team of unlikely monster hunters *were* inside the Canissphere.

"Oh, man. If they're asleep, we'll have to wait another twenty-four hours to get this. We need to do this *now*."

Her phone buzzed in her hand, and a robotic female voice not unlike the voice in the Starbucks train emerged from the device, which spilled out of Amanda's hand and toppled across the floor in her surprise.

"To send your message with top-priority urgent status, please confirm with voice recognition."

"What the hell?"

"Access confirmed. Message sent with top-priority urgent status."

"Wait, wait. Hold on." Amanda scrambled on her hands and knees toward the phone and snatched it up again. It had already sent the text, and a green light flashed across her screen.

Swiping her hair out of her face, she stared at the phone and drew a deep breath.

Great. I seriously hope top-priority urgent doesn't mean 'wake up the entire lab' because I accidentally sent a text through a screwed-up voice command. That's new.

A shrill *beep* from the phone made her jump again. Then an incoming text came through from Fiona.

Good work, kid. Never doubted you for a second. Maybe lay off the coffee. Your ideas are a lot better when you're not all jacked up.

"What?"

A second text came in from Bill.

Heading to Exam Room 4 now. Great idea to check her out at night, Amanda. I should've thought of it, but I guess this is why you're here. We'll get the song and dance recorded and can head out tomorrow. Hey, who wants to do the write-up for Caniss?

Amanda laughed and swiped her hair away from her face. "This is insane."

Better let the team leader do all the paperwork. You know. Her idea, her credit.

Good point. You got this, Amanda?

She quickly typed a reply.

Would either of you have to do it if I told you to right now?

Bill didn't answer, but Fiona's next message was eerily fast.

Not over text. Doesn't count as official correspondence, as far as paperwork's concerned. And I don't drink and plan.

Amanda rolled her eyes and hurried to her backpack. She pulled out a notebook and pen and sat at the desk to write up exactly what she'd found out. She included what she assumed Bill was doing right now with Spike and whatever recording devices they had and a loose plan for getting out to Virginia. Then she detailed how they'd use the recordings to call the creature's baby platypines to their fake mom so they could return them to their real mother here.

Only when she'd finished did she realize she'd written in "platypines" instead of the subject number Dr. Caniss referred.

Screw it. Might as well make the name official. If she asks, I'll say Bill and Fiona made a team effort.

CHAPTER TWENTY-SEVEN

Three days later, Amanda and her team stood in Exam Room 4 and watched the four baby creatures toddling around inside Spike's cage. The mama platypine hummed contentedly and shuddered whenever one of her young brushed up against her.

"I don't believe it." Bill chuckled and shook his head. "Two days without an attack or any aggressive behavior at all. And all we needed was to pretend to be mama."

"Yeah, keep telling yourself that, pal." Fiona snorted. "You'll probably have to make a few more changes to that fancy projector if you want anyone to call *you* mama."

"That was…easier than I thought." He set a hand on Amanda's shoulder and gave her a little squeeze. "Good thing one of us has trouble sleeping, right?"

"I guess. Hey, did Caniss say anything to you guys about the… damage to the jet?"

Fiona and Bill glanced at each other and tried to hide their amusement. "Nah." The redhead woman shook her head. "She won't say anything, either. What's a little acid through a fuel tank compared to maintaining the secrecy and anonymity of Omega Industries and the Coalition of Shifters?"

"Keeping the divergent species secret," Bill muttered. "That's all she cares about."

"Yeah. That's what I said." Fiona laughed and leaned toward the cage. "You guys are still a complete secret, aren't y—"

"Whoa." Bill and Amanda grabbed the woman's shoulders at the same time and hauled her back when Spike let out a low warning *hiss*. "Seriously. Stay away from the cage."

"Right. Yep. I'm done with those little twerps anyway." Widening her eyes, Fiona spun and headed for the door. "So. Looks like you're free to go back to school now, kid?"

Amanda smiled at Bill and reached out to shake his hand. "See you next time, I guess."

"Looking forward to it."

Then the shifter girl spun and raced after her mentor. "Fiona. Hey."

"Yeah?"

"That's it? I just get to go back?"

"I mean, Melody *would* keep you here if she could, but I'm pretty sure you have a few things to get back to at the Academy, right? And yeah, a hell of a lot cuter than baby turtle-bombs."

Amanda wrinkled her nose and tried to ignore the hot flush rising in her cheeks. "We're still not talking about that."

"Okay, yeah. Sure. Suit yourself. You have the rest of the semester to deal with *that* while everyone else holds down the fort here. Now you know how to get back whenever we need you. So, yeah. That's it."

"Like...right now?"

"As soon as you get your fancy new scooter down the tunnel and out of the lab, kid. Oh, hey. I almost forgot." With a self-conscious chuckle, Fiona reached into her back pocket and pulled out another black device, this time with a green button on top instead of red. "Can't exactly get outta here without D to C, right?"

"What?"

"It takes you back to the station under Denver, kid. Next time, leave the scooter."

With a snort, Amanda took the device. "You haven't tested this one out yet either, have you?"

"Nope. Happy teleporting." The woman clapped a hand on her mentee's shoulder and turned to head down the hall.

Amanda watched her for a moment, then spun and headed for the residential quarter to grab her things.

In twenty minutes, she'd packed everything into the rear compartment, said her goodbyes to anyone she passed in the central dome, and walked the scooter down the exit hallway until she passed through the wall at the end. She emerged in the cool, brisk air of the valley in the Rocky Mountains.

I get to go back to school. Finish up the semester like a regular senior. Deal with regular high-school things until the next time I have to pretend to be some divergent magical creature in the middle of the night.

A slow smile spread across her lips.

Yeah. Maybe go for another run with Matt.

She hopped onto her scooter, gritted her teeth as she grabbed the handlebar tightly, then looked down at the green-buttoned device that was supposed to work like the other teleporter, only in reverse.

Here we go.

Before she could press the button, a deafening alarm siren burst through the air behind her, followed by a flash of shimmering red light pulsing around the enchantment that made the entire Canissphere invisible. Amanda jolted and stared at the odd display. Then another obnoxious alarm rose in one endless squeal from her Coalition phone locked away in the rear compartment.

"Oh, *come on*."

She got off the scooter and rifled through her things for her phone. The screen flashed red as well, along with an alert that she was receiving an incoming video call. The only option available was to accept it. With a *hiss,* she stabbed the screen, and Dr. Caniss' face appeared.

"I see you haven't left yet."

"No. I'm right outside."

"Good. Get back inside and meet me in the strategy room. Right now."

Amanda swallowed. "What's going on?"

"That's the point of a briefing, Amanda. You don't have an excuse for being late this time, so don't make us wait."

"Hold on. Wait for—"

The call cut off a second before the alarm around the Canis-sphere did the same.

Amanda stared at the space where the pulsing red light had been, and a hard knot of disappointment and dread tightened in her gut.

No way is this good. I'm not going back to school, am I?

She turned the scooter around and headed back into the lab. The second she entered the tunnel, the shouted commands and clamor of urgent footsteps racing back and forth almost knocked her over. The central dome swarmed with Coalition employees running across the room to deliver printed reports or inform their coworkers of the next task.

Whoa. Something big just happened.

"Hey, kid!" Fiona shouted on the other side of the dome. "Don't just stand there. Come on."

Amanda left her scooter beside the tunnel entrance and wove her way through the mass of scurrying shifters before she reached her mentor. "You said I could go back to school."

"Yep."

"So why did Caniss call me to come back?"

"That's pretty obvious, don't you think?"

"No. Fiona." She grabbed her mentor's arm and turned the

woman around to face her. "I mean, yeah, it looks bad. But... I mean, do you know what happened?"

"Listen, kid. I'm as surprised as you are. Hence the whole 'let's hurry and get to the strategy room' thing happening right now, yeah?"

"Okay, but—"

"What are you guys doing standing there?" Bill shouted as he raced down the hall toward them. His eyes were wild as he tugged them along behind him and cradled a tablet in his other arm. "Let's go!"

"Go ahead, kid." Fiona gestured toward him as they hurried to catch up with the guy. "We both know you can't wait for a briefing anyway."

"Bill, what happened?" Amanda asked as she broke into a jog.

"We just got a massive frequency readout," he blurted. "Huge shockwave like I've never seen before. Yeah, it's all hands on deck for this one, Amanda. Sorry. I know you were ready to go home."

"Okay, well, how big?"

"Big-big."

She rolled her eyes. "Where?"

Bill skidded to a stop outside the strategy room, which was already full of more shifters than the room was supposed to hold. He glanced inside, then huffed out a sigh. "Right now, it's on the southern coast of South America. But it's moving fast, and I honestly have no idea where it's going or when it'll let off a giant blast like that again, so we should quit speculating and get inside."

He hurried into the strategy room, and Amanda looked up at Fiona with wide eyes. "South America?"

"Hey, look on the bright side, kid. Free international travel." The woman patted Amanda's shoulder, then slipped inside to take her place in the crowded room.

International? No, I was supposed to go back to school. I can't miss all the—

Her phone buzzed in her hand with a notification of an incoming email, so she tried to discretely open it up as she slipped into the room and waited with the rest of the giant team gathered inside for Dr. Caniss to give them some kind of explanation.

The email was from Principal Glasket.

Miss Coulier,

In light of the recent correspondence I've received from Dr. Caniss, this email is to inform you that I've approved an extended timeline for your finals this semester. Please return to campus before the start of your second semester. I'll provide you with a schedule for your final projects to be turned in to your teachers, including your second sparring session with Mr. Petrov. He was particularly disappointed to hear you will no longer be available the first week of November, as previously decided, but we all understand how important your work is.

Be safe. We're all pulling for you.

Dean Gladys Glasket

"Oh my God," Amanda muttered. She quickly closed her email and looked up, trying to peer around the sea of bodies crammed into the strategy room to get a glimpse of Dr. Caniss.

She already emailed Glasket and told her I'd be gone until winter break? What the hell is going on?

"Listen up!" Caniss' shout from the other side of the room brought all the commotion to a standstill. "Here's what we know. Anyone who can't save their questions until the end of this briefing needs to get out right now because we don't have time for interruptions."

Amanda swallowed and stared straight ahead at the back of the scientist in front of her.

Okay, now I get why she's such a hardass about being on time. Except for when it comes to my senior year of bounty-hunter school. Great.

As Caniss dove into her explanation of what their analysts were calling "the biggest ripple of magical activity they'd seen since the gates between worlds were fully open," Amanda tried to hide her phone so she could quickly type a text.

Something big just happened. I'm not coming back soon. If you don't hear from me again for a while, you can stay at my house over break.

Summer's reply was ridiculously fast.

You're killing me, shifter girl. Don't die.

Amanda cleared her throat and stuffed her phone back into her pocket.

Yeah. That's the plan. I seriously hope Caniss has a better one for this mess.

Get sneak peeks, exclusive giveaways, behind the scenes content, and more. PLUS you'll be notified of special **one day only fan pricing** on new releases.

Sign up today to get free stories.

Visit: https://marthacarr.com/read-free-stories/

AUTHOR NOTES - MARTHA CARR

AUGUST 3, 2021

Hobby: Something very individual that is done only for fun. Not to earn money or recognition or health. Just fun. It's my own definition and I'm sticking with it.

A hobby of any kind is also one of the first things we drop when we become adults. Our calendars become filled with jobs and friends and obligations and exercise and cleaning our nests. Then partners and children and pets and it seems like there is never enough time.

A hobby seems like an indulgent luxury.

Well, it turns out that having something to do that only incites fun is also a necessary ingredient to a happy and sane life. Don't make time for it and risk always feeling a little out of sorts. A little cranky. Or a little wistful. Like some important ingredient is missing.

There's a reason children's lives are mostly one giant hobby. They're learning so much at such a rapid pace from the moment they open their eyes for the new day. Interests are what guide them. In other words, hobbies.

Writing is not a hobby for me. I love doing it and find some peace and escape while writing but it's also how I earn my living.

Not a hobby. Neither is swimming or yoga because there's an element of exercise in there. I'm trying to de-stress and lose weight and get stronger. So many motives.

I mentor a lot of young women and one of the first things we look at is, where's the hobby? Some have a hard time even coming up with an interest. We start small with maybe dancing or take an art class. Somehow that gives the brain permission to start looking for other ideas.

A friend of mine has taken up drumming – like drum kit with cymbals and sticks. The whole deal, including recitals. Another tried trapeze and another hula hoops that are also set on fire. Yeah, that's a thing.

By being willing to let ourselves do something that will benefit only ourselves and the only benefit is fun, we are also saying that we are worth so much just because we're here. Worth is no longer earned – it just is.

So, what's my hobby. I've been asking myself that a lot lately. Particularly during quarantine when a good hobby or two would have been really useful. For now, it's gardening. I'm digging figuring out the best way to plant a seed and then watching the fragile tendrils pop through the soil and then become something sturdy that is beautiful to behold or great to eat. I forget about everything else while I'm out there and get lost with my hands in the soil.

Some days I can only find an hour to go putter and there are some days where even that gets squeezed out. But like any good hobby, it's waiting for me at a moment's notice.

Time to plan my fall vegetable garden and I've been eyeing a lot of dahlias lately, wondering if they'll grow in Austin.

Having this hobby makes everything else I do seem easier because I come back from it just a bit calmer, more centered – and feeling like a kid again. More adventures to follow.

AUTHOR NOTES - MICHAEL ANDERLE

AUGUST 5, 2021

Thank you for not only reading this story but these author notes as well.

While Martha and I haven't spoken about hobbies yet, that is a subject that has been on my mind. I don't think I have refined the definition down as tightly as Martha.

I was loosely defining it as something I wanted to learn more about. Unfortunately, it seems a lot of what I am looking into somehow gets tied back into work.

Thus, *not a hobby.*

I should probably figure out how to convince myself that puttering around the house and fixing the slight "issues" should be a hobby. It isn't focused on work, and I could probably listen to an audiobook while making it happen.

However, I've associated any fix-it stuff to work (ugh) in my life that I have an uphill battle with myself.

What would I do with "time?" Would I decompress enough that eventually I'd get bored and go find something else to create?

Probably.

But, given to flights of curiosity as I am, I'd like to spend time with 3D Animation, Music Creation, Cooking (which would be a challenge as I don't like fruits and vegetables...ok, maybe ½ Cooking... I'd skip the vegetables area) and some sort of flying w/ drones if they weren't such a pain on the legal front.

There are plenty of spaces around Las Vegas that I should be able to go flying with my drone, but it's so @E#%@#% HOT right now. Plus, I'm always jonesing for the next big thing in flying, which (for me) is the drones where you put on goggles to see as if you are in the drone, flying.

How cool is that?

My luck, I'd fly right into a tree and faint, thinking I'd knocked myself out. I'm that clumsy. No lie.

I need to BBQ more, actually. I have this great Traeger grill (over-bought a size too big for my wife and me), but damn, THAT would be something that has little work value.

Except, it does. EVERYTHING I do can be tied back into stories.

Which is true for Martha's gardening. She could easily create characters who love or love/hate gardening, and now her hobby is work-related.

Yeah, I'm not going to share that with her. It's hard enough to step away from our work without your collaborator @#%@# it up for you.

So, I'm off to take a nap. THAT is just for me, and work can't take it away from me. Maybe I'll become a hobbyist nap-taker. Since I'm getting closer to my mid-fifties, I think it might be time to admit this body likes a mid-afternoon siesta.

Hmmm... I'm going to go lie down and think about that ;-)

Ad Aeternitatem,

Michael Anderle

WAKING MAGIC

Solve a murder, save her mother, and stop the apocalypse?

What would you do when elves ask you to investigate a prince's murder and you didn't even know elves, or magic, was real?

Meet Leira Berens, Austin homicide detective who's good at what she does – track down the bad guys and lock them away.

Which is why the elves want her to solve this murder – fast. It's not just about tracking down the killer and bringing them to justice. It's about saving the world!

If you're looking for a heroine who prefers fighting to flirting, check out The Leira Chronicles today!

OTHER SERIES IN THE ORICERAN UNIVERSE

THE LEIRA CHRONICLES

SOUL STONE MAGE

THE KACY CHRONICLES

MIDWEST MAGIC CHRONICLES

THE FAIRHAVEN CHRONICLES

I FEAR NO EVIL

THE DANIEL CODEX SERIES

SCHOOL OF NECESSARY MAGIC

SCHOOL OF NECESSARY MAGIC: RAINE CAMPBELL

ALISON BROWNSTONE

FEDERAL AGENTS OF MAGIC

SCIONS OF MAGIC

THE UNBELIEVABLE MR. BROWNSTONE

DWARF BOUNTY HUNTER

MAGIC CITY CHRONICLES

CASE FILES OF AN URBAN WITCH

OTHER BOOKS BY JUDITH BERENS

OTHER BOOKS BY MARTHA CARR

OTHER BOOKS BY MICHAEL ANDERLE

JOIN THE ORICERAN UNIVERSE FAN GROUP ON FACEBOOK!

BOOKS BY MICHAEL ANDERLE

Sign up for the LMBPN email list to be notified of new releases and special deals!

https://lmbpn.com/email/

For a complete list of books by Michael Anderle, please visit:

www.lmbpn.com/ma-books/

CONNECT WITH THE AUTHORS

Martha Carr Social

Website: http://www.marthacarr.com

Facebook: https://www.facebook.com/groups/MarthaCarrFans/

Michael Anderle Social

Website: http://lmbpn.com

Email List: http://lmbpn.com/email/

https://www.facebook.com/LMBPNPublishing

https://twitter.com/MichaelAnderle

https://www.instagram.com/lmbpn_publishing/

https://www.bookbub.com/authors/michael-anderle

Made in the USA
Las Vegas, NV
01 March 2024